MY WAYWARD LADY

by
EVELYN RICHARDSON

CAMEL
PRESS

A Camel Press title Published by Epicenter press
Epicenter Press
6524 NE 181st St. Suite 2
Kenmore, WA 98028
www.epicenterpress.com
www.camelpress.com
www.coffeetownpress.com
For more information go to: www.RegencyReads.com

Published first by the Penguin Group Copyright © 1997 by Cynthia Johnson.

Cover design by Bethel Barban

my wayward lady Copyright © 2020 by Evelyn Richardson

ISBN: ISBN 978-1-60381-204-7 (Trade Paper)

Printed in the United States of America

Dedicated
To my inveterate cheerleader Christina Breslin.
Thank you for making me feel so valued.

Chapter 1

Alistair opened his eyes and stared groggily at the unfamiliar ceiling as he tried to figure out where he was. Certainly the rosy-cheeked cherubs who rioted above him had nothing in common with the severely classical frieze that graced his own bedchamber at his quarters in Mount Street. The bedclothes rustled beside him and, propping himself on one elbow, he turned to survey his still sleeping companion.

Her face, partially hidden by a mass of black hair, was pretty enough, but entirely unfamiliar. His eyes traveled down to the inviting curve of the hips and the long slim legs whose graceful proportions were obvious even under the sheet that covered them. Alistair grinned. Now he remembered. He was in Mrs. Gerrard's, a discreet but elegant establishment tucked among the clubs along St. James's and reputed to house the most beautiful bits of muslin in all of London. Definitely Kitty—at last he remembered her name— was no mean example of the delights that Mrs. Gerrard's had to offer.

The grin was quickly succeeded by a frown as Alistair recalled not only where he was but precisely why he was there. Tomorrow the announcement of the pending nuptials between Alistair Julius, Lord Chalfont, Marquess of Kidderham and the Honorable Alicia De Villiers was to appear in The Morning Post, and his evening at Mrs. Gerrard's represented one last moment of freedom, one last expression of his former reckless way of living before selling his soul to that great god of the ton, and the object of his future wife's devotion, reputation.

Most men would have been overjoyed. The Honorable Miss De Villiers had been hailed as a diamond of the first water since the moment she had come out nearly two years ago. Tall and stately, she was fashionably dark, with deep blue eyes and she possessed the retroussé nose and rosebud mouth so necessary in an incomparable.

In fact, she was so much the picture of feminine grace and loveliness that she might easily have stepped out from the pages of La Belle Assemblée. She also exhibited just about as much warmth and passion as those fashion plates, Alistair thought as the vision of his betrothed rose before him.

Other men might consider her a prize, but to Lord Chalfont she was, and always had been, his fate, just as his vast estates in Oxfordshire, his hunting box near Melton Mowbray, and the family town house in Grosvenor Square which was rented out while he enjoyed his simpler bachelor quarters in Mount Street. The De Villiers' land adjoined his in Oxfordshire, and for centuries there had been a tradition of alliances between the De Villiers and the Chalfonts. Alistair was no exception. Since he had been a boy, he had had the notion of Alicia as his future wife drummed into him by her father as well as his own ferociously respectable parents.

To a high-spirited lad, the prospect of a rigidly confining future had been daunting in the extreme and he had chafed mightily against such a dull and unadventurous existence. When his parents had died, both struck down by pneumonia within weeks of each other, he had seized the opportunity to purchase a commission in the Hussars and gone to the Peninsula in search of the excitement he craved.

Life in the cavalry had suited Alistair to perfection. Never one to revel in luxury, he had not minded the hard existence of campaigning. In fact, he had rather enjoyed the privation of long marches through a barren countryside, for it gave him a chance to prove himself in ways he never could back at home where his rank and possessions spoke so loudly to everyone he knew that the qualities of the man who possessed them were completely ignored.

His energy, fearlessness, and quick thinking soon earned him the respect of his superiors as well as his men so that by the time the conflict in the Peninsula was over he was a trusted member of Wellington's staff, his recklessness and daring remarkable even among men who were renowned for such things.

The Peninsula was now over, however, the troops were home, and there was no more putting off of the inevitable. Alicia had been too young for betrothal when he had left to join the army and after that, what with the threatening political situation there had been no question of his resigning his commission despite her objections that he was devoting his time and energy to his country instead of his intended. Of course she had made the most of his status as one of the heroes of the Peninsula, but the exhilaration over the glorious victory had soon died down, and being seen on the arm of a man in uniform lost the cachet it had previously conferred. Alicia had soon begun hinting— ever so delicately of course, for she never did anything that was not exquisitely conceived—that it was high time for the Marquess of Kidderham to settle down, take his proper place in the ton, and make her the most envied of women.

Being a man of honor, Lord Chalfont had kept his word, albeit reluctantly. As a dashing young-officer of considerable charm whose bold good looks had caused feminine hearts to flutter from Lisbon to Vienna, he had enjoyed numerous liaisons, some discreet, some not so discreet, with women of all ranks from princess to peasant, and he was not at all anxious to end this happy state of affairs, or even curtail it.

Though a supreme connoisseur of female charms, the Marquess of Kidderham had never been particularly attracted to those of his future wife. The Honorable Miss De Villiers's beauty, though undeniable and widely touted throughout the ton, was coldly exquisite. She exhibited the bloodless perfection of a marble statue—something to be admired from afar, but never touched. Alistair preferred his women to be real, passionate, and sensuous, women who enjoyed lovemaking as much as he did—women like Kitty here.

He looked down at the woman beside him and grinned as he recalled some of the more acrobatic moments of a few hours ago. No wonder she was sleeping so soundly now. Why even he, accustomed as he was to an active life of vigorous campaigning, was feeling pleasantly exhausted this morning and not a little dazed.

Alistair shook his head in an effort to clear the cobwebs from his brain. In addition to the rigors of passionate lovemaking, he had consumed quantities of port the previous evening, followed by equal measures of brandy and he was now finding it extremely difficult to marshal his faculties. However, he could tell by the sunlight filtering through the cracks in the curtain that it was high time he was up and on his way.

Little as he wished to face it all, he had things to do. Sliding from the bed he wavered unsteadily as he leaned over to gather the clothes scattered all over the room. His head swam unpleasantly as he bent to retrieve his breeches. This would never do. The sooner he got home to a pot of strong coffee, the better. Lord Chalfont hurried to tuck his shirt into his breeches, grabbed a fistful of coins from his pocket and poured them into a pile where Kitty would be sure to see them, pulled on his jacket, and made his way carefully to the door. In this state of mind he preferred to leave Mrs. Gerrard's as quietly and unobtrusively as possible. In the future he was going to have to offer up explanations to Alicia for every single thing he did and he did not propose to begin by having to explain this particular episode.

Making his way down a hall inadequately lit by a window at the end over the stair, Alistair crept quietly past the tightly closed doors on either side, down what appeared to be the back stairs, and then made his way to what he remembered as the front of the house. It was not as easy as he had expected for his memory of the previous evening was vague, to say the least. He recalled entering and being ushered into a brightly lit anteroom where the beauteous Kitty had hastened to greet him. She had led him off so quickly that he had not really had the slightest notion of where he was going beyond following this tantalizingly seductive young woman.

At the foot of the stairs he turned and headed toward what he thought was the entrance hall and turned the knob to open what he thought was the front door. Too late he heard the sound of voices droning on in a strangely repetitive manner, but before he could listen further to figure out what was transpiring in the room, the voices stopped, alerted to his presence by the click of the latch and the creak of the door. The damage was done. He was discovered and now his curiosity threatened to overwhelm him.

Alistair pushed the door wide open and boldly entered the room. Six faces, all extraordinarily pretty, swiveled to face him and six pairs of eyes ranging from deep brown to brightest green fixed him with inquiring looks. He stared back. For a moment the marquess thought he had stumbled somehow into another building next door to Mrs. Gerrard's, for the five demurely dressed young women, each holding a copybook, assembled in a row of chairs in front of another young woman who stood facing them, book in hand, looked like nothing so much as five schoolgirls and their instructress. However, a second glance at the ornate furnishings, the tasteful but seductive paintings and suggestive marble statues proved to Lord Chalfont that he was indeed still in Mrs. Gerrard's.

"May I be of some assistance to you, sir?" A cool voice interrupted Lord Chalfont's befuddled thoughts. He turned to look at the speaker addressing him from her place in front of the class. She was a diminutive young woman of slender build, but her air of self-possession and an energy barely suppressed made up for her lack of stature. Striking rather than beautiful, she commanded attention. From the riot of red-gold curls that peeked out from underneath the bonnet that proclaimed her an adherent of the Quaker religion to the dark fringed sapphire eyes, the young lady was someone who would be noticed immediately in any situation and not soon forgotten. The straight nose and firm little chin only added to the impression that this formidable person knew precisely what she was about and would brook no interference from anyone.

Intrigued as much by her distaste for his presence as by her obvious physical attractions, Alistair smiled lazily at her, his eyes glinting with amusement as he ambled over to an empty chair. "Yes, you may assist me. You may teach me whatever you are teaching them." He allowed his gaze to travel over the bevy of faces that were still regarding him somewhat suspiciously.

The young woman's spine stiffened visibly and the sapphire eyes darkened with annoyance. "You wish me to teach you to read?" There was no mistaking the frosty note in her voice. "Surely you have known to read this age, sirrah."

Alistair's grin broadened. What a little spitfire! "Nevertheless, I find I stand in great need of instruction. It has been years since I have done anything but fight the French and I fear I have become a trifle rusty." He coiled his prodigious length into the delicate gilt chair. "Do not let my intrusion interrupt such a worthy goings-on. Please proceed." He nodded and motioned to the young woman to continue.

There was a most unladylike snort beside him and Lord Chalfont turned to see that several of the pupils were desperately struggling to stifle giggles that threatened to overcome them. He winked at them and then turned back to the teacher, assuming an expression of innocent earnestness that was bound to provoke his lovely instructress.

Chapter 2

Lord Chalfont was entirely correct in his assumptions. Lady Harriet Fareham, for that was the name of the erstwhile Quakeress, longed to slap his handsome face, as his expression resembled nothing so much as her brother Charlie's when he was at his most provoking. Odious man! He knew very well he was upsetting the class and threatening her composure. Well, he was not going to get away with it. Lady Harriet Fareham was not going to allow some Bond Street beau to disconcert her by acting like a coxcomb.

Drawing herself to her full height, which she knew to be woefully short by fashionable standards, Harriet strode over to the marquess and handed her book to him. "Very well." She snapped. "We are at the top of page three. You may continue, ladies." And, refusing to be further disconcerted by the intruder, Harriet began to recite from memory the exercises they had been concentrating on before the insolent gentleman had so rudely disrupted them.

After the briefest exchange of a few sly smiles, the young women followed their teacher's lead and order was restored, at least outwardly. Inwardly, Harriet was fuming. How dare he burst into a private room in such a way, stare at her in the most impudent manner, and then force his presence on them? It was outside of enough! She darted a furious glance at the intruder only to discover that he was looking straight at her and grinning in the most impertinent way. Catching her eye, he raised one mobile eyebrow and slowly winked at her.

Oooh! It took all of Harriet's self-control to ignore him when she really longed to stomp over and strangle the man. It was only by exerting extraordinary concentration that she was able to recall the lesson that they were doing and continue on with her work. Despite her best efforts, however, her heart was not entirely in it and the schoolroom lacked the air of intense concentration that had existed before

Lord Chalfont's appearance.

Harriet sighed. The girls had been making such progress until this particular moment that she had truly been very pleased with herself and with them. In truth, she had not expected to discover anything half so interesting and rewarding during her stay in London as teaching the girls at Mrs. Gerrard's to read and write, and she devoutly hoped that the tall blond gentleman who had foisted himself upon them in such an unmannerly fashion was not going to ruin it for all of them.

For the moment he sat there, book in hand, not even pretending to follow along, a teasing light in his amber eyes and a smug smile of satisfaction on his lips that Harriet ached to wipe off. She detested such men—selfish pleasure seekers who flitted from one thing to another with never a thought for anyone or anything else beyond their own idle amusement.

Harriet had no idea how clearly these thoughts were mirrored on her expressive features. Her indignation was so intense that even the slight sprinkling of freckles across her nose seemed to glow with it. Alistair chuckled to himself. She was a spirited little thing, this Quakeress, a delicious change from all the marriage-mad young misses who were forever trying to attract his attention, and a definite contrast to the coolly elegant Alicia who simply assumed that he was hers to command. He wondered how so very proper a young miss came to be in an establishment such as Mrs. Gerrard's and what she thought of this sort of place. The marquess's eyes glinted with amusement as he resolved to follow her on her way out and discover the answer to his speculations.

Harriet glanced at the clock on the mantel behind the girls. At last the hour was up and she could put an end to this little charade that seemed to be providing so much diversion for their unwelcome visitor. Clearing her throat sharply, she said, "That will be all for to-day, girls. I shall be back again at—at— my usual time." And turning on her heel, she marched from the room without a backward glance.

Alistair grinned. She was a clever little thing all right and not about to acknowledge his presence enough even to retrieve her book, nor was she going to betray the time and date of her next appearance at Mrs. Gerrard's. With a conspiratorial grin at his fellow students, he rose and hurried out after her, reaching the hall just in time to catch the sight of a gray skirt whisking around the corner. He arrived at the door at the end of the hall to see her climb into a waiting hackney.

Lord Chalfont ran down the steps and tried to keep pace with the carriage as it moved out of Saint James's and into the press of traffic along Piccadilly. There it slowed enough for him to catch up with it before turning into Bond Street where it stopped in front of a most elegant millinery establishment.

Alistair frowned in puzzlement. From the little he knew of the Quakers, he would not have thought that the delights of Bond Street would have held any allure for the occupant of the carriage. But then, he had also not expected that a Quaker would be quite as spirited as Mrs. Gerrard's charming instructress.

The Quakeress and a maid alighted and disappeared into the shop while the hackney slowly moved off down the crowded street. Alistair waited for as long as he could without appearing to be a Bond Street lounger, but to no avail. It seemed as though the ladies were going to be occupied for some time.

At last he gave up, consoling himself with the notion of becoming a steady customer at Mrs. Gerrard's in order to encounter the intriguing young woman who, despite her reluctance to admit it in his presence, was obviously a regular visitor at the renowned establishment Alistair could not help but chuckle as he strolled along. Frequenting the company of beautiful women would not be so unpleasant after all, and his curiosity had been thoroughly aroused. In fact he could not think when he had been so interested in anything since he had returned from Europe.

Meanwhile his quarry, entirely oblivious to the heavy plotting she had inspired, was examining bonnets decidedly more frivolous than the plain one she now wore. She had been trying out the effect of the recently introduced Coburg bonnet whose narrow brim that turned off the forehead was excessively becoming and a delightful contrast to the unrelieved drabness of her Quakerish attire.

"What do you think, Rose?" Lady Harriet turned to her maid who had been examining some very enticing ribbons.

"Ooh, it is ever so lovely, miss, and the height of fashion," Rose exclaimed enthusiastically. The little maid was happy to see Lady

Harriet's thoughts traveling along less serious lines. Though devoted to her mistress, she did wish Lady Harriet would spend just a little more time and effort on taking her proper place in the fashionable world. Good works were all very well, but someone as pretty and lively as her Lady Harriet should be out finding herself a dashing husband instead of helping young women who were no better than they should be.

Little did Rose guess that this sudden interest in bonnets was all the merest pretense on her mistress's part. Harriet was more unsettled than she wished to admit, even to herself, by the attentions of the bold gentleman at Mrs. Gerrard's. Drat the man! His presence threatened to rob her of the one thing that she truly enjoyed in London and she fervently hoped he was not a regular customer. Calm down, Harriet, you are making a great piece of work over nothing, she chided herself. None of the girls seemed to know him after all. He must have been a newcomer to burst in on them like that. Undoubtedly, she would never see him again. In spite of this sound logic, however, she continued to fret over it during the ride home to Berkeley Square.

Lady Harriet Fareham had come to London under great duress for her one previous Season had shown her more than she cared to see of the frenetic and superficial world of the ton. It was only her elder sister's strong representations of the importance of her family's supportive presence that had convinced Harriet to return to the metropolis, leaving behind her happy existence in the country.

This show of support was critical to the future of Lady Elizabeth, for Harriet's sister was about to make a truly brilliant match—always a delicate affair—and one that required the utmost concentration from all members of the family. It was much to her credit that she had begun the process all on her own far away from the usual haunts of those bent on marriage.

Lord Rokeby had fallen in love with her the instant he had laid eyes on her as she emerged from a shop in the village. He had stopped at the George and Dragon in Thornby for a bit of refreshment before continuing on to London and had been strolling idly down the High Street when he had nearly bumped into the most beautiful young woman he had ever encountered.

The modest blush that had risen to her cheeks and her demure reply, "It is nothing, sir. Think no more of it," to his profuse apologies only confirmed for him that her loveliness was matched by her gentle nature. He would not leave Buckinghamshire until he had presented himself to her bemused father and asked Lord Fareham permission to pay his addresses to his daughter.

Lady Elizabeth had hardly been able to believe her good fortune and she was extremely anxious that her appearance in society as the affianced wife of Lord Rokeby not be marred by the slightest murmur. It was this concern for his happiness and reputation that had led the customarily mild-mannered young woman to issue an ultimatum to her younger sister.

With a determined look in her gentle blue eyes and an obstinate set to her sweetly rounded chin. Lady Elizabeth had announced her intention of going to London: "And the entire household must come with me," she had concluded with a significant glance in Harriet's direction.

Harriet had loathed the idea of leaving Buckinghamshire, her work among the poor there, and her quiet rides through the countryside, but knowing how important it was for her sister that they all be with her, she had acquiesced with creditable good grace. She had almost immediately regretted this move, however, for the moment they arrived in London her father, a longtime widower and reclusive at best, had retreated to the library with his books. Aunt Almeria had been called in to act as chaperon, and although she was a bluestocking of fearsome reputation who could ordinarily be counted upon for intelligent conversation and a complete lack of interest in the ton, she had thrown herself with such grim determination into her role that she had little time for anything or anyone except the bride to be. Thus Harriet was left with no one to talk to.

There was her brother Charlie to offer her company when he could, but as a captain in the First Guards living in barracks in Portman Street, he had his regimental duties to attend to and Harriet was left a good deal to her own devices. Accustomed to an active and productive life in Buckinghamshire, she had chafed at the enforced ease of London and longed for something interesting and worthwhile to occupy her time and energy. Fortunately for her and her family such a situation had presented itself before she could fall into a truly outrageous scrape in her search for some way to be useful.

The whole family had been waiting for their carriage at the opera one evening when Harriet, idly surveying the crowd, had suddenly caught sight of a familiar face among the brilliantly dressed throng leaving the theater. "Bessie?" she gasped incredulously.

Harriet's sister, whose attention was caught by this outburst, followed Harriet's gaze. "Bessie who? I do not recall anyone among our acquaintance of that name."

Harriet frowned and scrutinized the young woman in question more carefully. At first glance she had very nearly resembled the daughter of a local farmer in Thornby, the village near Fareham Park, but a closer inspection gave Harriet pause. Certainly the young woman possessed the same gold hair, corn-flower-blue eyes, and fair complexion that had set lads from miles around competing for her favors, but she lacked some of the softness of features and the open guileless countenance of the farmer's daughter. This woman had a knowing look in her eyes and wore a modish gown of grass-green crepe with the sophisticated air of one born in the metropolis.

As Harriet was debating all this in her mind, the young woman happened to glance in her direction. Her eyes widened and her full red lips formed an 0 of surprise as her eyes fell on Harriet. Quickly she turned away and began to head in the opposite direction, but it was too late.

Certain that her first impression had been the correct one and that the young woman was no other than Bessie Lopcombe, Harriet began to make her way purposefully toward her. It was extremely difficult for either of them to make any progress, the entrance being thick with opera-goers, but Harriet was less hampered by the crowd than was her quarry and she soon caught up with her.

"Bessie!" She panted, grasping the girl's arm. "Whatever are you doing here?"

The girl's face wore a curiously unreadable expression and Harriet, realizing that she must sound rather rude, hastily continued. "I mean, I am delighted to see you, but rather surprised. I had not seen you this age around the village, but now here you are safe and sound and I am very pleased at that." She stepped back to survey the young woman. "And not only are you safe and sound, but quite dashing as well."

This praise, however, provoked the oddest reaction from Bessie herself. Blushing she stammered, "Oh please. Lady Harriet, do not mention it to anyone. You must tell no one ..." Then, catching hold of herself, she stopped, gulped, tossed her head, and continued in a tone of false bravado, "That is, I am very well, thank you, but my companions will be missing me. I must be going."

She made as if to leave, but Harriet, her suspicions aroused by this sudden shift in attitude, laid a hand on her arm. "Stay a minute, Bessie," she begged. Then, in her characteristic, and what her family considered to be disastrously forthright, manner she shot a penetrating look at the uneasy Bessie. "I suspect that there is more to this than meets the eye. Something is amiss and I certainly cannot help you unless you tell me everything. Now what is it?"

No proof against the interest and concern in Harriet's eyes, Bessie dropped the brazen air of sophistication as quickly as she had assumed it and once more looked like the simple farmer's daughter that she was underneath the fashionable clothes she wore. " 'Tis nothing for you to concern yourself over, my lady," she began cautiously.

"But I wish to concern myself, Bessie," Harriet responded stubbornly.

There was no resisting Lady Harriet Fareham when she got that look in her eye and that determined set to her chin, Bessie thought. The entire village of Thornby knew that took well enough and it meant Lady Harriet was not to be dissuaded. Bessie had seen it when Harriet had snatched a whip from a villainous-looking tinker who was beating his horse unmercifully and another time when some of the boys had been taunting Ben, the blacksmith's simple son. That look meant that Harriet had seen a wrong she was bound to right and the rest of the world be damned.

"Very well." Bessie sighed. "But London is not like Thornby, my lady. You must be careful of your reputation, for no one here will care that you are Lady Harriet Fareham and you will be scorned by society if you concern yourself too much in my affairs."

"What ever are you saying, Bessie? If something is wrong, why naturally I shall concern myself."

"No! You must not." It was Bessie's turn to look obstinate. "See how people are already staring at us? You must not be seen with me."

Harriet glanced around. There appeared to be some truth in what Bessie said, for indeed, some of the town beaux who had been leaning idly against the nearby pillars of the porte cochere were regarding them with some amusement, and her elder sister, who had cast a nervous glance in their direction was tugging on the sleeve of their brother Charlie. "This is all the purest nonsense, Bessie. Why should we not be seen together?"

Bessie heaved an exasperated sigh. It appeared that Lady Harriet had not the least idea of what she had become or of her reasons for being at the opera. "It is not seemly, my lady. You are a lady and I... I work for Mrs. Gerrard as one of her, her..."

At last comprehension dawned in Harriet's eyes, but the stubborn set of her jaw remained. "We are old acquaintances, Bessie," she replied firmly, "and surely there is nothing wrong in old acquaintances discussing times past with each other, unless"—Harriet paused as she was struck by a sudden thought —"unless I am keeping you, er, from someone."

Bessie smiled tremulously. Lady Harriet had never allowed the prejudices of society to influence her actions even back in Buckinghamshire. She should have known that Harriet would retain that uncompromising attitude even in London. The lady was forthright and kind to a fault and Bessie's blue eyes filled with tears at the memories of home that came flooding over her. "No, my lady, you are not, but truly I must be going."

Observing Bessie's genuine distress, Harriet did not press any further, but she was not about to give up. Something disastrous must have befallen the girl and Harriet was not going to sit idly by when presented with such a situation, not if she could help. "Very well, but we shall talk more. What is Mrs. Gerrard's direction?"

Bessie's hand flew to her mouth. "Oh no, my lady, I could never—"

"Very well, then you must call on me. We are in Berkeley Square you know," Harriet replied reasonably.

Bessie shook her head sadly.

Lady Harriet's brows snapped together in a mutinous frown. "If you do not provide me with Mrs. Gerrard's direction, why then, I shall just have to discover it myself."

Worse and worse, Bessie moaned to herself. Even more disastrous than calling at Mrs. Gerrard's would be Harriet's revealing her awareness of the existence of such a place in an effort to find her. It was common knowledge in the village of Thornby that Lady Harriet's bright red curls had always meant trouble, and it was proving to be just as true in London as it had been in Buckinghamshire. Bowing to the inevitable, she murmured, "It is in St. James." Bessie blushed vividly. "And it is known as Mrs. Gerrard's." If Harriet was shocked, she certainly did not show it. But then, Bessie reflected. Lady Harriet was never disconcerted by anything.

"Very good," Harriet replied briskly. "And a late morning call would not be an, ahem, inconvenience, I trust."

Again Bessie shook her head.

Having won her point, Harriet smiled warmly at the girl. "Then you may expect me tomorrow." Not waiting for a reply she turned and made her way back to her anxious family.

Chapter 3

"Harriet, whatever possessed you to accost such a person?" her sister gasped when she had regained the group.

"She is not just a person, Elizabeth," Harriet replied firmly. "That woman is Bessie. I cannot believe that you have become so fine you would have me ignore one of our neighbors."

Lady Elizabeth bit her lip. "No, of course I would not, but neither would I encourage such a public display of friendship for someone who is ... who is ..." Lady Elizabeth's gentle countenance was the picture of consternation. "Who is unfortunate," her sister responded dryly.

"I know, I know," Elizabeth moaned, "but must you become involved in everything, Harriet? London is very different from Buckinghamshire. Reputation is everything here and ..."

"And we must do nothing to cause distress to Lord Rokeby," her sister finished, not unkindly. "I am aware of that, Lizzie, I truly am, but you would not have me be unkind, would you?"

Lady Elizabeth's soft blue eyes gleamed with unshed tears. "No, of course I would not, but—"

"Never fear. Lizzie. I shall not do anything that will compromise you in the least, but I must get to the bottom of this. Bessie left Thornby without a word and now suddenly, here she is and it is as plain as the nose on your face that she is not particularly happy about it. Something"—Harriet pronounced in a voice that informed one and all that it was useless to argue with her—"must be done."

Lady Elizabeth abandoned her efforts to save her younger sister from disaster. After all, with Harriet's reckless disregard for the world's opinion, disaster would most certainly befall her sooner or later; it was merely a question of when.

At last their carriage pulled up and all discussion of Bessie and her situation was put to an end, but Harriet's busy mind did not stop struggling with the problem of making her way undetected to Mrs. Gerrard's. It was a difficult task, though not insurmountable. Even someone with Harriet's pluck and her fine disregard for conventions would not venture to drive down St. James's. So how was she to get there? She could hardly walk boldly up to the front door even if she did have her maid with her.

Harriet sighed and stared blankly out the window as the carriage made the turn onto the Strand. She supposed she could disguise herself as a maid, and if she wore a bonnet that hid her face ... her thoughts trailed off busy exploring possibilities. A bonnet. Yes, that was it. Suddenly she had a mental picture of a deep-brimmed bonnet worn by the women in the small community of Quakers near them in Buckinghamshire. The pious Quakers were always involving themselves in good works. Surely it was not inconceivable that one would concern herself with the welfare of the young women at Mrs. Gerrard's and the costume would be sufficiently concealing that no one would recognize Lady Harriet Fareham.

Harriet grinned to herself in the darkness. It might take some doing to create the typical Quaker bonnet, but her maid Rose was a very clever seamstress. Undoubtedly between the two of them they could contrive a suitable costume. One of her old morning dresses would do well enough stripped of its few flounces and with a kerchief covering her neck. It was of a sober dove gray and simple design, plain enough for any Quaker miss once the trimmings were removed. She and Rose would take their carriage to Bond Street as though they were shopping and then send the coachman home. From there they could hire a hackney or walk if need be, donning their distinctive bonnets at the last moment. The chief thing was to enlist Rose's aid.

As Harriet had expected, the maid was naturally averse to a project that would be the instant ruin of her mistress should word of it ever get out, but she was no proof against Harriet's pleas. "Think if it were you. Rose, all alone and unhappy here in London. Would you not wish me to do the same for you?"

Rose did not think that she would ever find herself in such a predicament. She had a fair idea what had happened to Bessie Lopcombe and you would never catch Rose Marden allowing any man, young or old, rich or poor to turn her head as Bessie had allowed the squire's son to do. What with her ripe figure and flashing eyes, Bessie had always been one for the men and look what had come of it? However, Rose could not resist Harriet's genuine desire to help, and it did not take long for her mistress to persuade her. After all, the maid reasoned, when Lady Harriet was set on doing a thing, she was set on it and no one could sway her. She would do it alone if she had to, and Rose's presence would at least keep her mistress from embroiling herself in anything too outrageous.

Having consented to help her mistress. Rose set about it in her customarily efficient way and they soon produced creditable approximations of Quaker garb for both mistress and maid.

In fact, everything proceeded so smoothly that Harriet did not really stop to consider the full implications of her project until she found herself standing one morning on the steps of Mrs. Gerrard's and wondering just what sort of unspeakable things she was going to discover behind the discreetly elegant door. By then, however, it was too late to reconsider. Drawing a deep, steadying breath and squaring her shoulders, she instructed Rose to ring the bell.

They waited what seemed to be an interminable length of time before the door at last was opened by a sleepy looking footman who goggled blankly at Harriet's crisp request to see Miss Bessie Lopcombe.

He thought for several minutes—a process that appeared to demand a great deal of work and much frowning on his part— but finally he led them into a small simply furnished sitting room at the back of the house.

Glancing curiously into the ornately furnished rooms as they passed by them, Harriet was rather surprised at the austere appearance of the chamber into which they were ushered. The furniture was comprised of a serviceable-looking desk and two chairs, as well as some bookshelves that looked to be filled with account books rather than any of the more lurid volumes she expected.

Mistress and maid sat quietly for some minutes not knowing what to expect until at last there was a rustle of silk in the corridor and a tall, handsome woman with remarkable green eyes, exquisitely attired in a morning dress of French striped silk lavishly trimmed with lace at the neck and wrists, swept into the room.

"How may I help you, ladies?" she inquired in a low, surprisingly cultured voice as she disposed herself gracefully behind the desk.

Considerably taken aback by the elegant bearing of someone she presumed to be the owner of the establishment, Harriet, who had planned to make vociferous demands for Bessie's immediate release, sat silent for a moment before responding. "I believe you have, er, I mean, that an acquaintance of mine, Bessie Lopcombe, ah, resides here."

The woman on the other side of the desk held herself very still as she subjected her visitors to a scrutiny so intense that Harriet was vividly reminded of unfortunate incidents in her schoolroom days. "And just what is the nature of your, ah, interest in Bessie?"

The tone was discouraging enough to make strong men quake, but Harriet refused to be daunted. Looking her interlocutor straight in the eye she replied firmly, "I am concerned for her welfare. She left Buckinghamshire rather hastily and nothing was heard of her until I discovered her at the opera last evening. Being an acquaintance, I naturally wished to call on her. She gave me her direction and here I am. Now, I would appreciate your apprising her of my presence."

Mrs. Gerrard, or at least Harriet surmised that it must be the Mrs. Gerrard Bessie had mentioned, continued to regard her unusual visitor thoughtfully. It was quite obvious that there was no dismissing her. One had only to look at the defiant tilt of the firm little chin to know that. It was equally obvious from the quietly expensive pelisse and bonnet and the proud bearing that she was a lady of quality, but what did she really want with Bessie?

A sly look gleamed in Harriet's eyes. "If you are unwilling to tell her of my visit, then I must assume that she is not here of her own free choice and naturally I shall take steps to insure that she is given that choice."

An ironic smile glimmered at this threat before the proprietress responded. "No. She is not here of her own choice, but then, none of us is." There was no missing the sarcastic note in her voice. "I see you look surprised. Do you honestly think that any of us would wish to do this if we had any alternative?"

Somewhat taken aback, Harriet stammered, "Why—no, I suppose not, but then I know very little of such things."

"Fortunately for you," her hostess remarked dryly. "Bessie was forced into this, er, choice by the time I met her. I merely assured her her safety and well-being by offering her my protection."

"Your protection?" Harriet echoed stupidly. Truly, things were not going at all as she had anticipated—not that she had known precisely what to expect, but she had certainly not thought to find that the owner of such an establishment would resemble a respectable merchant's wife more closely than she did anything else. Indeed, nothing so far had given the slightest indication that this discreetly elegant house lived up to its reputation as the most sought after seraglio in London.

Mrs. Gerrard continued to survey her unexpected visitor, her rather severe expression softening a little. Certainly the young lady seemed genuinely concerned for her friend from the country, and there was not the least hint of condescension or condemnation in her charming countenance, which expressed nothing so much as lively curiosity.

"Yes, protection. You see, I know what a difficult life one like Bessie's can be—disgraced and abandoned, forced to earn your own living. With no one to help you or to give you references there is but one thing to do and that leaves you at the mercy of your, ah, patrons. I give girls like Bessie a decent place to live and provide them with a background that is exclusive enough so that they only meet people of quality."

Something in Harriet's face caused Mrs.Gerrard to lean forward, her voice low and earnest. "I assure you, I found Bessie on the streets where she had been plying her trade for some time before I met her. But perhaps you would now like to speak with Bessie yourself." She reached up and gave the nearby bellpull a vigorous tug.

Bessie must have been waiting very nearby for the door opened almost immediately and she appeared in a demure morning dress of primrose jaconet with a delicate fichu and a lace collar trimmed with matching ribbon. She smiled shyly at Harriet as she took her seat. "Good day, my lady. I knew how it would be and I warned Mrs. Gerrard that you would visit."

Harriet leaned forward. "You look very well, Bessie. Are you happy here?" A shadow flitted across Bessie's face, but she answered readily enough. "Oh yes, my lady. We are all well looked after and Mrs. Gerrard is ever so good to us." The grateful look she directed at the proprietress left no doubt in the visitors' minds that Mrs. Gerrard at least had nothing to do with any unhappiness that Bessie might be suffering.

At this moment Mrs. Gerrard, apparently having assessed the situation to her satisfaction and concluding that Bessie's welfare was not threatened in the least by her surprise caller, rose and, smiling graciously at Harriet and Rose, prepared to depart. "I can see you are anxious to discuss old times and share news of mutual acquaintances so I shall leave you to yourselves. I shall have Jamison bring you some refreshment. Do ring for more if you wish." With that she closed the door behind her leaving the three women alone to a rather awkward silence.

Chapter 4

Harriet was the first to recover herself and she proceeded straight to the question in her customarily blunt manner. "Bessie, what ever are you doing in a place like this? This is not like you. Why I had thought you hoped to marry and have a farm of your own someday. London is quite a long way from that."

Bessie's eyes filled with tears. "And so I meant to, my lady. Do not be too hard on me, I beg of you. Things—things happen to a girl that... that change her mind, so to speak."

"What things?" Harriet fixed her with an intensely questioning gaze. After all, she was not one to sit idly by and watch someone give up her dreams.

"Oh, a girl grows up, learns about life, and changes her mind." Bessie gave a toss of her head trying for a tone of airy insouciance that failed miserably.

It did not fool Harriet in the least. Laying a gentle hand on the girl's shoulder she smiled sympathetically. "Now, Bessie, you know as well as I do that this is so much nonsense. Do tell me what went wrong."

"Oh, my lady," the young woman whispered. She gulped several times, fighting for control. "I was that much a fool. I— I mean it was ... it was Mr. George," she blurted out at last.

"What? Squire Westcott's son? I suppose I am not surprised," Harriet responded dryly. "He certainly has an unsavory reputation where women are concerned. But I am surprised at you, Bessie. I would not have thought you would fall for his empty promises."

"Oh no," Bessie hastened to assure her. "I did not. I would never believe such things and I have always done my best to ignore him though he does put himself in one's way, if you understand me."

Harriet nodded grimly. George Westcott's reputation as a predator on attractive young women was well known in the surrounding countryside. Certainly someone as pretty as Bessie would have caught his eye long ago. "Go on," she commanded grimly.

"It was last Midsummer's Eve during the festivities and I was walking home across the fields. He was drunk and kept asking me to give him a kiss. I tried to laugh it off and keep going, but he would not let me. At last he grabbed me. I managed to break free from him and I ran. I would have escaped because he was too drunk to chase me very far, but my foot got stuck in a rabbit hole. I stumbled and fell and he caught me." She finished with chilling finality. "There was nothing to do. I hoped and prayed that nothing would come of it, but—"

"But did you not tell someone, complain to your family?" Harriet interrupted.

"Who would I tell? What would they do? They could do nothing and they would blame me. Everyone knows what George Westcott is. They would say I should have known better and stayed out of his reach and the fact that I did not must have meant that I wished for it," Bessie replied simply. "When my father found out I was with child, he threw me out. What was I to do except what I have done? I could not work as a maid or a seamstress for I had no references, so I came to London. I was alone here on the streets picking up what work I could before I was too far along when Mrs. Gerrard found me. She guessed my story—it is common enough after all— and made me come home with her. I did sewing and light work for her until my time came and since then I have done all that I could to repay her for her kindness."

Harriet, who had sat quietly during this sad recital suddenly found her voice. "What... what happened to the baby?"

"It never drew breath, poor little thing. It was born blue and so tiny it was a mercy it died." Bessie replied softly. "Mrs. saw that I was well taken care of and that it got a proper funeral."

"Could you not have gone home then? Surely your father would have forgiven you."

Bessie shook her head firmly. "No. He said I was no longer a child of his and that I was never to see any of them again." The resignation in her voice made Harriet want to cry out, or, at the very least, murder both Bessie's father and George Westcott. "I miss the little ones,"

Bessie continued, "and I wish I could get word to my mother that I am well cared for."

"I will write a letter for you," Harriet volunteered. "I shall send it to the vicar and he can let your mother know that you are well."

"Could you, my lady?" Bessie's face lit up with a sudden smile. "It's knowing that they're worried—or at least my mother is—that is the hardest to bear. I could rest easy if I knew they were assured that I was safe."

"But what will become of you?" Harriet wondered aloud. "Surely you cannot continue on like this."

"It is not so bad, my lady. In many ways I am freer here than I would be if I were a maid in a respectable establishment. I have a room to myself and I have become friends with some of the girls here. Of course Mrs. Gerrard does try to find us other employment because she has only so much room and she is always trying to save others like me, but it is not easy discovering people who will take us. When you saw me the other night I was out looking for any poor girl who needed help. One of our girls had met a very kind gentleman who set her up as mistress of her own establishment in Marylebone so we had space for someone new and it was my turn to go look for someone."

Harriet was thoughtful for a long time. "This Mrs. Gerrard appears to be a singularly kind individual. I would not have expected that in such a person."

"Oh, she is indeed a most wonderful person." Bessie was quick to rush to her benefactress's defense. "She was a respectable governess herself until her master forced himself on her. The mistress found out about it and she was let go without a reference. She started Mrs. Gerrard's to help people like herself and here we are."

Harriet had listened to this tale attentively, but with a fair amount of healthy skepticism. There was a good deal missing and she was not so convinced as Bessie was of the purity of the proprietress's motives. Harriet was not about to leave until she had assured herself to her own satisfaction of Bessie's continuing welfare. However, it would not do to let on to Bessie that she harbored any reservations about the entire arrangement. "It is a most fascinating story. I find I should like to know more of Mrs. Gerrard. Perhaps she could favor me with a little more of her time."

Bessie jumped up. "I am sure she could. I shall fetch her and you will see for yourself." She hurried from the room leaving Harriet and Rose to their own devices.

"I don't like it, my lady," Rose began as soon as the door had shut behind the girl. "It is not a place for a respectable young lady."

"But that is just the point, Rose," Harriet responded reasonably. "In the world's eyes Bessie was no longer a respectable young lady when she came here."

"And you won't be either, if you continue to stay here," was the grim rejoinder. Rose opened her mouth to say more, but was cut off by the sound of someone at the door.

"Bessie informs me that you wish to speak with me further."

"Yes." Harriet straightened and composed her ordinarily sunny features into what she hoped was an impressively severe expression. "I am concerned for Bessie. This is no life for a young girl from the country. It may do very well for the others you have saved, but Bessie is not that sort of girl. She is different."

"My dear young lady, we were none of us that sort of girl. We are all different, but circumstances have forced us into a common situation." Mrs. Gerrard did not bother to hide the irony in her voice.

"But she cannot remain here. She has the rest of her life to consider." Harriet came to a sudden decision. "I shall take her back with me. She does not need references to do that. I shall make her my—" Harriet caught sight of the horrified expression on Rose's face and hastily amended her plan. "I believe I can find a place for her as an upstairs maid at Fareham Park."

"And force her to return to the scene of her disgrace?" Mrs. Gerrard inquired scornfully. "She would never consent to it."

"But she cannot stay here," Harriet protested. "With the exception of one unfortunate incident she is a respectable young girl and this is not, is not..."

"A respectable profession?" Mrs. Gerrard's voice dripped sarcasm. "And tell me, my dear young woman, how is it any less respectable than journeying to London every Season in search of an advantageous match? Is Bessie doing anything so very different from the young miss who contracts an alliance with a man she barely knows and whose desirability depends on the number of carriages and amount of pin money he can provide her? Are the young women showing themselves off at Almack's so very different from the ones parading their wares in Covent Garden?"

Harriet stared at the woman on the other side of the desk. She had never precisely thought of it in those terms, but now that she did, she had to agree that Mrs. Gerrard did have a point. Certainly Harriet herself had been disgusted during her first Season by the girls who spent their days dressing and flirting in an attempt to catch the interest of the most eligible parti. She had been appalled in particular by the bevy of beauties who had thrown themselves at one man who was so ill favored and lacking in charm that only his rank and an income of thirty thousand a year recommended him. Yes, it had been the very venality of the ton that had made her resolve never to participate in it again, yet here she was in London, much against her own wishes, constantly being forced to be on her best behavior—always a struggle for Harriet—simply because her sister was bent on making her own brilliant match. At least Elizabeth seemed to be genuinely fond of Lord Rokeby, but Harriet had occasionally wondered whether she would have been quite as fond had he not offered her the possibility of being the wife of such a highly respected husband and mistress of such a fine estate.

But then Harriet had never been able to understand Elizabeth's relish for the role of wife and mother. For Harriet marriage did not offer inducement attractive enough to assume so many added responsibilities or to give up her own independence. True, married women were accorded a greater degree of freedom than a single young lady, but not enough to tempt Harriet into spending the rest of her existence with some man who would consider it his right to order her life. Now that she thought about it, Harriet realized that Mrs. Gerrard's assertions did not seem so very farfetched. "I suppose that there is some degree of truth in what you say," she conceded slowly, "but the woman who marries is at least securing her future in society while your girls are subject to the whims and tastes of their, er..."

"Patrons." The establishment's proprietress finished for her. "That is so, but at least my girls have some control over what they earn which is more than can be said for a wife. Besides, I do try my best to make sure that they advance in their profession if they cannot find employment elsewhere that will outlast their, ah, more transitory charms."

"And what constitutes advancement in the profession?" Harriet wondered aloud.

Helen Gerrard shot a quick, suspicious glance at her visitor, but saw no hint of condemnation in the dark blue eyes, only curiosity. "A generous patron who sets one up in a house of one's own and takes care of all the annoying expenses of life," she replied. "I see you are skeptical. Believe me it is quite possible. It was just that sort of arrangement that allowed me to do what I am doing today—running a business instead of selling myself and, I hope, helping others along the way."

"But that is still—" Harriet began.

"One can make it a life of one's own," Mrs. Gerrard responded fiercely. "My girls have been taught to make sure that they use their compensations—whether they be jewels or carriages, or finery—to make themselves financially independent. Some of them remain mistresses to this day. Some of them have used their money to purchase their own shops. Some of them do as I do and put their earnings in the consols, but we all of us are working to make sure that we can take care of ourselves and never fall victim to the prejudices of society again."

Struck by the passion in the woman's voice, Harriet studied her as she spoke. In spite of herself and the unpleasant suspicions she had first harbored toward the mistress of the establishment, she liked what she saw. There was character in the straight, dark brows and finely chiseled features, pride in the way she carried herself and in the air of confidence that surrounded her. She was a person who had lived through a great deal. One could sense that in the depths of understanding in the brilliant green eues and the alert, observant expression. Yet she had survived it all, whatever it had been, and had even prospered if the fine quality of her clothes and the furnishings in the house were any indication.

Harriet could not help feeling drawn to the woman. Here was someone who had led a life so different from her own, but who appeared to share with Harriet the same desire to be mistress of her own fate. Suddenly, even before she knew what she was about, Harriet found herself saying, "I would like to help you if I could."

"What?" Helen Gerrard snorted. "How could you possibly help me?"

Harriet colored. Accustomed to being more intelligent, more forceful, and more daring than those around her, she was not used to being dismissed so scornfully, but she took it in stride. If nothing else, she possessed a sense of humor, not to mention a lively appreciation of the ridiculous and she did see how absurd it must appear for a member of the ton, albeit a reluctant one, to be offering assistance to a person whose existence most of Harriet's acquaintances would not even be aware of, much less acknowledge. But Mrs. Gerrard's outright incredulity challenged her to prove herself and Harriet had never been one to resist a challenge. She was determined to show this amazingly capable woman that she too was a person who took charge of her own life, thinking and acting deliberately and independently instead of slavishly accepting the role society had decreed for her. "I could teach." Harriet spoke with a quiet resolve that caught the older woman up short.

Mrs. Gerrard stared. The chit was actually serious! There was something about the look of steely determination in those dark blue eyes and the set of her chin that made the proprietress believe her. "And what would you teach that could possibly help my girls?" The words were skeptical, but the tone of voice was softer now.

Harriet squared her shoulders. "For one thing, I am a gentlewoman and though I am disinclined to do so, circumstances beyond my control require me to mingle with the ton. This allows me to help you in two ways: firstly, I can teach your girls to act like ladies which is always valuable when one is wishing to become a maid or even a ... a companion to a fashionable gentleman; and secondly, I can possibly provide references for those of your girls who wish to go into service. Beyond that I could help your girls to learn to read and do their sums—skills they will always find useful no matter what they do."

There, that should wipe the doubting expression off the proprietress's face and make her see that Lady Harriet Fareham was not just another milk-and-water miss with no thought in her head but the next gown she was to wear. Why she wished to prove herself to this woman Harriet no idea, but she did.

And apparently she had, for a slow smile swept across Mrs. Gerrard's rather severe features, allowing Harriet a glimpse of charm beneath the competent exterior. "Perhaps you can be of some assistance," she acknowledged carefully. Her brows drew together in a thoughtful frown. "But why would you wish to?"

Why did she? Harriet considered carefully before replying. Her response to Mrs.Gerrard had been almost instinctive and thus very difficult to articulate. She felt that she wanted to help more than she actually understood why she wanted to, and it was a moment before she could marshal these impulses into thoughts or words. "I am not precisely sure," she admitted honestly, "but I think it is because I find being a female rather confining myself and I, at least, am possessed of an independent income left to me by my mother. Moreover my father is too interested in his studies to interfere in my life. This gives me a degree of freedom not available to other young women, but even I am not as free as my brother and father are, for example. But I know of no other female who is allowed to live as I do and enjoy the independence I do. Most of them are forced to find a man to take care of them and look after them. In return for this they must subject their wills to their husbands'. So many women are at the mercy of men who are anything but kind to them. You appear to offer protection to some women who have suffered the most. Even more importantly, you appear to be trying to insure that such a thing does not happen again. I believe that women should be mistresses of their own lives." Harriet grimaced ruefully. "And until now I have not met another woman who agreed with me on that except my Aunt Almeria who avoids the question altogether by burying her head in her books and ignoring the world as much as possible."

Mrs. Gerrard listened intently, scanning the vivid face in front of her. Her visitor's voice rang with the strength of her convictions. It was clear to see that she had given these matters a good deal of thought. It was also clear that this was a passionate nature longing to express itself in worthwhile endeavors. She smiled. "Very well then. I suggest we put your thoughts into action. If you will agree to instruct my girls in their letters and show them how to go on, I shall be most grateful to you. I promise you, you will feel most rewarded by all that you can do for them. Assuredly I have felt so for these past several years. Now I think it high time you return home before your family becomes too concerned with your whereabouts. Though I feel certain they are accustomed to your independent ways I would not want them to worry unduly. If you can arrange to visit us perhaps once a week in the morning, we would be most grateful."

With that Mrs. Gerrard rang the bell for the footman, who appeared with more alacrity than he had when they first knocked on the door. If he was curious as to the identity of this unusual caller, however, he gave no sign, having been well trained in discretion by the mistress of the establishment.

Chapter 5

And so it was that Harriet became a regular visitor to one of the most select bawdy houses in all of London. If Harriet's family had not been so preoccupied with other things they might have wondered at a sudden interest in the modistes of Bond Street being demonstrated by a person who hitherto had only one requirement for her wardrobe—that it be comfortable.

However, Lord Fareham was far too busy rendering translations from the medieval texts he had managed to acquire for his burgeoning library, and Elizabeth's thoughts were all of balls and routs and proving herself worthy to be called Countess of Sandford as she dragged the reluctant Aunt Almeria all over London in pursuit of this goal.

Charlie, though he called in Berkeley Square whenever he could, lived in the barracks with the rest of his regiment and was occupied with regimental duties and therefore was not around enough to notice that something havey-cavey was going on with his younger sister. And Rose, though she did not approve of her mistress's visits to a house of ill repute, was too loyal to Harriet to betray her secret, besides which she was loathe to do anything to upset Lady Harriet's newfound interest.

Anyone who cared to could see that Harriet's visits to Mrs. Gerrard's brought her a great deal of satisfaction. She had lost the restless air that reminded Rose of a caged lion she had once seen at a traveling show. Now she spent a great many hours poring happily over volumes of educational theory from the Edgeworths' Practical Education to Keyne's On Classical Instruction to the latest edition of Thomas Smith's book on teaching, which she rejected as being too mechanical.

These volumes were all very stimulating, but nothing seemed to apply to her particular case so Harriet was compelled to come up with her own ideas. At last she decided upon employing a combination of advertisements from The Times and articles from La Belle Assemblée and Ackermann's as supplemental texts to Thomas Smith's reader that would capture the interests of her pupils.

Having heard from Bessie a thorough catalog of Harriet's many talents, chief of which was a burning desire to eradicate any injustice, real or perceived, her pupils greeted her gratefully, if skeptically, the first morning she appeared clutching a stack of newspapers and fashion plates. Harriet's true identity had been kept secret and she was simply introduced as Miss Harriet, a gentlewoman who had taken a serious interest in the ladies at Mrs. Gerrard's.

These ladies, attired in the most modest gowns they could find, greeted her in a sitting room at the front of the house, which had been arranged to approximate a schoolroom, with rows of chairs facing a small table at the front. To be sure the voluptuous paintings of nymphs gaily cavorting in forest glades and scantily clad marble statues placed in a corner here and there afforded an atmosphere that was in distinct contrast to the soberness of the gathering, but no one appeared to think it at all strange.

Noticing the blatant skepticism in the faces assembled before her, Harriet discovered herself to be rather nervous. It had seemed such a good idea at the time, but now, confronted with these young women who had been betrayed by so many people thus far, she began to doubt herself. However, an encouraging nod and a bright smile from Bessie, seated at the back of the room, made her square her shoulders and plunge in.

As Harriet explained what she planned to do and showed them the newspapers and the fashion plates she intended to help them read, she felt a stirring of interest and hope among her prospective pupils. "Oooh, miss, you mean I could even tell what them words means?" a saucy-looking raven-haired girl gasped, her dark eyes sparkling with sudden enthusiasm.

"Yes," Harriet responded with more assurance than she actually felt. "I am also going to teach you to speak like ladies so that gentlemen of the first stare will not be ashamed to be seen in public with you, and I shall start by saying those words instead of them words." Realizing how pompous she must appear, Harriet frowned. "Oh dear. I do sound altogether too much like a schoolmaster already. I apologize. What is your name?"

"It's Fanny, miss," the girl responded, suddenly shy now that the lady was actually paying attention to her.

"Well, Fanny, it may seem rather unreasonable for me to tell you to say those instead of them when it is quite obvious that I can understand perfectly well what you mean, but I assure you that it makes a difference to the rest of the world and people will treat you ever so much better if you learn to speak properly. I shall do my best to help all of you understand how to do that, though I expect my task will be an easy one because Mrs. Gerrard assures me that you are all very bright young ladies, which I can see for myself. Before we begin I would like to know a bit about each of you. Let us start with Fanny here and proceed around the room giving your names and telling me what you would like to do if you could do anything in the world."

"Anything, miss?" Fanny's eyes were wide with astonishment.

"Anything." Harriet responded firmly.

Fanny thought hard for a moment. "I would like to have my own shop in a nice little village somewhere, a village just like Bri ..."—she stumbled over the name that was too painful to reveal, then caught her breath and continued—"but never mind, a nice little village where I could sell all sorts of things and people would come in and chat with me."

The wistful note in her voice made Harriet's heart ache for the girl. She was so lovely and looked so worldly, yet she longed for the simplest of things. In that moment, Harriet caught a glimpse of just how isolated and how lonely these girls' lives truly were and she became even more determined to help them.

As she listened to them, Harriet's wish to teach Mrs. Gerrard's ladies soon expanded mightily into a burning interest in them and their lives. One by one she listened to their tales— all sadly similar— of seduction and betrayal. Over the course of a few lessons she came to know each one of the girls, her hopes and her dreams, and each time Harriet left Mrs. Gerrard's she did so with renewed resolve to help each one gain her wish.

It was only by exercising the greatest restraint on her part that Harriet did not call at Mrs. Gerrard's every day, armed with her educational materials, but she knew that such frequent disappearances from the Fareham residence in Berkeley Square would arouse the suspicions of her family. Furthermore, as Rose carefully pointed out, the girls did have work, other than their lessons, that commanded their attention. So she was forced to confine herself to fewer visits than she would have liked in order to insure that she could continue her work undetected and undisturbed.

Now, with the unforeseen appearance of the insolent gentleman who had caused her such aggravation, even these few precious hours a week with Mrs. Gerrard's ladies, as they called themselves, were threatened.

Harriet had comforted herself with the thought that perhaps the unknown gentleman was not a regular visitor and therefore would not reappear to annoy her further. A few discreet questions posed to her pupils at their next session confirmed this. None of them had ever seen the man before the morning he had erupted into their schoolroom.

"And we would certainly not forget a top-of-the-trees gentleman like him," Violet, one of her most promising students, had responded slyly. "Would you like us to discover more about him?"

Harriet's brusque, "No. I have not the least interest in such a vulgar person," fooled no one. However, beyond exchanging knowing glances with each other, the girls pretended it had.

What the girls refrained from mentioning to Harriet was that the gentleman they now knew as Lord Chalfont, though he had been unknown to them before his appearance in the schoolroom, had become a frequent caller after his encounter with Harriet. He had been only a little less circumspect in his inquiries as to the identity of the enchanting instructress than she had been.

After Lord Chalfont's initial reappearance Bessie had assembled the girls and lectured them thoroughly. "Now we will not tell Miss Harriet of this lest we cause her alarm. She does not need to know that Lord Chalfont has been asking after her." Bessie's tone was decidedly fierce as she had laid down the law to her fellow students.

"Yes, but what if he is courting her?" Violet had piped up. "He is such a handsome gentleman and a lord besides. What is the harm in throwing them together?" Violet had done a little investigating on her own and Lord Chalfont's title, his ancestry, his income, and his properties were known to one and all.

"Miss Harriet is a lady who has a most superior mind and she does not intend to waste it on such foolishness," Bessie had pronounced loftily. "She is dedicating herself to higher things than hunting for a husband and you would do well to remember that, Violet."

"Very well." Violet had agreed meekly enough, but she had not entirely given up. She had seen the way the sparks had flown between Lord Chalfont and Miss Harriet during their first encounter and she knew enough to recognize two people who were drawn to each other, even if it seemed to be in mutual dislike. If Miss Harriet had not been so very pretty and so ready to challenge his presence, Lord Chalfont would never have teased her the way he had. And if Lord Chalfont had not been so very dashing he would never have been able to provoke her in the first place. Miss Harriet simply would have ordered him out of the room or rung for Jamison to show him the door, but she had not.

Violet chuckled to herself. Oh yes, there was something between the two of them all right; it just wanted a little encouragement, and she, for one, was going to give it any encouragement she could. For all that her mind was on higher things, Miss Harriet was too attractive and too lively a person not to have a handsome man like Lord Chalfont looking after her.

Though Lord Chalfont had become a frequent caller at Mrs. Gerrard's, he missed Harriet's next visit. It was by sheer bad luck that the auction of the Duke of Morley's beautifully matched grays required his presence at Tattersall's the next time that Harriet was due to appear at Mrs. Gerrard's, and thus she was allowed to hope that his presence the first time had been an unfortunate accident and nothing more.

In fact, Harriet had almost succeeded in putting the disturbing gentleman completely out of her mind when he appeared the week after that looking far more alert than he had been at their first meeting.

His unusual amber eyes were more focused and there was none of the redness that indicated a night of carousing, but the same sleepy smile lurked in their depths as, calmly taking his place at the back of the class, he held up a package. "I have brought my own book this time." Without further comment he proceeded to unwrap his parcel and, to Harriet's considerable astonishment, pulled out the very reader she had been using.

She could have sworn he had been too castaway at their first encounter even to remember her presence at all. Quite obviously she had misjudged the man. He was more determined than she would have given him credit for, but what was he determined upon? That was the question. Harriet was not about to give him the satisfaction of letting him see her surprise. "Very well." She acknowledged his presence with the briefest of nods. "Then you, sir, may begin where we left off."

She was testing him, the little witch. Well, she would see that the Marquess of Kidderham was no empty-headed Bond Street beau. Alistair grinned and opened to the page on which they had concluded the lesson he had last attended and began to read.

The wretch! He remembered exactly where they had left off at his last visit and he was taunting her with it. She was not going to let him get the better of her. No one got me better of Lady Harriet Fareham, especially not some worthless tulip of the ton. Fuming silently Harriet allowed him to continue for a few minutes before interrupting. "Thank you. Now I believe it is Fanny's turn." She directed a significant look at Fanny, hoping me girl would be clever enough to follow the gentleman's lead without letting on that the class had met since he had last been there. She had no intention of letting him learn when and how often they met.

Alistair eyed the teacher speculatively. Little as he was accustomed to dealing with those of the Quaker faith, he did know that they addressed each other as thee and thou, something which this attractive young woman definitely did not do. He also believed Quakers to be rather modest, humble folk. There was nothing the least bit humble in the haughty air the pretty instructress adopted toward her newest pupil. Her short, slender frame was stiff with outrage and she made no attempt to disguise the hostility in her tone.

Alistair grinned. She was a taking little thing with huge dark blue eyes, a slight dusting of freckles across her pert little nose, a determined set to her delicately sculpted mouth, and a riot of red curls framing her face—pretty rather than beautiful—but she was definitely no Quaker, of that he was now quite certain. If she was not a Quaker, then who was she? She was obviously someone who did not want to be discovered at Mrs. Gerrard's, of that one thing he was sure.

Alistair leaned back in his chair examining her in a more leisurely manner. Her graceful movements and cultured accents as well as her proud carriage proclaimed her a lady, and a lady accustomed to commanding the respect of those around her. Oh, she was gentle and encouraging enough as Fanny stumbled over a word and he could see from the way her students responded that her kindness and interest in them had won their trust. But the flash in her eyes whenever they fell on him and the resolute lift to her chin left him in no doubt as to the strength of her character. She was not someone who allowed herself to be influenced by others, and he, Alistair, was most decidedly affecting her, he noted with satisfaction.

Well versed in the ways of women. Lord Chalfont could see that she was seething under the rigid calm she was so desperate to maintain. Her cheeks were delicately flushed, and the rise and fall of her bosom under the demure muslin kerchief that covered it betrayed her agitation. Lord Chalfont smiled broadly and chuckled to himself. He hadn't had such fun since he had sold out and returned to England.

Unbidden, the image of his betrothed rose before him and he thought of the contrast she afforded to this young woman. Forever cool and calm, the Honorable Alicia De Villiers never allowed herself to become the least bit discomposed. In fact, now that he stopped to consider it, Alistair realized that she never reacted to anything, certainly not to him. He hastily banished all thoughts of his prospective wife as he concentrated on the expressive face of the young lady in front of him. He liked the fire in her eyes and the passionate undertones in her voice. Yes, he definitely liked all of her, even the mystery surrounding her—a mystery that he intended to solve or his name was not Alistair Julius Augustus Chalfont, seventh Marquess of Kidderham.

There was no denying it. The intruder assuredly had an effect on her, Harriet grimly admitted to herself as she struggled to regain control of her breathing. She could not understand it in the least. After all, she had grown up the constant recipient of her brother Charlie's teasing, and this gentleman, lounging back in his chair, arms folded across his broad chest, was no more provoking than Charlie ever had been, at his most irritating. Long ago she had mastered the trick of ignoring even Charlie's most exasperating behavior, but she was not having any noticeable success where this man was concerned. All her standard tactics were of no avail. Harriet was still uncomfortably conscious of those tawny eyes fixed so steadily on her, the unnerving smile that hovered around the mobile mouth, the lines of amusement etched in the deeply tanned face. Oh, he had an effect on her all right. Furthermore, he was well aware of it and, what was worse, he was thoroughly enjoying it.

With a supreme effort, she forced her mind to attend to the matters at hand. "That was excellent. Fanny. Just be sure to pronounce each word slowly and distinctly. You have a tendency to speak hastily and all the sounds become jumbled together. The more carefully you speak, the more people are likely to listen to you."

Harriet could not help glancing in the direction of a hastily muffled cough from the back of the room. It was a mistake. One dark brow shot up and the gentleman grinned in a way that very nearly overset her. She tossed her head and continued. "Now Violet, do carry on."

Somehow, though she was not quite sure how, Harriet managed to get to the end of the lesson for the day without further incident. After the cough, the gentleman remained quiet, offering no further provocation beyond his intense scrutiny of her as she listened to the others performing their readings.

At last every girl in the room had recited and Harriet was free to go. Hastily she donned her bonnet and pelisse and hurried toward the door, but it was too late. The intruder reached it before she did and effectively blocked her escape as, leaning one broad shoulder against the doorway, he offered to conduct her to her carriage.

"That will not be necessary," Harriet snapped, thoroughly exasperated. She wished for nothing more than to leave her tormentor behind, but there was no way of getting past him without indulging in an unladylike shoving match which she was not about to do.

Taking pity on her, for after all he had done his best to provoke her, Alistair at last relented. Stepping aside to let her pass, he murmured apologetically, "I do beg your pardon. I am behaving badly when what I really wish to do is to convey my deepest admiration to someone who has the courage to involve herself in the lives of those less fortunate than she, to sympathize with them and to help them."

That stopped Harriet more effectively than blocking the doorway had. Her eyes opened wide as she gazed up at him in astonishment. For once the mocking smile was gone. Not a trace of guile showed in the handsome face. The amber eyes were warm with appreciation, and the tone of voice was sincere rather than teasing. Her anger evaporated and she was left with nothing to say. "Why—why, thank you," she stammered, mesmerized by the expression in those amazing eyes.

Then, realizing that she was gawking up at him like a perfect ninny, she blushed furiously, ducked her head, and hurried out to the waiting carriage. What was wrong with her she wondered as Rose closed the door behind them and she leaned back against the cushions. Ordinarily she was never flustered. She had managed to ignore the rude heckling of the stranger in her classroom, yet when he had spoken kindly to her she had fallen to pieces. You are turning into a ninnyhammer allowing someone to overset you like that, Harriet, she scolded herself. Shaking her head at her own weakness, she resolved not to let such a thing happen to her again.

Chapter 6

Meanwhile, the disconcerting stranger was subject to his own unsettling reflections. The blush had thrown him as it transformed the feisty little Quakeress from a tigress into an adorable young woman. Those eyes, so dark a blue that one could drown in them, had stopped him dead in his tracks. Their overriding expression had been one of surprise, but underneath that was intelligence and curiosity. Truly the force of her character was reflected in their sapphire depths.

Alistair had encountered many people in the course of his varied and colorful existence and he had gazed into the eyes of countless women, but he could not recall ever before having felt that he was seeing so much of the person behind them. In fact, he was so struck by the thought that for some moments he completely forgot his intention to follow her and discover more about her.

Rousing himself from his reverie he rushed to the outer door, but the carriage had disappeared from view. Blast! For an experienced soldier he was making a very poor job of attaining his objective and learning the identity of the fair teacher at Mrs. Gerrard's.

He would just have to keep patronizing Helen Gerrard's elegant establishment until he did discover who the Quakeress was. Lord Chalfont grinned at the memory of Kitty sprawled seductively across the bed this morning as he had bid her good-bye and headed downstairs. Not for her the lessons being taught in the opulently decorated sitting room. Kitty was not the least bit interested in bettering herself. "I like my life the way it is," she responded simply on being questioned about the entire project. "Not that Miss Harriet isn't as kind a lady as one could hope to meet—offering to help us and all, but I don't wish to be helped. I like what I do." She grinned saucily at him.

"And you do it so well too." Alistair chuckled as he traced the outline of one dark curl draped provocatively over a plump breast.

"With a gentleman like yourself, sir, it is a pleasure." Kitty's eyes drifted hungrily across the broad chest covered with tight gold curls and down to the flat stomach. She sighed with contentment. She was indeed fortunate. Lord Chalfont was so skilled a lover she sometimes felt as though she should be paying him instead of the other way around. "Now with the others it takes more art."

"Oh?"

"Yes. Take, for example. Lord Sherburne—an ugly little man if there ever was one, and so shy. That wife of his is as cold as a block of ice. I saw them together at the opera once. She is handsome enough, but so prim and proper she could freeze the blood in your veins. Poor man. No wonder he comes here where he can find a bit of warmth and comfort."

At her words the vision of Alicia's coldly perfect features and flawless complexion rose before Alistair, but he banished it as quickly as it had come, focusing instead on Kitty's entrancingly full lower lip which gleamed deliciously as she ran her tongue slowly over it. "He is most fortunate to have you, Kitty, to, ah, warm him up."

"I know." Kitty smiled. "I am very good at what I do." She reached for him. "And I could be very good to you again, my lord."

"Thank you." Alistair grabbed his shirt, buttoning it hastily. "I have a mind to see what this Miss Harriet can do."

Lord Chalfont had enjoyed his night with Kitty very much indeed and in addition she had been able to offer him a little more information about the elusive Quakeress. The girls of Mrs. Gerrard's had been told that she was to be called Miss Harriet and nothing more. She came once a week on Tuesdays and was helping the girls to learn to read so they could better themselves and would not be forced to depend on a livelihood in which they were valuable only as long as their youth and beauty lasted. Kitty, whose mother before her had plied the trade, had chosen her profession, but she was unique among Mrs. Gerrard's ladies. Most of the others had had it forced upon them by unfortunate circumstances and they longed for nothing more than to find a way out of it. Not only had Miss Harriet promised to teach them to read, do sums, and speak and act like ladies, but she had also offered her assistance in finding them positions as maids or shop girls when they had mastered their lessons.

Kitty appeared to have the utmost confidence that Miss Harriet would be able to accomplish all of this. "For she has a fearful amount of energy, that one," Kitty averred. "Why already Fanny is giving herself airs and talking like a lady, not to mention forever practicing her lessons. She is constantly poring over those fashion plates Miss Harriet brings in—says Miss Harriet is going to find her a place in a fine establishment on Bond Street or maybe a position in a shop in her village."

"Ah." Absorbed in tying his cravat, Alistair had barely been listening to her idle chatter, but his ears had pricked up at this information. "And which village is that?" Undoubtedly a person as forceful as Miss Harriet would be well known in any village she frequented and, if he did not miss his guess, she was probably a member of some rather influential family whose principal seat was in the village's vicinity.

"I do not know. Fanny did not say, just that Miss Harriet knew of one. And she also has a friend who might need Violet as a nursemaid. Violet is ever so fond of children and was, I believe, a nursemaid before the master of the house got her with child. She was desperate to have the baby in spite of everything, but the poor little thing was born dead. Which is all to the good if you ask me for Violet was in dreadful condition when Bessie found her, so thin she was nothing more than a bag of bones."

"This Miss Harriet of yours seems to be nothing short of a sorceress if she can bring about all she promises," Lord Chalfont remarked idly as he shrugged into his coat which he had refused to let fit as snugly as the tailor had wished, insisting that he preferred his coats loose enough so he could don them without requiring the assistance of a valet.

"That she is." Kitty responded. "The girls fair dote on her for she is ever so quick and knows so much about everything, but she is not the least high in the instep."

"A most unusual female, in fact," the Marquess of Kidderham agreed as he glanced quickly in the looking glass to give a final twitch to his cravat.

That morning's little discussion with Kitty had only whetted his appetite for information about the fair schoolteacher and now, malingerer that he was, he had let her get away and lost his chance to discover her identity until next week. Shaking his head in disgust Alistair stepped out into St. James and headed toward his chambers. He had rather a full day in front of him what with his appointment to escort Alicia and her mother to the park and later to a performance of The School for Scandal.

Alistair sighed. His life was not his own any longer. Even as an aide-de-camp, subject as he had been to the orders of Wellington and the other commanders, he had possessed more freedom than he did now with what was expected of him as the future husband of an incomparable. Alicia was never openly demanding—she was never so ill-bred as to be that— she was merely serenely confident of the attention that was her due and expected nothing less from him. His duty was very plain however unstated. Sometimes Alistair wished she would come right out and order him around; then he would have felt at least a little freer to refuse her. As it was now, if he failed to respond with sufficient enthusiasm to some plan of hers, she merely looked pained and withdrew into a reproachful silence that made him feel a perfect beast for not leaping to fulfill her every wish.

Alistair shook his head as he turned the corner into Piccadilly. It was unlike him to indulge in such an orgy of self-pity. His responsibility was plain. He had a role to play that had been clearly laid out for him since infancy and now it was time to play it. He had never been under any illusions as to what was expected of him and he had always been one to honor his obligations. Buck up man, he admonished himself severely, you have never been one to complain about what life has in store for you. You will do your duty like a man. Stop dwelling on any misgivings you might have, and make the best of it.

And thus it was, fortified by this bracing little speech to himself that he was able to ride alongside the De Villiers' barouche that afternoon with all the proper attentiveness required of a fiancé. In truth, he told himself, he was a lucky man. Alicia did look ravishing in a primrose carriage dress of jaconet muslin ornamented with bows of palest pink. A fetching Polish cap completed the ensemble that was responsible for envious looks cast in her direction by the occupants of several other carriages.

Alistair consoled himself with the thought that it was not so much the idea of Alicia that he was having trouble adjusting to as it was the whole concept of marriage and settling into a dull respectable life full of fashionable routs and dinner parties and the inevitable duties of a country landowner.

He could always depend on her to present an exquisite appearance and to behave with the utmost propriety, and he could count himself lucky that she did not chatter nor was given to gossip overmuch as so many women were. Few of his friends could expect to find so much in a wife and he should consider himself fortunate in the person who was the other half of the long-standing arrangement between the two ancient and distinguished families, the De Villiers and the Chalfonts.

The fact that Alicia lacked passion and enthusiasm was a small price to pay when he was gaining a wife who would always do him proud in the eyes of the fashionable world, while someone like the spirited Miss Harriet would continually have him on tenterhooks wondering which cause she would take up next and who she would dedicate herself to rescuing.

Lord Chalfont stopped his horse dead in its tracks and blinked in astonishment. Now where had the idea of Miss Harriet come from? But now that it was there he could not rid himself of it. Taking up the reins he resumed his pace and, glancing down at Alicia who sat serenely in her place acknowledging acquaintances now and then with a gracious nod, he pictured how Harriet would be, the sun gleaming on her red curls, her face bright with interest as she surveyed the passing scene. In all probability, however, she would not be sitting tamely in a barouche. From the little he had seen of that lively young woman, he was relatively certain that she would ride her own horse or drive herself in some dashing vehicle.

"... make Lord Chalfont known to Lady Kilbride." His fiancée's well-modulated voice intruded into Alistair's thoughts and he looked down to see Alicia waving to a stately looking dowager nodding to them from an approaching landau.

"So very happy, such an honor, so delighted for dearest Alicia," the lady gushed enthusiastically, inspecting him as critically as anyone he had ever seen examining the prime bits of blood at Tattersall's. Indeed, Alistair felt like nothing so much as a prize hunter or a beautifully matched team as they greeted Alicia's various acquaintances. Many of these were already known to him, but those who were not scrutinized him with the same degree of interest that one might accord a prized piece of livestock. At least, he muttered bitterly to himself as another barouche of town tabbies bade farewell to them, they appear to think she has done well for herself. I suppose I should be grateful for that.

But he was not. And Alistair returned to his quarters in Mount Street in a savage mood, thoroughly disgusted with humanity in general and the ton in particular. In fact, the only thing that truly cheered him was the prospect of returning to Mrs. Gerrard's next Tuesday to discover more about Harriet. At least she was a woman who demanded nothing from him except his absence. He chuckled at the thought of how very put out she had been when he had reappeared in her class and how very hard she had tried to hide it.

The marquess could hardly wait to put her out all over again, but he was forced to contain his impatience for an entire week as best he could, enduring tame excursions to Hyde Park at the fashionable hour and even tamer appearances at the plethora of balls and routs for which Alicia and her mother required his escort. Alicia's father, lucky dog, had managed to have himself urgently recalled to the country the moment he had established his women in London.

Thus it was that no matter how often Lord Chalfont frequented Brooks' or Tattersall's or Gentleman Jackson's in an effort to enliven his existence and balance out his days with a little companionship, time hung heavy on his hands. In a word, and for the first time in his life, the Marquess of Kidderham was bored, utterly, thoroughly, and completely bored, with no hope of relief in sight, except for next Tuesday.

Harriet, on the other hand, was finding herself to be far more entertained than she had hoped to be in London. By day she pored over all the educational texts she could lay her hands on, only allowing her sister to drag her for an occasional drive in the park. In the evenings she dutifully made her appearance at the various functions that Lady Elizabeth and Lord Rokeby were attending. Once there, she devoted much of her time and energy to conversations with various highborn ladies about their servants and the possibility that they might want a likely looking young person to act as an upstairs maid or an abigail for one of their daughters. One thing she was discovering, however, was the almost universal prejudice against pretty girls, no matter how bright or eager they might be.

"They are forever after the gentlemen in the house," one hatchet-faced woman, happening to overhear her conversation, complained shaking her head so vigorously that her diamond earrings danced. "You have no notion of the maids I have had to dismiss because they would throw themselves in my husband's path." She pursed her thin lips in disgust, an expression that only made her face appear even more like a hedgehog's.

It was with great difficulty that Harriet refrained from making a tart retort, for the woman's husband was well known as a lecher even among the gently bred ladies of the ton who had been forced to endure his lascivious looks and conversations full of improper innuendo. From the little she had learned at Mrs. Gerrard's, Harriet knew that things were more likely to be quite the other way around. A girl who depended on a life in service for her livelihood was far from inclined to risk soliciting masculine attention no matter how attracted she might be to the males in the household, for to be caught in a compromising situation almost certainly meant dismissal and the elimination of all prospects of similar employment elsewhere.

It took only a few conversations for Harriet to realize that the hope of placing Mrs. Gerrard's ladies in genteel households was impractical. She regretfully discarded it in favor of seeking out possible positions as assistants in the various establishments in Bond Street. This plan won a great deal of favor from Rose who very correctly pointed out that in order to accomplish anything in this direction her mistress needed some influence with the proprietresses of these establishments. "And the way to gain influence is to patronize these shops, my lady, which is something your wardrobe could use a great deal of," the maid pronounced firmly as she gazed critically at an outmoded walking dress she had pulled out for inspection.

Harriet wrinkled her nose. "I expect you are in the right of it, but I do find it so boring, what with the endless fittings and poking and prodding and everyone aghast if you are wearing a gown of the poplin that was popular last Season instead of the striped one which is the favorite during this one, or if one continues to wear a pelisse when mantles have become all the rage. I ask you, if something is comfortable and serviceable and shows no signs of wear why should a person not don it more than one Season in succession?"

"Oh no, my lady. That won't do at all, especially not here in London." Rose was horrified at such a heretical speech. "It would never do for Lady Elizabeth's sister to be considered démodé. Why what ever would Lord Rokeby think?"

"In my opinion we all give entirely too much thought to what Lord Rokeby thinks. If his regard for my sister is so tepid that he can be made to cry off because his future sister-in-law is a frump, then we are well rid of him. And he will be lucky if that is all I am," Harriet responded darkly. "If I have to mind my ways so carefully for fear of offending him, I am likely to do something far more outrageous than being seen in a quiz of a bonnet."

"No, miss, of course not." Recognizing from long experience the unfortunate circumstances that could arise from such a conversation. Rose hastened to intervene. "But you do owe it to the, ahem, your students to acquire some ascendancy over at least one or two of the fashionable modistes in order to be able to find positions. After all, you did promise to do what you could to help."

"Yeees," Harriet agreed slowly. "And in spite of my lack of a la modality, I am better acquainted with fitting rooms than I am with taprooms."

"Taprooms?" Rose's jaw dropped in astonishment.

"Yes. Lucy would like to own her own tavern someday and I have absolutely no knowledge in that area whatsoever. I do not have the slightest idea how to proceed in helping her."

"I should think not," the maid snorted in disgust. Sometimes she was inclined to agree with her mistress's sister, the angelic Lady Elizabeth, that Lady Harriet needed to be watched constantly. There was no predicting what sort of scrape she would get herself into. Her lively curiosity and generous nature were inclined to overcome her good sense more often than not, and if her family and friends were not careful to keep an eye on her, she could soon find herself in a compromising situation. In Thornby where she was well known and the family highly respected, this was not so likely, but here in the metropolis where one's reputation could rise or fall on a single word it was dangerous business indeed. Rose did her best to steer her mistress toward more acceptable lines of thought. "Now as to the shops you should patronize ..."

"But if that is what Lucy wishes to do, then—" Harriet would not be diverted.

"Then you can ask John Coachman to recommend her at the Rose and Crown in Thornby," her maid interrupted her. "Heaven knows he should have enough influence there. No one could be a more regular customer than he is. But you, my lady, must concentrate on the shops you know best such as Madame Celeste's."

And thus it was that Harriet, spurred on by her own noble projects, began to acquire such a distinct air of fashion that even her sister was moved to remark in considerable surprise one morning as Harriet was departing to spend a pleasurable hour among the books at Hatchard's, "What a charming ensemble! Is that the new Charlotte pelisse I saw described in Ackermann's? It is vastly becoming."

Indeed it was, for the green sarsnet shot with white brought out the rich red highlights in Harriet's hair, while the fullness at the back emphasized the gracefulness of her slight figure, making it appear taller than usual. "Er, yes it is," Harriet admitted sheepishly as she waited for the next remark that would compare it to her usual mode of dress or the drab gray gown she seemed to wear so frequently, but none was forthcoming. Beyond directing a quizzical look at her sister, Lady Elizabeth said nothing further, merely smiling as she continued, "I am so looking forward to Lady Walsingham's musicale this evening. Lord Rokeby has promised to take both of us. I do hope you will like it, Harriet. I feel certain you will find it more to your taste than you have found the affairs we have been frequenting of late."

Elizabeth directed an anxious glance at her sister. Much as she wished to please Lord Rokeby by making this Season absolutely perfect, she did not wish to do so at the expense of her sister. Harriet could be outrageous, to be sure, and Elizabeth did not always understand her sister's madcap behavior, but she knew it sprang from nothing more than high spirits coupled with a genuine desire to do good, and it never caused any really serious trouble.

Though Elizabeth herself was thoroughly enjoying the splendid routs and balls, she could appreciate just how tedious they must be for someone like Harriet who was never so happy as when she was galloping about the countryside around Thornby or reading the plethora of newspapers and journals to which she subscribed.

At least Charlie was home from the wars and here in London. As a child, Harriet had always been more her brother's playmate than her sister's even though she and Elizabeth were closer in age. Charlie had allowed his lively younger sister to follow after him on the condition that she keep up with him and not whine or cry when she hurt herself. They had made an odd pair as they tramped across the park in search of adventure, he so tall and fair and she so short, running along to keep up with his long strides.

Harriet had missed Charlie desperately when he had gone away to school and lived for his vacations when they could go off exploring. She had written him constantly while he was off fighting in the Peninsula and existed for his letters which, though briefer than hers, were packed full of exciting detail about the long marches across barren, inhospitable countryside or bloody clashes with the French. More than once Harriet had looked up from one of his travel-stained missives, her eyes shining with excitement and longing to remark, "Oh how I wish I were a man!"

In truth, Elizabeth knew Harriet found very little about being a

woman that interested her. She was utterly bored with the feminine
chatter of their neighbors in the country. She did not long for babies
or a home of her own, and at the local assemblies she was far more
likely to chat about farming or politics with her dancing partners
than she was to flirt with them. More than once she had been heard
to declare that she would rather have a brother or a friend like Charlie than a husband.

Yes, Elizabeth could see why London, aside from such obvious
attractions as the theater, the opera, and some of the historic sites,
would hold no attraction for her sister. Indeed, at the outset of their
sojourn in the metropolis Harriet had seemed to have lost her usual
sparkle. Of late, however, some of that appeared to have returned.
And now here she was dressed in the first stare of fashion. Was it
possible that she was at last becoming a young woman of the ton
instead of the sad romp she had always been? Lady Elizabeth admitted to herself that she would miss that, for outrageous though
she might be, Harriet inevitably enjoyed life to the fullest. She was
always brimming over with energy, vitality, and a natural warmth
and generosity that made her an interesting, though somewhat unsettling companion, and a loyal sister. For Harriet's sake, however,
Elizabeth hoped that this new look signaled an acceptance of the ton
because she wished to see her sister welcomed into that world and
appreciated instead of being labeled a bluestocking and relegated to
the lonely position of an eccentric.

It was not that Harriet intended or even wished to be at odds
with the fashionable world; indeed life would have been a great deal
pleasanter if she could enjoy it as her sister did, but she could not.
When Harriet had come to London for her first Season she had expected to be overwhelmed by the wit and charm of those among
the Upper Ten Thousand, but to her intense disappointment she had
discovered that the topics of conversation were no more elevated
in London than they were in Thornby. The women, though more
worldly than the squire's daughters and Lady Marcus and her two
daughters, were just as obsessed with who wore what and who had
danced with whom as the women of Thornby were.

To Harriet it appeared that society in London was no more enlightened or interesting than it was in Buckinghamshire, merely on a

larger scale and more competitive. She had been as bored by the ton's most glittering balls as she had been by the local assemblies.

For most young women, the prospect of catching a husband outweighed any of the possible discomforts of the Season— the fear of being left partnerless at a ball, the dreadful possibility of being labeled a quiz or, worse yet, a bluestocking, the agony of having the same goal as all the other young women, many of whom were more wealthy or more beautiful or both. None of these common afflictions had bothered Harriet in the least because she had never entertained any idea of finding a husband.

The first time she had revealed this singular point of view to her sister, Elizabeth had been shocked beyond words. For a full minute she had gazed at her sister, her blue eyes wide with horrified dismay. "Not want to be married!" She gasped. "What ever will you do?"

"I shall stay here and take care of Papa and keep house for Charlie until he marries and then I expect I can move to the dower house," Harriet had responded simply.

"But, I mean what will you do without a husband, how ever will you manage?" Elizabeth was unable to comprehend such a fate.

"I shall manage the same as I always have. I shall be me and not someone who is at the beck and call of another person who would probably be a great deal less intelligent than I am. Look at poor Lady Winslow, worn to a shadow by that worthless husband of hers who runs through her inheritance and does nothing but drink and ride to the hounds. And then there is the squire's wife who not only has to contend with her loutish husband, but with son who is a boor as well. And what have they gotten for their pains—the respectability of being married women. No thank you. I would prefer to be disreputable and free."

"But what about love?" her sister protested. "Do you not long for a handsome man to admire you and take care of you"—her eyes grew soft and dreamy—"and give you babies?"

Harriet snorted in a most unladylike fashion. "Love? Maybe someone could love you for you are soft and pretty and biddable. I am not at all like you. No, I think love is as unlikely as marriage for me. I am just not that sort of person. I am not at all romantic or silly like the Marcus girls, who are forever giggling over one handsome face after the other or filling their days with foolish novels from the circulating library and lessons in dancing, music, and anything else that they hope to use to catch a man."

"But how lonely you will be." Elizabeth remained unconvinced.

Harriet smiled. After all, her sister truly was concerned about her welfare and was trying to insure it the only way she knew how. "You will have lots of babies and I shall come and visit them from time to time and question them fiercely about how they are doing in their lessons as Aunt Almeria used to do. Remember?"

Elizabeth, who had never been much at schoolwork, shuddered. "Yes, I do. It is all very well for you to remember such things because you were her favorite. You were always so much quicker than Charlie and I despite your being younger. But you do not wish to be like Aunt Almeria with her scholarly meetings and—"

"Why not?" Harriet broke in. "She seems to be perfectly content with her life in Bath and never appears to lack for friends or amusement."

"No?" Elizabeth was uncertain. For some reason, she could not say quite what, Aunt Almeria's well-regulated way of life was not the one she would choose for her vibrant younger sister. To be sure, Harriet's keen mind, which she never made the least attempt to hide, made gentlemen uneasy more often than not. And her sense of the ridiculous, which endeared her to her family, did not have the same effect on dancing partners determined to cut a dash. Nor did her outstanding equestrian ability recommend her to men who were only too aware that she could best them at almost anything. Still, Harriet was warm and loving to her family, generous and concerned with the welfare of everyone in the neighboring countryside. No, she was not at all like Aunt Almeria, who was kind enough to her immediate family but had not the least use of anyone else, while Harriet was eternally curious about the lives and hearts of everyone she met.

She knew the names of all the members of the burgeoning Lopcombe family and all its various branches, as well as the ages of the blacksmith's children, which of them could say their letters, and who could be depended upon to carry a message. She visited the bedridden, listening to their reminiscences and complaints with a sympathetic ear, never missing the chance to help if she could. And she was fierce in the defense of those who had been done an injustice even if it forced her to behave in a most unladylike manner. No, Harriet was not like Aunt Almeria who, in spite of her burning intellectual interests and her loyalty to her brother's family, was a rather dried-up old thing. Harriet was passionate and lively, and ripe for adventure. Elizabeth could not envision her sister retiring tamely to Bath. In fact, she was not precisely sure what sort of life she pictured for Harriet, but she knew it would be as unusual as Harriet herself was.

Chapter 8

The very next day Harriet's life took a turn toward the unusual—too unusual even for her comfort. She had appeared at Mrs. Gerrard's in her customary manner and was conducting a lesson which was going extremely well. Violet was piecing together a few words from an advertisement in The Times and much to Harriet's delight the disturbing gentleman, who had been intruding entirely too often in her thoughts since their last encounter, had not appeared. It was during a pause while Violet was puzzling out the word engage that the silence was broken by a piercing scream. Harriet looked up in alarm as the first scream was followed by another and another.

"I think it's Fanny, miss." Lucy leaned forward listening intently. "Yes, it's Fanny."

Not in the least reassured by this, Harriet hurried toward the door of the schoolroom. "We must do something."

"But what?" Violet wanted to know. The girls sat there, curiously unquestioning and passive.

"I am not sure what, but we must. Follow me." And Harriet headed out the door and up the stairs without looking to see what effect her words had had on the others, if any.

They had. Led by Bessie, the others charged up the stairs hanging close behind her as Harriet stopped at the first door, listened, shook her head, and proceeded to the next. Finally at the third door she heard the crash of a chair being overturned.

That was all Harriet needed and she burst into the room which was the scene of considerable disarray. The bedclothes were torn from the bed and hurled all over the carpet, and there was a heavy brass candlestick flung to the floor in addition to the overturned chair. Over to one side by the fireplace, a swarthy man, his thick hands fastened around her throat, was shaking a half-clothed Fanny and shouting furiously, "You bitch! You'll do as I say and like it!"

"Unhand the girl, sirrah!" Harriet shouted as she sprang into the room. The gentleman did not even look up. "Get out of here, you interfering trollop," he snarled as he continued to tighten his fingers around Fanny's neck and she, too weak from lack of oxygen, stopped struggling, using her strength instead to gasp for air.

A red mist of fury rose before Harriet's eyes as she glanced around, desperately searching for a weapon of some sort to threaten him. Aha, she thought as she spied the poker. Grasping it firmly, she swung it with all her might against the assailant's right arm. She would have preferred to use it on his head, but much as she wished to kill the man, she knew that such an act would only bring trouble for everyone at Mrs. Gerrard's.

With a yelp of pain the attacker dropped his victim and turned his attention to Harriet. Fanny sank to the floor in a dead faint and Bessie, bolder than the rest who clustered in the doorway transfixed with horror, rushed to her side.

"So, you have spirit do you?" the man growled as he lunged for the poker. "There's nothing I would like better than to tame a little spitfire like you."

Gritting her teeth Harriet swung the poker again, but she was no match for a powerfully built man who was taller than she was. With one hand he grabbed the wrist that held the poker, pulling her toward him as he wrapped his other arm around her waist. "So you think you are a match for Sir Neville Fletcher, do you my pretty one. We shall see about that," he panted.

A wave of nausea swept over Harriet as his hot breath blew in her face and his fingers dug into her ribs. She tried to ignore the greedy look in his eyes as she fought for control. I must not faint, I must not faint she told herself over and over as she struggled in his grasp.

It was a terrifying experience. Harriet had always been strong enough to do anything she wished to, in fact had scorned those who regarded females as the weaker sex, but now she was fast beginning to learn that men, or at least this particular man, truly were a good deal stronger than women. She was powerless against her aggressor who was not only stronger than she, but larger. He seemed to be all over her everywhere. Her heart began to pound and she gasped for breath.

"Unhand the lady!" the words were spoken quietly enough, but there was a deadly menace in the cool voice. Both Harriet and her attacker stopped dead in astonishment and looked up as Harriet's unknown gentleman strode into the room.

"She is no lady, just a damned interfering trollop and this is none of your business, Chalfont," Harriet's assaulter snarled.

"It is the business of any gentleman to protect any lady. Now let her go."

For a moment, Harriet's captor remained still, uncertain as to what to do next. That second's hesitation was all her rescuer needed as he delivered a punishing left to the jaw which sent Sir Neville crashing to the floor at the feet of Lord Chalfont. Stepping over him without a downward glance, Alistair gathered Harriet's hands into his warm, comforting grasp. "Are you all right?"

Too stunned to speak, Harriet nodded dumbly, her brain in a whirl. To think that she would actually be glad to see her tormentor from the schoolroom! He had his arms around her shoulders now and they felt so strong and reassuring, but not as reassuring as the look of concern in those unusual amber eyes. If she had had her wits about her, she might have wondered what it was that made her instinctively trust and draw closer for comfort and protection to a man who heretofore had done nothing but tease her. But she was not thinking clearly. Reacting to her jangled nerves, she only knew what she needed and nothing else.

Gazing down into the dark blue eyes still wide with horror and disgust, Alistair gave her an encouraging smile. She looked so fragile and helpless now when just moments before she had been fighting like a tigress. She was a courageous little thing, his Quakeress, no doubt about that. He had arrived just in time to see the poker being wrested from her clutches and had had no need of the chorus of voices to tell him what had happened. Somehow he had known she would rush to the victim's defense without a thought for her own safety.

"What a little fire-eater you are to be sure. It is a good thing I arrived when I did or who knows what you would have done to poor Fletcher here." He prodded the inert gentleman on the floor with the toe of one gleaming Hessian.

Harriet gave a weak laugh. Some of the color had returned to her face and her breathing was coming more regularly now.

"That's my girl." Alistair beamed at her, relieved to see that she was more the thing now. He longed to do nothing so much as wrap her in his arms and hold her until the trembling, now detectable only as a slight tremor in the hand that pushed a wayward curl from her forehead, had completely subsided. But of course he could do nothing of the sort with the audience they had. "I am exceedingly sorry you had to have anything to do with Fletcher here. He is a very nasty piece of work." Lord Chalfont nodded in the direction of the man on the floor who was now sitting up and shaking his head groggily.

"That he is. And he is no longer welcome in this establishment," an imperious voice broke in.

Harriet looked up to see Mrs. Gerrard, framed by two brawny footmen, standing just inside the doorway. "Help him to his feet and see him to the door," she commanded. The two footmen leaned down, and each grabbing a shoulder of the unwelcome customer, helped him to rise. "I run a respectable house that caters only to gentlemen and you, sir, are no gentleman." Mrs. Gerrard turned on her heel and swept from the room leaving the others to gape after her.

The prisoner was the first to recover. "I'll see you ruined, madam!" he spat as the footmen led him to the door. "And you"—he shouted over his shoulder at Harriet—"I'll teach you to interfere in something that is none of your affair. You're a fighter. I like 'em that way, hot and fiery and all the better to tame." And he leered at her in a way that made Harriet's blood run cold.

"The welfare of another human being should always be the affair of another human being," Harriet shot back with a good deal more spirit than she was feeling. Instinctively she moved closer to her protector who again smiled comfortingly at her.

"Do not worry," Alistair reassured her, "I shall not let anything happen to you. Sir Neville Fletcher is a low, scoundrelly sort of fellow, but he only picks on those weaker than he is. He is not very good ton though he desperately tries to be, so you can be assured that he will do his best to keep quiet about an incident that does not redound to his credit. His reputation is unsavory enough as it is; he will not take any chances on its being made any worse. If he does make the slightest move to bother you in any way, you must call on me. I am Chalfont, by the way, and my lodgings are in Mount Street. You have had quite a day. No one else I know would have done such a brave thing, and I am honored to make your acquaintance. Now, may I see you home?"

Chalfont. Harriet's brain was in a whirl. Where had she heard that name? It sounded vaguely familiar, but she could not place it, certainly not at the moment when her thoughts were considerably disordered. She shook her head. "No thank you. I am quite recovered." Glancing around to see that the others, with the exception of her maid Rose, were all clustered around Fanny, she hastened from the room before Alistair knew what she was about. Her retreat was so precipitous that by the time he gained the street she and her maid were already climbing into the waiting carriage.

Blast! Was he never to discover anything more about the woman except that she appeared to be devoted to helping others, even at the risk of considerable danger to herself? How fierce she had looked even as Sir Neville forced the poker from her grasp. What a woman! She had been half the man's size and, from the look of horror and disgust in the depths of her eyes, had never been in that sort of situation before, yet she had fought gamely on, her cheeks burning with exertion, her lower lip firmly clenched between her teeth.

More than anything he wanted to take her home, to reassure himself that she was suffering no ill effects from the encounter, to promise her that he would personally see to it that she never had to see Sir Neville again. Actually what he wanted was just to be with her. She was so vital, so filled with an energy and purpose Alistair had not seen in anyone since he had left the army. In her presence he felt more like his old self—the bold and daring Major Lord Chalfont who had led his men into battle against incredible odds and delivered messages behind enemy lines, not the idle useless Lord Chalfont who had no other purpose in life than to escort the Honorable Alicia De Villiers from one ton event to another.

And now, even if he had known where and how to pursue his mysterious Quakeress he could not for he was due at the modest house in Hanover Square that the De Villiers' were renting for the Season. His betrothed had made it quite clear that his presence was expected not only for the requisite ride in the park and any entertainment she was attending that evening, but she also expected his escort on any other errands she and her mother might wish to accomplish. In particular she had mentioned that this morning she wished to discuss with him some patterns she had chosen for the refurbishment of the hangings in what was to be her new bedchamber and other various schemes she had dreamed up for the improvement of her new home.

Alistair let out a sigh of resignation as he began to make his way back to his chambers. There was nothing for it but to wait with as much patience as he could muster until the Quakeress's reappearance next week, if she did reappear. His heart sank at the thought that she might no longer visit Mrs. Gerrard's, but surely a woman who had exhibited such spirit this morning would not allow one unfortunate episode to deter her from her mission. No, not she.

In the carriage Harriet was also reliving the entire momentous scene and coming to the rather uncomfortable conclusion that the most upsetting thing about the entire episode was not the horrible way Sir Neville had behaved, but the surge of happiness and relief that had swept over her when Chalfont had come to her rescue. Harriet was not fainthearted and she had never before found herself in a situation she could not manage, so why now should she have been so relieved and happy at the glimpse of broad shoulders filling the doorway as he had stormed into the room? Even worse, why had she clung to him like a ninny even after he had summarily dispatched Fanny's attacker? More mystifying still was the lingering wish that he was still there with his arm around her, solid, safe, and comforting. She had never needed reassurance before, why should she suddenly long for it now, especially from someone who had done nothing before this but tease her, someone who was precisely the useless sort of rake and wastrel she despised?

Of course Harriet did not know for sure that Chalfont, as he had called himself, was a wastrel, but certainly someone who frequented Mrs. Gerrard's as much as he appeared to was not involved in much activity of a productive nature. And though it was well enough known even among the young misses of the ton that men did occasionally need to relieve their primitive urges at establishments such as Mrs. Gerrard's, Harriet did not like to think of her rescuer as doing such a thing.

Lord knows she was no prude—quite the opposite in fact. Elizabeth was forever being shocked by her younger sister's free and easy ways, her cavalier dismissal of society's intricate rules and regulations, her insistence on associating with people like Bessie, for example, regardless of their reputations. Why should she now be made uncomfortable by the fact that Mrs. Gerrard's ladies appeared to be on excellent terms with the man she had come to consider as her rescuer?

Enough. Whatever the reasons were, Harriet did not wish to dwell on them. Resolutely pushing all thoughts of Chalfont from her mind, she concentrated instead on how she was going to persuade Madame Celeste to take Fanny on as an assistant. In all probability, the best way to approach it was to have Fanny trim a bonnet for her or make up something that would show off the skill she claimed to have as a seamstress. Certainly after today she would be more eager than ever to leave Mrs. Gerrard's and find employment elsewhere.

The unfortunate incident had only strengthened Harriet's determination to help the girls find some other means of livelihood. In Harriet's opinion women in general were too dependent on men for their welfare, and the women who had no families to turn to should some man mistreat them, no friends to help them when times were hard, were at more of a disadvantage than the rest. This opinion, unfortunately, was not widely held, and Harriet was only too well aware that she was quite alone in her view of things.

Her sister and her schoolmates at Miss Drew's, the select seminary in Bath to which she had been sent to complete her education, looked upon men as their destiny and their salvation. Men, as husbands, were the opportunity for freedom from all the strict rules governing the conduct of a proper young lady. Men offered a woman an establishment of her own, a chance to repair the family fortunes or to improve her position in the ton.

In fact, Harriet's schoolmate, Alicia De Villiers, had summed up their collective opinions quite nicely one day when Harriet, the only girl not set wholeheartedly on marriage, had pointed out to those who were sighing over the handsome dancing master and the dashing heroes in the novels smuggled in from the circulating library, that women rarely married such romantic but uncertain people and were far more likely to wind up with the very dull but eligible son of long-standing family friends. Fixing Harriet with a scornful glance Alicia had pronounced in withering tones, "Harriet, you are a simpleton. A woman is nothing without a man." Certainly Alicia, who used her charms to entrance every male in her vicinity from the aged émigré who taught them French to the dancing master, and even the

vicar at the church where they attended service, took this philosophy
to heart as she used this power to her best advantage.

Harriet's outraged reply, "Well, this woman is going to be something without one," had merely provoked derisive laughter. It was
all very well for the young ladies at Miss Drew's Select Academy to
believe that once married they would be in command of ample pin
money and adoring husbands, but Harriet had looked closely at the
world around her and knew that things were otherwise more often
than not.

Her own father, though charming enough when he stopped to
notice anyone, was so wrapped up in his studies that he was oblivious to all else. From the little she could remember of her mother who
had died when Harriet was five, the Countess of Thornby had been
largely ignored by her husband, who often confounded her with his
absentmindedness and total lack of interest in such practical but
necessary aspects of life as rents, repairs, and the management of the
estate. In fact, when he did emerge from his fits of abstraction the
results were usually most disconcerting, if not downright inconven-
ient. Harriet vividly remembered times when her father had suddenly decided to take over the running of daily affairs. The consequences
were always disastrous, since he had no head for business and even
less for dealing with people from solicitors to servants. The end result was that he soon flew into a towering rage of frustration over
some rather everyday complication and retired, fuming, to his study.

Then there was the squire, a man as brutal and selfish as his son
was. Completely disregarding his wife and daughters except when he
wanted to be fed, he gallivanted about the countryside hunting and
drinking, with little regard for anyone else.

From what Harriet had seen, most men were somewhere in between her father and the squire, but in the main, all of them were
oblivious to the needs of women. Even her beloved Charlie was quick
to forget her when a mill, a war, or some other sort of male excitement caught his attention. Certainly Harriet had never come across
an approximation of the romantic heroes that the young women at
Miss Drew's dreamed about. Unbidden, the image of the man who
had just rescued her rose before her eyes. He had rushed to her defense in a manner entirely appropriate to the most romantic of he-

roes and had been as tenderly solicitous of her welfare as any of the men her schoolmates had sighed over. However his mere presence in a place such as Mrs. Gerrard's, rescue or no rescue, was a fair indication as to the unheroic aspects of his nature. Fortunately for Harriet's peace of mind, the carriage drew up in front of Madame Celeste's, putting a halt to further disquieting speculations.

The proprietress of that exclusive millinery establishment was delighted to see the young lady who had become such a good customer of late and who had a sister on the verge of becoming the Countess of Sanford. She was not quite so delighted, however, at Harriet's proposal to add to her workforce. "I would have to see her work, my lady," she demurred cautiously. It would never do to offend a patroness of Harriet's potential. "As you know, I run a most select establishment and I simply could not employ a seamstress who could not produce work of a most superior quality."

"I quite understand," Harriet reassured her quickly, afraid that it might occur to Madame Celeste to wonder where Harriet had encountered the young woman she was recommending. But the proprietress, who was really the erstwhile Sally Brimblecombe, an enterprising young lady from Dover who had acquired her French style and accent from her lover, a French chef to the Marquess of Moresby in whose household she had been an upper housemaid, was the soul of discretion who would never have run the risk of alienating such a generous patroness by questioning her.

"I shall bring you some of her handiwork the next time I come for a fitting. At the moment, however, I should like to see some designs for ball gowns as I have nothing to wear to the Countess of Rotherham's ball," Harriet continued, chuckling to herself at the absurdity of her taking an interest in any gown, much less a ball gown. But she wanted to keep the idea of Fanny as an assistant in Madame Celeste's mind and the best way to do that was to link discussions of Fanny to Harriet's expensive orders from the modiste. After all, Madame was a businesswoman above all else.

To be honest, Harriet was rather enjoying herself. One thing about masquerading as a Quakeress was that it gave one an appreciation for all the frills and trimmings available to the ladies of the ton. Holding up a piece of silver tissue over the white satin Madame Celeste had brought her, she surveyed herself in the looking glass and wondered irrelevantly what Chalfont would think of the prim little Quaker miss if he were to see her in a ball gown.

Thoroughly annoyed at herself for this absurd thought, Harriet pushed the unwelcome notion aside, concentrating instead on deciding what sort of project she should commission Fanny to do for the modiste's perusal. Perhaps she should ask her to do more than trim a bonnet. She had been immediately taken by the stylishness of Fanny's own garments which the girl had assured her were both of her own design and construction. It might be sufficient to bring in one of the girl's own gowns though they tended to be rather more daring than those customarily worn by the belles of the ton. Yes, that was it, she would commission Fanny to make something for her with the proviso that it be sufficiently demure for her to wear to church.

Her mind made up on that score, Harriet casually pointed to one of the figures in La Belle Assemblée and, holding out the tissue and satin in front of her again for a quick inspection, remarked, "Yes, I think I should like something like this in these materials." She drew on her gloves and headed toward the door.

"But, my lady, you have not settled on the trimmings! Would you like a flounce of French lace at the hem of the skirt or a rouleau of satin entwined with pearls? Do you wish the sleeve to be slashed or decorated with knots of ribbon?" The modiste was aghast at her customer's cavalier attitude.

"Whatever you think best. I trust your taste implicitly. Just inform me when you wish to do a fitting. Thank you." And with that breezy dismissal of a process that absorbed the entire lives of most of her fashionable peers, Harriet departed, leaving Madame Celeste and her assistant to wonder aloud at a young woman who could order a very expensive ball gown without the blink of an eye and who could remain so uninvolved in its creation.

"However she is always agreeable and such a pretty thing too— never in the least demanding, not like some." Miss Milsop, the assistant, rolled her eyes in the direction of a stout red-faced woman swathed in purple who was berating another assistant to the verge of tears.

"Yes. But why she must always appear in that plain gown when we have made her at least one delightful carriage dress, I do not know. At least her bonnet was more the thing," the proprietress replied, little suspecting that Harriet had been so immersed in thought over the recent incident at Mrs. Gerrard's that she had very nearly forgotten to exchange her Quaker bonnet for the more fashionable one she always carried in a bandbox.

Fortunately, Rose had caught her mistress at the last minute just as she was about to emerge from the carriage and enter the shop. "Oh, my lady, your bonnet!"

Harriet had smiled ruefully. "Too much woolgathering. Thank you. Rose." And she had hastily bent over to reach into the bandbox, hoping to hide the telltale blush that had crept up into her cheeks. It was bad enough for Harriet to be aware that her thoughts were dwelling entirely too much on the mysterious Chalfont who had rescued her, but she was bound and determined that no one else, especially the sharp-eyed Rose, should think that anything was amiss.

Nor did the mysterious Chalfont fade from her thoughts as the days passed. Harriet kept telling herself that her continued preoccupation with him was the natural response of a person trying to establish the identity of someone whose name was familiar but whose face was not by attempting to recall the context in which she had first heard of Chalfont. However, she was forced to admit to herself that she spent far more time remembering the mixture of admiration and concern in his amber eyes than she did trying to remember the precise circumstances in which she had heard his name mentioned.

Much as she wished to discover the identity of the unknown gentleman who had come to figure so largely in her thoughts, Harriet deemed it prudent to avoid appearing at Mrs. Gerrard's until she could be sure that it was entirely safe from further visits by Sir Neville. Consequently, she sent a note around to Mrs. Gerrard informing her of her decision. The proprietress's reply was gracious enough, but left Harriet in no doubt that her presence would be sadly missed by the girls who had come to look forward to their weekly lessons.

Harriet smiled as she read the reply. She too would miss their Tuesday morning meetings for she had come to feel very much a part of the lives of Mrs. Gerrard's ladies. Their stories of faithless suitors and unforgiving families made her prize all the more the freedom she was fortunate enough to possess. To be sure, society did not allow her the latitude it granted to her brother Charlie, He could go anywhere and do anything without thinking twice while she was confined to a few respectable occupations such as shopping, riding in the park, or attending ton functions and always in the company of a maid at the very least.

In fact, if it had not been for Charlie, Harriet would have been nearly suffocated by the boredom of her daily routine which was now devoid of the stimulation formerly offered by the lessons at Mrs.

Gerrard's. Charlie, however, knowing full well how his younger sister chafed at life in the ton, and thoroughly aware of her propensity for falling into a scrape when life became too dull, was careful to take her riding in the park as often as his guard duties permitted. A captain in the First Guards, Charlie was accustomed to a life of hardship and adventure in the Peninsula. Now suffering the tedium of mounting guard at Saint James's, he could sympathize wholeheartedly with his sister's frustration at the flatness of her existence.

Knowing Harriet's dislike for the tame pace maintained by those who rode in the park at the fashionable hour, he took Harriet with him for his early morning rides when the only occupants of the park were military men like himself bent on exercising themselves and their mounts.

It was during one such ride, on a remarkably fine morning, that the eyes of both brother and sister were caught by one rider in particular. Both man and horse were equally magnificent specimens. The gentleman, a man of soldierly bearing, was well over six feet, with broad shoulders and a slim waist, while his horse, a magnificent gray, was nearly seventeen hands and as powerfully built as his master.

"What a superb animal!" Harriet exclaimed and then caught her breath as the rider glanced in their direction. She should have known who it was the instant she laid eyes on the pair but she had been so taken with the horse at first that she paid little attention to the rider. Now that she looked more closely, however, she realized that there was no mistaking the blond hair and dashing manner of her erstwhile tormentor and rescuer from Mrs. Gerrard's. Hastily changing the subject she continued, "But no horse could be more splendid than my own dear Brutus. Do you not think his manners improved? Why now he hardly takes any exception to those nasty cart horses or the press of traffic in the streets."

But Charlie, who had also been regarding horse and rider with admiration, was not to be so easily distracted. "Yes, by Jove, they are a remarkable looking pair. Now where have I seen them before?" He reined to a halt and considered for a moment while his sister, in acute discomfort, pulled her hat down on her head and tried to look as unnoticeable as possible.

"Ah, now I have it!" he exclaimed with some pleasure. "He is one of Wellington's aides-de-camp. I knew I had seen him with the duke somewhere. I before that at the battle of the Pyrenees the gentleman's colonel declared a retreat. He refused to listen, jumped off his horse, grabbed his regiment's colors, and scaled the wall to get the infantry to follow him. His conduct must have impressed Wellington enough that he made him one of his aides. I must speak to him and tell him that I saw his splendid performance in the Peninsula." And much to his sister's dismay, Charlie headed his mount in the direction of the solitary horseman, while Harriet, ordinarily delighted by her brother's open and friendly ways, cursed him silently for being so forthcoming with someone to whom he had not even been introduced.

She reached up to jam her hat even farther down, but it was no use. The stylish creation had been designed to look particularly jaunty and therefore had barely any brim at all with which she could conceal her face. Even had she been able to accomplish that, nothing could be done about the red-gold curls that peeped out becomingly from underneath it. At any rate, she had no choice because by this time they had reached the horse and rider and her brother was greeting the former soldier in his usual ingenuous fashion."

"Hello, Fareham here. I saw you at the battle of the Pyrenees and thought you were a regular Trojan leading the chaps along like that. Saw you on the Peninsula—no mistaking a mount like yours."

If the rider was taken aback at being addressed so unexpectedly, he gave no sign of it, but scrutinized Charlie's uniform, then grinned and extended his hand. "It's good to see another military man, especially one who has the good fortune to be a soldier still. I am Chalfont. I remember you fellows in the Peninsula. The Guards were certainly in the thick of it at the end there. I am pleased to see that you came out of that carnage unscathed. But may I be introduced to your fair companion?"

"Oh, I beg your pardon." Charlie glanced around in some surprise to find his ordinarily friendly sister cowering behind him in what appeared to be a most uncharacteristic fit of shyness. "This is my sister. Lady Harriet Fareham. And you must be Lord Chalfont, Marquess of Kidderham, I believe?"

Alistair nodded as he bowed low over the gloved hand extended so reluctantly to him.

Her heart thudding, Harriet kept her eyes lowered demurely, hoping against hope that she was unrecognizable in her fashionable slate-gray riding habit and dashing high-crowned hat. It was a vain hope, quickly shattered by the rider's low chuckle. She looked up in alarm to see the amber eyes, alight with mischief, gazing at her with a wealth of significance.

She held her breath as Lord Chalfont opened his mouth to speak. What would Charlie say when he heard that his favorite sister had been a regular visitor at London's most exclusive brothel? Her brother was well known for his free and easy ways, but he would most certainly draw the line at this. It would definitely be the end to all her plans for Mrs. Gerrard's ladies and the only worthwhile thing she had found to amuse her in all of London.

"I am charmed to make your acquaintance. You must be most grateful to have your brother back home unhurt after his years fighting the Corsican monster." There was nothing in the marquess's voice or words that gave the least hint of their prior acquaintance. Even the closest observer would not have known that he had ever laid eyes on her before, much less come to her rescue in the most compromising of situations.

Faint with relief, Harriet let her breath out slowly. He was not going to betray her after all. Following his lead she replied with as little self-consciousness as she could muster. "Yes, I am delighted to have Charlie home, though I know he finds guard duty excessively dull after his exploits in the Peninsula and the recent events in Belgium." At last she dared glance up at him again. It was a mistake for he gave her a conspiratorial wink that very nearly overset her.

"We are all finding life rather quiet after the years spent campaigning," Alistair continued smoothly, and then he turned back to Charlie. "Tell me, were you at the siege of Bayonne or were you part of the group that chased Soult back to Toulouse?"

And with that, Harriet's presence was entirely forgotten as the two soldiers compared notes about crossing the Adour, foraging for food in the harsh countryside, and the unreliable nature of the Spanish troops. Though she could not help feeling the tiniest bit miffed at being so quickly and so easily forgotten, Harriet was happy to see Charlie enjoying himself so thoroughly.

It was also the first opportunity she had had to observe Lord Chalfont without his being aware of it. So immersed was he in the discussion of past exploits that she was entirely at liberty to examine the lean, tanned face with its high cheekbones and aquiline nose, the broad shoulders and powerful physique hardened by years in the saddle that quite set him apart from most of the men of the ton who seemed pale and soft by comparison. There was an air of command about him that she had not noticed before. He carried himself with the unconscious pride of a man who had seen a great deal of life and dealt with all of it—so very different from the men of fashion who were constantly on the alert, looking nervously around to see if anyone else had a better cut coat, a more intricately tied cravat, or Hessians more highly polished than theirs.

Examining him, Harriet was assailed with an odd breathlessness that had been troubling her ever since the latest incident at Mrs. Gerrard's. It appeared to come over her whenever she relived that scene—Lord Chalfont knocking down her assailant. Lord Chalfont with his arm around her shoulder studying her with eyes full of concern. And here was that fluttery feeling again as the sun glinted on the golden highlights in his hair, making him look like some Greek god astride that magnificent horse of his.

Harriet shook her head in an effort to clear her rapidly deteriorating mind. What had come over her? Ordinarily it never occurred to her even to consider a man's appearance. To her men were just men—exercising no more effect on her than women did. Now, however, all she could think about was what a singularly attractive man the Marquess of Kidderham was. Lord, she was no better that Alicia De Villiers and all the silly schoolgirls at Miss Drew's who sighed over every handsome face their eyes happened to light upon. What a lowering thought!

The marquess and Charlie were deep into a discussion of battle strategies, hashing out mistakes that had been made, rating the various commanders on their strengths and weaknesses and, in general, thoroughly appreciating the chance to talk over such things with another person knowledgeable about the bitter struggle that had been the Peninsular Campaign. As Harriet watched them conversing she thought how different Lord Chalfont appeared here in the park talking with Charlie than he did at Mrs. Gerrard's.

To be sure, he was no less attractive, but here he was all energy and animation while there, though he was interested enough to poke into her affairs, he did so with an air of lazy amusement, as though he had nothing particularly compelling to keep himself occupied. She had resented his teasing pursuit of her and his intrusions, until the last time that was, when she had been more than grateful for his presence. Now she understood the motivation behind his presence at Mrs. Gerrard's.

Put quite simply, the Marquess of Kidderham appeared to be bored and she, Harriet, had offered him a diversion of sorts. That was certainly clear enough now. Was his patronage of Mrs. Gerrard's merely the result of an active restless spirit forced to endure the dull and constraining world of the ton upon his return from the wars? If it were, then she could most definitely understand his presence there. After all, she had ended up at Mrs. Gerrard's herself for the very same reason, well, perhaps not exactly the same; after all, she was educating the girls and he was—Harriet did not care to contemplate what he was doing. But at least now she had a better comprehension of it all.

Harriet shook her head. What did it matter what he was doing at Mrs. Gerrard's? She could not fathom this compulsion on her part to explain away Lord Chalfont's frequenting of Mrs. Gerrard's. Why should she care whether or not he was a sad rake? The only men whose welfare was any concern of hers were Charlie and her father. How Lord Chalfont spent his time was immaterial to her.

But Harriet reluctantly acknowledged to herself that it did matter. Much as she pretended to be annoyed by Lord Chalfont's insistence on attending her classes, she could not help but admit that his presence added a good deal of spice to these sessions and, annoyed as she was at him, she did take some perverse pleasure in resisting all his attempts to disconcert her. For some reason she felt challenged by him and she simply could not help rising to that challenge. She had a sneaking suspicion that he felt much the same way about her.

It was this rather combative camaraderie that made her wish to think well of him, to believe that he was something more than a Bond Street beau, and it made her question her brother later as they rode home about the exploits of the Marquess of Kidderham.

According to Charlie, these were many and varied. "Now mind you," Charlie insisted on pointing out, "he never blew his own horn, but I was present at many of the engagements he mentioned and I know he was in the thick of it. You don't get made a member of Wellington's staff unless you have proven yourself."

Harriet listened carefully as he described some of Lord Chalfont's narrower escapes. Somehow she had known he was more than just an idle lounger of the ton who spent his days drifting from Tattersall's to his club to Mrs. Gerrard's. From the start Harriet had been conscious of a suppressed energy, a barely contained thirst for excitement. Perhaps it was because she was blessed—or rather cursed, for such characteristics were definitely not acceptable in a young woman whether she was in the center of the fashionable metropolis or rusticating—by the same traits in her personality that made it so easy for her to recognize them in someone else.

Yes, Harriet thought as she thanked her brother for escorting her to the park, there was more to the Marquess of Kidderham than met the eye. She had already seen several different sides to him: the careless, insouciant frequenter of Mrs. Gerrard's, the man sensitive enough to appreciate what she was trying to do for Mrs. Gerrard's ladies, the bold defender who had rushed in to rescue her from Sir Neville, the discreet gentleman who gave not the slightest hint that he recognized her as the instructress at Mrs. Gerrard's, and now, according to Charlie, a brave soldier and hero of the struggle against Napoleon.

Much as she had wished to, Harriet had never been able to dismiss the unknown gentleman from her thoughts entirely. Now she began to wonder if she could think of anything else, so frequently did he seem to appear in her life. No, she told herself resolutely, now that she knew his identity that was no longer to be the case. There was no further need for speculations about the Marquess of Kidderham and at the moment she had far more serious things to occupy her time, serious things such as finding suitable positions for Fanny, Violet, Bessie, and the others.

While Harriet was doing her best to direct her attention elsewhere, Alistair was very much enjoying concentrating all his on her. Lady Harriet Fareham! He smiled slyly. He had known all along that the fiery little schoolteacher was far too spirited to be a Quakeress—not that it was not a clever ruse, but it was totally out of character. Yet, as he considered it, Lady Harriet Fareham must feel as out of place in the world to which she had been born as she was in the persona she had chosen to adopt. She was no more the model of the self-effacing propriety expected of a fashionable young miss of the ton than she was a modest and demure Quakeress.

Alistair's thoughts turned involuntarily to someone who was the epitome of the successful belle—his fiancée. Nothing could be more different from Alicia than a girl who cared enough about the welfare of women whose existence she was not even supposed to recognize that she offered to help them while risking that most precious of possessions, her reputation. Why Alicia would have swooned at the mere mention of Mrs. Gerrard's ladies and here was Lady Harriet, not only teaching them and involving herself in their lives, but endangering her own by coming to their defense.

He had sensed she was special from the moment he had seen her at the head of her unusual class, her expressive little face alight with interest and enthusiasm for the task at hand. He had been doubly intrigued by her successful resistance to all his attempts to disconcert her. There was no doubt that Lady Harriet possessed the courage of her convictions in abundance. Lord Chalfont had never before encountered a woman like that. He found it oddly attractive and most definitely intriguing. Unlike the other members of her sex, Lady Harriet improved upon acquaintance. Instead of rapidly becoming bored with her as he had with every other woman he could remember, no matter how beautiful or how seductive, he only wanted to know more about Harriet with each encounter.

The marquess chuckled to himself as he recalled the pleading expression in the dark blue eyes fixed so intently on him when they met one another in the park. She had been desperate to keep her secret and he had been delighted to oblige. The look of gratitude that had flooded across her face when he treated her as a perfect stranger had sent a wave of pleasurable warmth over him that the most seductive glances of raving beauties, the most languorous sighs of practiced flirts had failed to inspire in him. There was something about sharing this particular secret with this particular woman that made Alistair feel closer to her than he had to many women with whom he had enjoyed far more intimate relations.

He grinned remembering how she had looked in the awkward Quaker bonnet whose deep brim all but obscured her face, except for the unruly red curls that escaped in spite of her best efforts. The jaunty little hat she had been wearing today was much more the thing to set off the glorious hair and the vivid little face, as was the tightly fitting riding habit. She was a tiny thing, but perfectly proportioned, with a figure that quite took his breath away, now that it was no longer hidden by an unfashionably outmoded gown and numerous shawls.

Lady Harriet was not precisely beautiful: her face was far too full of character, her mouth too generous, her chin too determined for the classic loveliness required in an incomparable. But there was something infinitely appealing about the deep blue eyes fringed with thick dark lashes, and the straight little nose with its sprinkling of freckles. One felt upon looking into those expressive eyes that one was looking into her very soul—a soul of great depth, and so unlike the many vain and shallow ones he had come across lately. Yet there were tiny crinkles of laughter at the corners of her eyes that showed that Lady Harriet Fareham, though she might throw herself into life's difficulties headlong, did not take herself so seriously that she could not see the humor in it all. Having met Lady Harriet, one was unlikely to forget her, and, if one were Lord Chalfont, one wanted to know more about her.

Fortunately, now that he knew her true identity, the marquess could arrange to encounter her at functions she was likely to attend.

He grinned. Who knew, now he might actually enjoy accompanying Alicia and her mother to the ton parties she insisted he escort her to. Lord Chalfont felt oddly cheered as he finished his morning ride. All of a sudden he had something to look forward to besides brief sessions on Tuesdays with a mysterious Quakeress. Knowing that Lady Harriet was part of the world he now inhabited made that world, which hitherto had been so excruciatingly dull and uninspiring, at least palatable. Now Alistair could be reasonably certain he would see her again in the near future. Certainly he intended to ride in the park every morning on the off chance that her presence there this morning meant it was part of her daily routine.

In fact it was not in the park but in the Countess of Rotherham's splendid ballroom where Alistair next laid eyes upon Lady Harriet Fareham, thus fulfilling her quickly suppressed wish that he could see her in the ball gown Madame Celeste had created.

The gown was so exquisite that even Harriet's sister had been moved to comment on it. "Why, Harriet, you look vastly elegant this evening," she had exclaimed in some surprise, for it was rare that her sister put any effort into her appearance, especially for an event such as the Countess of Rotherham's ball, which was sure to be a sad crush. Elizabeth was particularly delighted with Harriet's appearance this evening since she and her betrothed had hatched a scheme to introduce Lady Harriet to Lord Rokeby's longtime friend Lord Aylward, Earl of Woodbridge. The Countess of Rotherham's affair had seemed the appropriate place and Elizabeth was highly gratified to see her sister in such looks.

Indeed Harriet was rather pleased with the effect herself as she had surveyed her image in the looking glass one last time before departing for the countess's imposing mansion in Grosvenor Square. The silver tissue frock exquisitely fitted over the clinging white satin slip lent her gown distinction, separating it from the requisite white attire of the young miss, and softening the effect of her hair which generally appeared so deep a red as to be seen as carroty. The silver lent an air of sophistication and sparkled against the creamy skin of her neck and shoulders. The short waist, combined with elegantly draped skirt made her appear taller than usual, while the heavy trimming of silver roses along the hem weighed it down enough so it revealed the long slim lines of her body when she moved.

Pearls at her neck and threaded through her hair completed the ensemble, and Harriet grudgingly admitted to herself that she did look rather fine. Even though she usually could have cared less about her appearance it was nice to see the admiration in her sister's eyes. Lady Elizabeth, with her golden hair, blue eyes, and rosebud lips was always the picture of feminine grace and beauty and Harriet had spent a lifetime feeling somewhat unkempt, slightly awkward, and always less attractive than her exquisite older sister. Therefore, she could be pardoned for the small surge of satisfaction that rose within her as she thought that for once she was equal to Lady Elizabeth in a la modality.

This heady feeling was not dispelled as they mounted the impressive marble staircase at the Countess of Rotherham's. Even Lord Fareham, pressed into service for the occasion, blinked in surprise as he became aware of his youngest daughter's presence. "Have you done something different, Harriet? You look very fine," he commented vaguely.

"Why, thank you. Papa," Harriet replied with considerable astonishment. She must be looking splendid indeed if the sight of her was enough to shake her absentminded father out of his usual abstraction.

"Harriet always looks most presentable." Aunt Almeria sniffed, coming to her niece's defense. "Just because she is a sensible young person who does not waste her life on the fripperies of the moment does not mean that she does not have a neat appearance."

Lord Fareham had retreated again into his customary fog, but Harriet shot a grateful look at her aunt—not that she agreed with her. Aunt Almeria's concept of a pleasing appearance was vastly different from the rest of the world's, but Harriet appreciated her support.

At the moment, however, she wished to be more than presentable for they had reached the top of the stairs and the first person Harriet caught sight of as she surveyed the glittering crowd in the enormous ballroom was Lord Chalfont. Even in the crush of people he towered over the crowd, his proud, unself-conscious bearing setting him apart as much as his prodigious height and athletic physique. Disgusted at herself for doing so, Harriet strained to see his companions. He was most definitely escorting someone and Harriet was consumed with curiosity. What sort of woman would command the attention of the dashing, not to mention rakish, Marquess of Kidderham?

At last there was a break in the press of people around them and Harriet was able to distinguish a tall, elegant, dark-haired woman who bore herself with the natural assurance of a great beauty. Alicia De Villiers! Harriet would have recognized the regal bearing of her old schoolmate anywhere. Now she knew where she had heard the name of Chalfont before. Alicia had been forever boasting of the great wealth and impeccable lineage of the man she had been betrothed to since birth. Alistair, Julius, Lord Chalfont, seventh Marquess of Kidderham, Harriet murmured to herself; she had heard it often enough. To be sure, this long-standing arrangement had not kept Alicia from trying to reduce every male in her orbit to slavish admiration, from the dancing master to the gardener, but it had given her an air of superiority to have her future so brilliantly assured when her less fortunate schoolmates had to look forward to the struggle of making a suitable match.

Of course Harriet had not paid much attention to Alicia's frequent enumerations of her betrothed's many enviable attributes, but she did recall one afternoon when Alicia, after discussing his vast estates and the extremely favorable mention of his lordship in the most recent dispatches, began to describe his person in terms that would have been excessive for a Greek god.

Harriet had been able to stand it no longer. "Do stop, Alicia. No one is such a paragon and well you know it. Why I am beginning to think he is naught but a figment of your imagination." The others had laughed and Alicia had stomped off in high dudgeon, but now Harriet admitted grudgingly to herself as she observed the gentleman in question, that her former schoolmate's imagination had not been so overheated as Harriet had thought it to be. The Marquess of Kidderham was a man among men, even apart from the exalted rank and enormous fortune that were so important to Alicia.

Fortunately Harriet was able to banish these unsettling reflections from her mind as they moved slowly along to be greeted by their hostess who had warm words of welcome, especially for Elizabeth.

"Rokeby. Such an estimable man, my dear. You are fortunate indeed! Young women have been throwing themselves at his head this age. But it is easy to see why he renounced his bachelor status when he met you—so lovely, the perfect countess for him." Elizabeth flushed with gratitude at these words, and then, catching sight of her fiancé as he made his way toward them, she flushed even more deeply with a glow of happiness so apparent to everyone that even Harriet, as skeptical as she was where love, romance, and marriage were concerned, could not help feeling the tiniest pang of envy.

Chapter 12

But these feelings were quickly dismissed as Harriet realized with dismay that Lord Rokeby was not alone. At his elbow and a few paces behind followed a gentleman with a pleasant open countenance, a man who in many ways resembled Rokeby himself. He was of medium height, and medium build with brown hair, regular features, elegantly but quietly dressed in dark evening clothes with nothing distinctive about them to set them apart. In fact, there was nothing in the least remarkable or even interesting about him. A hideous premonition seized Harriet and she darted a suspicious glance at her sister who had the grace to look somewhat self-conscious as she greeted the two men.

"My lord." She smiled fondly at her fiancé. "How fortunate that you found us so quickly in such a sad crush. Lord Aylward, what a pleasure it is to see you again. I would like to make you known to my sister. Lady Harriet. Rokeby tells me that you keep a magnificent stable and that you are to have a horse running at Newmarket this year," Elizabeth continued, darting a meaningful glance at Harriet. "My sister is a most devoted horsewoman."

"Do you have a horse in London, then. Lady Harriet? I myself find it rather tame after the countryside and there is so little space really to give one's mount its head." Lord Aylward spoke in a tone of such pleasant interest that Harriet had no choice but to respond with equal enthusiasm in spite of her urgent wish to strangle her sister. So, not content with dragging her to London and ton parties, Elizabeth was now going to throw respectable prospects in her way. She would not have it! Inside, Harriet was positively fuming, but she managed to keep her anger contained. After all, poor Lord Aylward was only an unsuspecting pawn in this game and he was perfectly harmless as he did his best to make conversation on topics that would be of interest to her.

Actually he turned out to be quite nice, and the only things that Harriet could truly find to hold against him was that Elizabeth so obviously meant for the two of them to become an item, that and the fact that compared to Lord Chalfont. Lord Aylward, seemed hopelessly dull.

However they chatted pleasantly enough about country matters. As the Earl of Woodbridge, Lord Aylward owned several large estates and was surprisingly knowledgeable about such things. He actually turned out to be more interesting to talk to than most men. In fact, Harriet might have enjoyed their discussion had she not been constantly aware of her sister's eyes upon her and the complacent expression in them as they observed Lady Harriet and Lord Aylward deep in conversation. Harriet even went so far as to allow the earl to lead her onto the dance floor in a quadrille, but it was with some relief that she returned to her party, hoping all the while that the gossips would not read more meaning into their conversation than there actually was.

Fortunately for Harriet, by the time the dance was ended, her brother had arrived. Charlie could always be counted upon to rescue her and to take a turn around the ballroom with her to give her a respite from conversing with or assiduously avoiding boring partners.

It was as they were making their way slowly around the perimeter of the brilliantly lit ballroom, chatting about an auction Charlie had attended at Tattersall's that morning that they very nearly bumped into Lord Chalfont, freed for the moment from his duties as escort while Alicia danced with the Duke of Staunton and her mother exchanged the latest on dits with her cronies.

"Ah, Fareham," he greeted Charlie with pleasure. "Did you purchase the hunter that caught your eye today? He was superb."

"Yes he was, and far too rich for my blood." Charlie grinned. "Buying him is one thing, feeding him would be quite another. What about you? I hear you have a place near Melton Mowbray, lucky devil."

"So I do. You must visit me there sometime. It offers one of the few rewards for being back in England and enduring this forced inactivity."

Lord Chalfont might have been speaking to the brother, but his attention was all on the sister. Lord she was a taking little thing! In that filmy shimmering material and with that vivid hair she looked like a sprite from some magical world, all bright energy and an intensity that made the other women in the room seem dull and lifeless. Alistair wanted to reach out and touch her and absorb some of that zest into his own jaded spirit.

The orchestra struck up a waltz and, without stopping to consider, Alistair offered her his arm. "May I have this dance. Lady Harriet?"

Now Harriet knew why she had endured the endless evenings at Almack's. Its august patronesses had given her permission to waltz and she was able to respond without hesitation, "Why thank you. I should enjoy that."

They were silent at first, gliding around the floor enjoying the music and the motion together. Lady Harriet was certainly a tiny thing, the marquess reflected as he laid his hand on her slender waist. Her head barely reached to his shoulder and the hand in his felt like a child's, but there was a firmness and strength in the slim body and she moved with the grace and control of a born athlete whose life had been spent in rigorous exercise.

A slight cough awoke him from his reverie and the marquess looked down to discover a distinct twinkle in the blue eyes fixed on him. "Ah, er, I beg your pardon. I was ..."

"Woolgathering, my lord?" She inquired with a laugh. "Not a recommendation for the attractions of your partner. If I were not made of sterner stuff, I should very likely go into a decline."

It was Alistair's turn to chuckle. "I apologize profusely. Now what was it that you were saying?"

"I merely wished to thank you for not betray—er, for not implying to my brother that we had met before our introduction to each other in the park."

"Aha. So the estimable Charlie is not aware of his sister's campaign to save Mrs. Gerrard's ladies. I rather thought not. And if Charlie lives in happy ignorance of this program, I feel certain that the rest of your family has not the slightest inkling of it."

A vivid blush stained her cheeks, but the chin rose defiantly as Harriet replied, "No, they do not and—"

"They will not be enlightened by me, I promise you." Lord Chalfont smiled reassuringly at her.

"Oh, thank you. I—" Harriet began.

"On one condition," he interrupted her smoothly.

Dark brows snapped together and a frown wrinkled the smooth white forehead. "And pray, what is that?" She demanded suspiciously.

"That you tell me why a lady of gentle birth who should have nothing more serious on her mind than the trimming of her bonnet is concerning herself with the welfare of th inhabitants of Mrs. Gerrard's."

"Of all the—" Harriet gasped in indignation.

"No. Do not fly up the boughs at me. I did not say you thought of nothing but the trimmings on your bonnet. I merely said that most young ladies did. I have seen enough of you to know that you are no such young lady. In fact, you are quite extraordinary, which is why I am trying to discover more about you."

"Oh." Harriet responded in a mollified tone. "Well, you see, I encountered Bessie one evening outside the opera and..."

"Bessie?"

"Surely you know her. She is one of Mrs. Gerrard's ladies. They all know you so I assumed ..."

"You did nothing of the sort, you little wretch." He grinned at her, for he saw the twinkle in her eye and he rather liked it. No lady he could remember had ever twinkled at him, and certainly none of them had ever dared to tease him. They had all been too intent on winning something from him—money, jewelry, his name—to risk annoying him.

"Bessie is the blond one and she used to live in Thornby not far from Fareham Park. She was a dairymaid, that is, until the squire's son ruined her and her father refused to have anything further to do with her. She came to London and was on her own, practically starving, when Mrs. Gerrard found her and rescued her as she has so many. The night I recognized Bessie she was at Covent Garden looking for other poor unfortunates who were in the same dire straits as she had been. I made her tell me where she was staying and the next day I went to visit her."

"All alone?" Alistair could not hide his surprise.

"I had my maid with me," Harriet responded a trifle defensively.

"And I did disguise myself."

"Ah yes, the unlikely Quakeress."

"It was a very good imitation of a Quaker bonnet," she protested.

"But you, my girl, are nothing like a Quaker."

Harriet opened her mouth to disagree, but he cut her short. "You are far too spirited, which is not all that unattractive, you know. It just does not happen to be what one would find in a Quakeress."

"And what experience of Quakeresses do you have, pray tell?" Harriet could not help asking in patent disbelief.

"Touché." Lord Chalfont chuckled. "I admit I have very little, if any, but you have an air about you which could only belong to someone who is accustomed to ... er ... to command, shall we say."

"To getting my own way, is what you mean." Harriet shot back at him.

"Well, yes," Alistair conceded. "But as your way seems to involve doing what you think is best for others without a thought for its cost to yourself, I see nothing wrong with it."

"How do you know all that about me?" Harriet demanded suspiciously. Truly the man seemed omniscient.

"Call it the result of experience. I have led a life that has thrown me constantly in the company of a great many different men ..."

"And women," Harriet supplied sardonically.

"And women," he agreed, raising a quizzical eyebrow. "And from it I have gained an ability to read a person's character within a few minutes of making his or her acquaintance. Yours, being something quite out of the ordinary, took longer than most, but I think I am correct in my assessment, am I not? You do tend to rush to the defense of those less fortunate than yourself without stopping to consider the cost of your involvement, do you not?"

"It is of no consequence." Harriet scornfully dismissed such a churlish attitude. "If one has made up one's mind to do what is right, why, then, one must do it."

"And in your case, it is without any hesitation, I'll be bound." He chuckled.

"Delaying only weakens one's resolve," Harriet responded firmly.

Lord Chalfont shook his head in admiration. "Not only do most people lack the courage to do the right thing, they usually fail to see

what the right thing is in the first place. I gather you are not afflicted
with such convenient blindness."

"Not usually."

"And I would be willing to hazard a guess that this clarity of vision and purpose makes life rather uncomfortable for those around
you."

Harriet had the grace to look slightly self-conscious. "I never fall
into any truly bad scrapes," she protested.

The amber eyes gleamed with amusement. "I can see, Lady Harriet, that you are a rare handful. I rather suspect that Charlie was not
your companion in the park as much as your keeper. If I were your
brother, I should lock you up."

"Of all the—you would not dare." She sputtered.

The marquess laughed. "No. I should not dare, nor would I ever
hinder the impulses of someone who has brought so much hope into
the lives of others."

"Really?" Surprised, Harriet glanced up at her partner, but there
was not a hint of mockery in the eyes that gazed intently into hers.
"Why—why, thank you," she stammered, suddenly breathless. "I had
wanted ... that is, I had hoped I was helping, but one never knows. I
could simply be seen as meddling."

"No gesture that is made from the heart, as yours is, could be
seen as meddling," Alistair responded gravely. "However, I know"—
here the marquess looked slightly self-conscious himself—"from, er
talking to Kitty that your visits mean a great deal to Mrs. Gerrard's
ladies. Even if you are unable to do anything to change their lot, your
interest and concern have made a vast difference in their lives. They
no longer feel so abandoned by the world."

It was Harriet's turn to look grave. Truly the Marquess of Kidderham was turning out to be the most surprising sort of person and not
at all the irreverent rake she had first judged him to be. "I am glad.
Their fate has been a cruel one. All women's lives are so dependent
on male whims, and these particular women have paid dearly for
it. There is little one poor girl can do to change the inequities of the
world, but at least I can help those who have suffered from them."

"Oho. Then are you one of those terrifying females who espouse
the teachings of Mary Wollstonecraft?"

Lord Chalfont's tone was a rallying one, but there was a gleam in his eye that Harriet was hard put to interpret. "Whatever one thinks of the question of the rights of women, one cannot condone deception and cruelty which is what the ladies at Mrs. Gerrard's have been victims of."

The gleam in Alistair's eyes was distinctly appreciative now. "Very clever. So you will not say, my fiery reformer, how you feel about the delicate subject of the equality of women? My guess is that in your experience, most men you encounter are not only not superior, but considerably inferior to you." One look at her expressive face told the marquess all he needed to know. He laughed. "I thought as much. But then, you are a very superior person for a female, or a male, for that matter."

The music ended and Lord Chalfont glanced across the floor to see his betrothed, now returned to her mama, regarding him in a most significant fashion. "And now I must return you to your family, but I wish to thank you for a most enjoyable conversation."

There was such a wealth of meaning in his tone that Harriet looked up in some surprise. Such seriousness did not accord with her previous impression of the devil-may-care Marquess of Kidderham, but then, most of their discussion had caused her to reexamine her conceptions about this man.

"You may stare, but believe me, I speak in all sincerity. I have not felt this inspired since I left the army. No one has spoken to me of things that truly matter since my days in the Peninsula and I wish you to know how much pleasure it has given to me."

By now they had reached the little group that included Lord Fareham, Aunt Almeria, Lady Elizabeth, and Lord Rokeby. Lord Chalfont nodded to Lord Rokeby and his fiancée and then directed a devastating smile toward Aunt Almeria, who was frowning ferociously at him. "I count myself fortunate to have had Lady Harriet as a partner. It is so rare to encounter intelligent conversation anywhere these days, particularly in a ballroom. Do you not agree?" Without giving her a moment to answer, he continued, "And judging by appearance, which of course one should never do, I would say that it must be your influence that has made her the clever and informed young woman that Lady Harriet is. She does great credit to you." Alistair concluded this brazen little speech with another brilliant smile, bowed, and strode off in the direction of Alicia and her mother, leaving both Aunt Almeria and Harriet to stare after him.

There was a silence for a moment as Aunt Almeria recovered from such unexpected remarks and then she nodded decisively. "A bold young man, to be sure, but a direct and honest one—perceptive too." She shut her jaw with a snap and turned back to the argument over the significance of the Cluniac reforms in which she and her brother had been immersed since their arrival at the ball, leaving Harriet to her own considerably confused reflections.

Chapter 13

For Harriet, the rest of the evening passed in a fog of insipid conversation and even duller partners. Perhaps this was a rather harsh judgment of the inoffensive young men who tried to amuse her after her waltz with Lord Chalfont, for compared to the Marquess of Kidderham almost any man was bound to appear colorless. To Harriet's mind the marquess dwarfed everyone else in the room both mentally and physically, yet she still could not decide whether she liked the man or not. Of course she admired anyone as bold and seemingly unconcerned with the conventions as he was, but she could not help remembering their encounters at Mrs. Gerrard's.

In the first place, though she was not a prude by any means, she did wonder about a man who was so intent on his own pleasure that he was a regular patron of Mrs. Gerrards establishment. Secondly, she mistrusted his provoking behavior toward herself. Why had he teased her so? Had he been goading her in the hopes of making her lose her composure so he could flirt with her? Had he been so unable to accept the thought of a woman who did not fall at his feet that he resolved to prove to her and to himself that he could affect her enough at least to unsettle her? Certainly that was how Harriet had viewed his initial behavior toward her. Now, she was not quite so sure.

She leaned back against the squabs of the carriage as they made their way back to Berkeley Square. Her sister was chattering happily about the evening: it had been a brilliant affair, a sad crush to be sure, but most enjoyable, nevertheless, and they had been in their best looks for she and Harriet had not been left to stand out more than one dance apiece. Lord Rokeby had been so pleased with their success, dear man.

Harriet paid no attention except to nod and smile now and then. She was happy at her sister's pleasure in the evening, but at the moment she wished to be alone with her thoughts, to revisit her waltz with Lord Chalfont and examine all its unexpected revelations, the most disturbing of which was that she had enjoyed their dance very much indeed.

Although Harriet had waltzed often enough with a variety of partners, she had never before been so aware of the intimacy of the dance. This time, however, she had been intensely alive to the closeness of her partner. The warmth of the marquess's hand on her waist through the thin material of her gown had almost felt as though he were caressing her bare skin, and though he held her at the proper distance, she had had the not entirely unpleasant sensation of being crushed against his broad chest. Odd how she had never really paid the slightest attention to men or their physiques until she had met the Marquess of Kidderham, and now Harriet found she could hardly take her mind off his tall, powerfully built body.

He had moved superbly with the assurance of a natural athlete. No padding was needed to enhance the massive shoulders. In fact even the dark broadcloth of his jacket did not quite conceal the muscles that rippled underneath it as he had held out his arms to lead her onto the floor.

It did not help either that Harriet had been privy to the comments of the ladies at Mrs. Gerrard's. It was difficult to know precisely how many of them had seen him in what state of undress, but they had all pronounced him to be a splendid specimen of the masculine sex. Kitty even going so far as to describe in some detail his expertise at lovemaking. Harriet blushed in the darkness at the thought.

Ruthlessly she tried to push all treacherous thoughts of Lord Chalfont from her mind and concentrate on the rest of the evening instead, but she was not entirely successful, for the remainder of the Countess of Rotherham's ball had been something of a blur. She had been conscious of the marquess's returning to Alicia's side and had then spent an entire set of country dances nodding occasionally to her partner while wondering how it happened that a gentleman as lively as Lord Chalfont appeared to be betrothed to the coldly perfect Alicia De Villiers.

Of course, theirs was an agreement of some duration between the two families, but this was an enlightened age and few parents now were so gothic as to force their children into marriages they did not want. Perhaps the Marquess of Kidderham wanted this marriage; after all, Alicia was undeniably beautiful. But Harriet could not picture the laughing, teasing, provoking man she had come to know spending the rest of his life with Alicia. Why, he would be bored within a minute while she would be thoroughly disgusted by his irreverent view of life.

Harriet had tried to keep herself from looking for the two of them as she whirled around the dance floor with one partner after another, but her curiosity had gotten the better of her and her eyes had followed the two of them everywhere.

Alicia had looked as lovely as usual in a white lace dress over white satin slip ornamented with knots of pale blue ribbon and pearls. It was the perfect gown to set off the delicate complexion and dark hair, while the touches of blue complimented the blue of her eyes. There was no doubt that she drew envious looks from the women and admiring ones from the men; however, as far as Harriet had been able to tell. Lord Chalfont had remained unmoved by such dazzling beauty.

His behavior to his betrothed had been everything that was correct and attentive, but he had looked like a man performing a ritual while his mind was elsewhere. Harriet did not think she was being presumptuous in thinking it, but it did seem to her that the marquess had appeared more animated in conversation with her than he was at any time with Alicia.

Well, it was assuredly none of her affair, Harriet thought as she alighted from the carriage and followed her sister up the stairs, nodding absently at the footman who sprang to open the door. Undoubtedly the two of them deserved one another. The Marquess of Kidderham would get a compliant wife whose manners were too perfect to allow her to take notice of the women he might consort with and who could be counted on to be the perfect marchioness at all times. In return, Alicia would have a wealthy husband whose rank and style would strike envy in the breast of every female in the ton.

It would have astounded Harriet to know that at that very moment someone else was also comparing the charms of Alicia De Villiers with those of Lady Harriet Fareham and Alicia, toast of the ton, was coming off second best.

Having tossed down one glass of brandy handed to him the moment he entered his chambers by Richards—batman, valet, and general factotum—Alistair had thrown himself into a comfortable chair in front of the fire and was now well into his second glass. It always took at least two glasses before he was able to recover his equanimity after attending these ton affairs with Alicia, where somehow he always seemed to feel like one of the trained horses at Astley's Amphitheatre being put through its paces. While Alicia never actually demanded anything of him, she always conveyed the sense of her high expectations for his behavior. If perchance he happened to fall short of these expectations, she never was so vulgar as to reprimand him; instead, she would wear a look of hurt disappointment or of pained resignation as though she knew very well that he would never measure up to her exquisite sensibilities, but she accepted this as a cross she had to bear.

Actually, when he stopped to consider it, Alistair did not think he was all that bad. Other women appeared to like him well enough. He grinned as he thought of the lascivious looks Sally Jersey had been tossing in his direction all evening or the subtle way Lavinia de Montfort had kept lessening the space between the two of them as they had waltzed together. These women certainly had not objected to him—far from it—but somehow Alicia always seemed to find him lacking.

Lord Chalfont told himself that he did not care, that to him the petty rules and overly refined manners of the ton were ridiculous. Long ago, disgusted by this pettiness, he had left the fashionable world behind and gone in search of real challenges and real life. Still, it irked him that Alicia assumed her views to be so vastly superior to his without even bothering to discover what his were. The fact that she would have thought it vulgar to discuss anything deeper or more personal than the latest fashions or on dits only made it worse. Undoubtedly she would have been horrified at the intimacy of his latest interchange with Lady Harriet.

Alistair took another swig of brandy and chuckled as he remembered the look on Harriet's face when he had implied that she should be concentrating on trimming bonnets rather than trying to improve the lot of Mrs. Gerrard's ladies. She had been outraged, and rightly so. What a little fire-eater she was, and how lovely she had looked this evening, all liveliness and energy, her eyes sparkling with interest as they surveyed the dance floor. How refreshing her expressive face was and what a contrast it offered to the carefully assumed masks of boredom and indifference that everyone else wore.

He wondered if she would be in the park the next morning or if he would have to wait until Tuesday for her visit to Mrs. Gerrard's, if she came at all. His face darkened as the picture of her struggling with Sir Neville came back to him. Damn the man for the nasty piece of work that he was, and for the look of distress he had brought into those dark blue eyes, and into the eyes of all Mrs. Gerrard's ladies. Alistair had the uneasy feeling that they had not seen the last of the man, but he was bound and determined that Sir Neville would cause no more trouble for the ladies of Mrs. Gerrard's, or Harriet, for that matter.

Funny, he felt more protective toward her than he did toward Alicia when of the two of them, Harriet obviously possessed a great deal more courage and more resources. But she was vulnerable in a way that Alicia was not. Her passion for life, her interest in and concern for others were indicative of a warm heart that could most definitely be hurt. Alistair doubted very much if Alicia cared enough about anything to be affected in such a way. Yes she might be annoyed or disgusted by events or people who did not conform to her rigid idea of propriety, but she would never be personally involved enough to suffer the way Harriet would.

Alistair took a last swig of brandy and set the glass down with a snap as a grim vision of the future rose before him—escorting the ever fashionable, always beautiful Alicia to one ton party after another, endlessly replaying the scenes of this evening with the same people, and nothing to vary it except that a different color would be all the rage, or there would be a new way of tying a cravat or a slight variation in waistcoats.

And why was he condemned to this life of stultifying boredom? It was all for the sake of a woman who cared very little, if at all, for who Alistair Julius Chalfont was as a person, but was very concerned about what the Marquess of Kidderham represented to fashionable society. Alistair sighed. How had he gotten himself into this dilemma? How had he, a man who had thrown himself single-handedly into the breach against the French at the Battle of the Pyrenees, been unable to tell a mere woman that he had no wish to marry her and become yet another accoutrement in her perfectly ordered existence?

Alistair's features were set in such grim lines that even the flickering firelight failed to soften them or warm the bleak expression on his face. He knew the answer to his question lay in his damnable sense of honor, the same honor that had refused to give quarter to the French, that had driven him to dismount in a hail of fire at Vitoria to rescue a wounded comrade, that made him abide by an agreement made years ago between two ancient families.

Oh yes, he would abide by it, but how was he going to be able to bear the thought of endless dull evenings spent at Alicia's side as her ever attentive escort with the only hope of satisfaction being more evenings spent at Mrs. Gerrard's? At the thought of Mrs. Gerrard's select establishment, the image of Harriet's bright face rose again before him. Just the idea of her, her refusal simply to accept the role life had cast for her made him feel better. Why most women in her station would not even have recognized women such as Bessie, Kitty, Fanny, Violet, and the others, much less cared enough to help them. But then, Harriet appeared to be intrigued by anything and everything. He remembered reminiscing about the war with her brother Charlie while she sat silent on her horse, blue eyes bright with interest. Even at the Countess of Rotherham's ball where one bejeweled beauty closely resembled the rest and the turbaned dowagers were virtually indistinguishable from one another she had looked around her with wide observant eyes alight with curiosity. She, like he, had been bored with the idle chat of ballrooms, and had readily dispensed with it in favor of more serious conversation which Alistair had thoroughly enjoyed.

The marquess lay back in his chair shutting his eyes wearily. He might be condemned to the enervating existence of a member of the beau monde, permanent consort of an incomparable, but it was reassuring to know that people such as Harriet and his few close friends from the army did exist, that there were others besides himself who occupied their minds with something besides the cut of their coats or the latest rage in bonnets. And at least he would be able to see one of these people very soon. After all, Tuesday was not so very far away. A smile smoothed out the harsh lines of his face as the Marquess of Kidderham drifted off to sleep in his chair.

Chapter 14

As luck would have it, Alistair was not forced to wait until Tuesday to see Lady Harriet for he encountered her in the park the very next morning. Feeling hemmed in and confined by the suffocating rituals of society so vividly brought to mind by the previous evening, and suffering from the general restlessness incurred when one accustomed to an energetic existence is forced to suffer long periods of inactivity. Lord Chalfont was up betimes the next morning and looking forward to the peace of a deserted park. He had barely had time after entering it to feast his eyes on the vast green expanse when he caught sight of another horse and rider followed at a respectful distance by someone who could only have been a groom. Alistair did not need a second glance to know that the solitary rider was Lady Harriet. There was no mistaking the straight little figure or the powerful black horse she was controlling with such ease.

Even though he had been looking forward to seeing her again, the marquess was himself surprised at the current of excitement that ran through him the moment he recognized Harriet. It had been a long time since anyone's presence, even that of the most beautiful and wanton of his female admirers, both in and out of the ton, had inspired that son of reaction in him. Alistair felt his senses quicken in expectation—expectation of what he did not know, but Harriet was bound to provide something of interest and amusement; she always did, and it was always a surprise.

He dug his heels in his mount and hurried to catch up with Brutus and his mistress as they indulged in a highly improper gallop across the thick carpet of grass.

Harriet heard the pounding hooves behind her, but instead of reining in her horse, as any respectable young lady would, she leaned over Brutus's neck and urged him to put forth even greater speed. The hoofbeats behind her increased in rhythm, but she refused to look back until the powerful gray shoulders of Lord Chalfont's Trajan were equal with Brutus's.

Somehow Harriet was not surprised to discover the identity of her pursuer. Even though men were accorded far more latitude in society than women, few men would have joined her in such an undignified dash across the park, and even fewer would have been abroad at such an early hour after an evening of revelry. She could not help wondering if Lord Chalfont had capped off an evening spent dutifully escorting his betrothed with a rousing visit to Mrs. Gerrard's. Hastily she suppressed such a thought as being none of her affair, though she could not help but wonder. Certainly Alicia was a cold fish if there ever was one, while Mrs. Gerrard's ladies were a lively bunch and more likely to appeal to someone who possessed the zest for amusement and adventure that the Marquess of Kidderham apparently did.

He definitely looked to be full of energy and ripe for anything this morning. The golden eyes looking down at her were alight with enjoyment of the day, the exhilaration of their gallop, and something else that Harriet could not quite identify, a warmth that seemed to be especially for her. How could that be? Surely she was mistaken.

But Lord Chalfont's greeting confirmed her intuition. "Lady Harriet, this is a delightful surprise. I had not dared hope to see you about at such an early hour. Any other young lady who had danced until all hours would not arise until well after noon. However, I am learning that you are not just any young lady and that I am constantly underestimating you."

Harriet dismissed the habits of other young ladies with a contemptuous snort. "Pooh. Dancing is not so very exhausting, and I find the fresh air and lack of people in the park most reviving after an evening wast—er, spent, in a crowded ballroom."

The marquess's eyes gleamed. "So you too consider these gala affairs to be a waste of time. I rather thought you might."

"I did not say it is a waste of time, precisely." Harriet hastened to explain herself. The man was entirely too quick. No one else she knew would have noticed her slip of the tongue. "It is just that I fail to find such affairs as enthralling as the rest of the world appears to. After one has danced several dances and discussed the weather thoroughly, there is nothing much more to do. I try my best to enjoy them, but I fear that I am not like the other people who find such things entertaining."

Alistair chuckled and nodded in agreement. She was far too intelligent and inquisitive a person to be satisfied with such bland amusements for very long; however, there was a hint of wistfulness in her tone that he found oddly touching. "Yet you were never lacking for partners last evening so you must have appeared to enjoy yourself with great success."

Harriet looked up in some surprise. So he had been as aware of her after their waltz together as she had been of him. "I do try," she answered gravely. Then responding to the look of understanding in those penetrating eyes, she continued in a confiding tone, "You see, it is not for myself that I attend such functions, but for Elizabeth."

"Your sister?" He asked in some surprise.

"Yes. She is betrothed to Lord Rokeby and is most anxious that the family appears to its best advantage. If it were not for that I should not be here at all for I have not the least use for such things."

Lord Chalfont raised a quizzical eyebrow.

"Well, you see," Harriet went on to explain, "one only attends such functions as the Countess of Rotherham's for three reasons: to see, to be seen, or to catch a husband. As I care very little for all three, I really have no need to spend my time prancing around in all my finery."

"Though you did look extremely fine," his lordship could not help interjecting. "But tell me, why do you have an aversion to catching husbands? I thought all young ladies aspired to them."

"Why should I spend my life working to gratify the whims of someone who, from what I have seen of most gentlemen, would not be interested in anything that I am and would be a great deal stupider as well?" Harriet demanded somewhat pugnaciously.

"Why indeed?" Lord Chalfont murmured, his eyes dancing. Yes, as he had always suspected, Lady Harriet Fareham was quite refreshingly different from every other woman he had ever met. "But what does your father have to say to all this?"

"Papa? Why, if he notices I am there at all, which is only occasionally when he emerges from the library, it is to make sure that I am healthy and furthering my own education. "The life of the mind, Harriet,'" she intoned in a deep voice. " 'must be constantly culti-vated, else we are no different from the beasts in the fields.' And Aunt Almeria feels much the same way: any time spent away from her studies is time wasted. But she has a strong sense of family duty and thus devotes herself to Elizabeth's needs until she is happily married and we can all return to our own particular interests."

"You are most fortunate in your family. Lady Harriet."

The bantering tone had gone from the marquess's voice. In fact, there was a serious note that Harriet had never heard before and she looked up in some surprise. Lord Chalfont's expression was grave to the point of regret as he gazed off over the park. For a moment he was lost in his thoughts—and not very pleasant ones at that, Harriet thought as she tilted her head curiously, studying him carefully. This was a very different man from the insouciant rake who frequented Mrs. Gerrard's. She wondered at it, wondered which was the real Lord Chalfont. Was it the reckless libertine who appeared to care for nothing, or the man who had served his country so well that Wel-lington had made him one of his own inner circle?

But before Harriet could marshal her thoughts, he had turned back to her and smiling wryly down at her, broke the silence. "For-give me, my wits are wandering and it is not good for the horse." He was entirely correct in this for they had slowed to a halt while talking and both Brutus and Trajan were tossing their heads impatiently.

Harriet glanced up at the sun. "Yes. And just look at the time. Why even Aunt Almeria will begin to wonder if I am absent this long." And with a nod to her groom and a flick of her heels, she had wheeled and began heading back toward Berkeley Square where, contrary to what she had led Lord Chalfont to believe, the sole oc-cupant of the morning room when Harriet entered was surprised to see her return so quickly from her morning ride.

"Back so early?" Aunt Almeria barely looked up from the book in which her nose was buried before lapsing into silence again. Her devotion to Elizabeth's routine left her very little time for her own studies, so she seized every available moment not spent shopping, driving in the park, or chaperoning her charge at fashionable affairs to read.

"Oh, not really."

Harriet's tone was one of such studied casualness that her aunt glanced up sharply to discover the faintest of blushes tinge her niece's cheeks. Now what was the child about this time? she wondered. It was not like Harriet to act self-conscious. Ordinarily she had not the least compunction about revealing whatever outlandish scrape she had fallen into. It was a highly unusual circumstance when Harriet betrayed any signs of deviousness. This bore some watching, the older woman thought as she returned to her book while her niece rang the bell for more chocolate.

Her aunt's scrutiny was not lost on Harriet and she sank into her place at the table deep in thought. What was it about the Marquess of Kidderham that commanded so much of her attention? Ordinarily she would not waste a second thought on a man such as he but now she found herself puzzling over him a good deal of the time. He was such a strange mixture, with his apparent disregard for most of the things members of the fashionable world treasured above all else such as respectability and reputation. Yet he demonstrated a real concern for other things most people would have been horrified even to mention, such as the lives of Mrs. Gerrard's ladies. For quite apart from his obvious enjoyment of what they had to offer, he seemed to take a genuine interest in them and to approve most heartily of Harriet's projects to improve their lives.

And today Harriet had come across yet another contradiction in the man. She sensed a sadness or ennui. There had been pain in his eyes as they had surveyed Hyde Park during their conversation, a pain that seemed out of place in the dashing character her brother had described or the amorous adventurer that Mrs. Gerrard's ladies drooled over.

What was it that was wrong? Harriet could not pinpoint it exactly, but her curiosity was piqued. Though she did not like to think of Lord Chalfont as being a regular customer at Mrs. Gerrard's, she did rather hope she would encounter him there again on her next visit. The man was a puzzle to her and Harriet could not resist a puzzle.

Chapter 15

Harriet also could not resist remarking several days later to Lord Chalfont as she looked up to see him leaning casually against the door of the schoolroom after Rose and her class had departed, "I would think that a gentleman who had spent so much of his life defending his country would have something better to do with it now than idling it away at Mrs. Gerrard's." Harriet could not have said what devil prompted her to make such a remark, for ordinarily she disliked people who meddled in her own life so much that she was careful to refrain from doing so in other people's. But the idea of a former hero of the Peninsula lounging aimlessly about irked her somehow. It seemed such a waste of a life that had until now been well spent, if half the stories her brother had been telling her were true.

Lord Chalfont's eyebrows rose in surprise and he regarded Harriet with faint hauteur. While it was perfectly true that he had little patience with the overly refined but meaningless phrases of fashionable intercourse, he was not accustomed to such plain speaking and it set him back a bit. "I apologize if my ways are so offensive to you, madam," he began with icy politeness.

But Harriet, now fully aware of how impertinent she must have sounded, pressed one hand to her mouth in dismay. "No, I apologize," she muttered through her fingers. "It is my wretched tongue. I have no place criticizing you in such a fashion."

A wry grimace twisted his lips as the marquess replied. "On the contrary, you of all people have every right to reprove me. You who are actively doing something to make the world a better place are quite justified in censuring those of us who are not." He smiled grimly. "At one time I could have said the same thing of myself, but now you are in the right of it. I am turned into a useless fribble and am likely to remain so—a perfect example of a man of the ton."

He sounded so bitter that Harriet could not help laying a consoling hand on his sleeve. "No, do not say such things. I am persuaded that it does not need to be so."

A grim laugh was his only reply as he stood there staring unseeingly at a marble statue of a nymph trying not very hard to escape the clutches of a satyr.

Harriet regarded him with a puzzled frown. It was not at all like Lord Chalfont to be at a loss for words. If anything, he usually erred on the side of having too much to say, and it was usually provocative at that. Alistair glanced up to see her staring at him curiously. "Pay no heed to me, Lady Harriet. I am an ungrateful wretch. Any sane man would be delighted to be returning from war to a peaceful existence and living out his days on his own estate with a lovely wife and nothing to worry about but amusing himself. Only a fool would be a blue-devilled at such a prospect."

He turned as if to go, but Harriet detained him. "No, pray, do not leave. Surely you need not give in to it all so tamely. While it is true that there are no military battles to be fought at the moment, there are many political ones."

"Political?"

She hastened to explain. "Yes. There are all those soldiers who fought alongside of you now returned to a nation that has quite forgotten the sacrifices they made, a nation where there is little way for them to earn the food that is becoming increasingly dear."

Seeing that she had caught his interest, Harriet warmed to her theme. "They need someone in the government to remember their sacrifices, to speak for them, to insure that the way of life they fought to protect does not pass them by. You could be such a person. In fact, you are the perfect person. You have power and position. There are very few great landowners among the Opposition, and now that the price of corn has started to rise again, the agricultural interests are much less inclined to agitate for change than when corn had fallen to little more than fifty shillings a quarter. But the plight of the laborers has only worsened, and many of those laborers were the very men who fought for so many years to save England. The government is already borrowing in order to maintain what army there is left; who knows what will happen if that money is cut? There is a great deal to be done, and in my opinion the country is as much in need of your services now as it was when you were scaling walls under enemy fire in the Peninsula. Why not offer those services to England again?"

Whew! Harriet paused to catch her breath. Where had that speech come from? she wondered. And what had made her think that a devil-may-care rake such as the Marquess of Kidderham would listen to it, or care?

But he had listened to it. The tawny eyes focused on her intently and there was a curiously arrested expression on his face as he murmured softly, "Why not indeed?" He was silent for some time, considering.

It had been quite a moment as she confronted him, eyes flashing with righteous indignation. Alistair had never known a woman could look so fierce, or at least a woman as gently bred as Lady Harriet Fareham. He had seen peasant women in the Peninsula defending their homes and families against the foreign invaders and admired their spirit, but that had been different; their whole way of life was being threatened. Here was someone who had not the slightest reason to defend the poor and the downtrodden, beyond her own natural humanity, turning on him as if he were the veriest laggard. She was truly magnificent.

And almost as impressive as her passionate plea to help those in need was her grasp of the political situation right down to the price of corn. Alistair was both inspired and humbled—inspired by her very idealism, and humbled by her knowledge and willingness to consider some of the most pressing issues of the day, issues that were defeating far more experienced politicians than Lady Harriet.

"I know," a soft voice interrupted these thoughts. "It is all very well for me to speak. After all, I am not trying to convince Parliament to act. I should do something myself to tackle these problems instead of urging someone else to do so, but I cannot stand up for Parliament."

"And a good thing too." A lopsided grin tugged at one corner of Lord Chalfont's mouth, softening its grim expression. "They are not ready for a spitfire such as you."

"Spitfire!" Harriet was indignant. "I am no such thing. Why, I am just—"

"A milk-and-water miss," the marquess continued smoothly with only the faintest touch of irony. "A milk-and-water miss who throws herself into the defense of a group of people most gently bred young ladies do not even know exists, or at least do not admit to knowing exists. No, Lady Harriet, that won't fadge. Why you're as ardent a spirit as Brougham himself, perhaps more so. The government should count itself lucky you are a woman. You would make mice feet of poor Parliament in a day were you to be elected to its august membership."

A reluctant chuckle escaped Harriet. "I should certainly try," she admitted, "but even though I cannot, I feel that someone should. And I can think of no one better than you. After all, you never seem to have the least regard for anyone's sensibilities, and—"

"Whoa, there, my girl." The marquess held up an admonishing hand. "How can you say such a thing after our perfectly unexceptionable waltz the other evening? Why I was a model of decorum and gentlemanly behavior."

"Which I never would have guessed existed in you had I been left to form my impressions of your character after our first few encounters."

Lord Chalfont shrugged and grinned. "I had to discover more about you. You were so confoundedly prim and proper that the only thing to do was to throw you off your guard which, I might add, was impossible to do."

"Precisely what I am talking about. Just proceed the same way in Parliament as you did with me and you should do very nicely," Harriet retorted.

"If I am not called out first."

"You were the one who implied that your life was lacking in challenge and adventure."

Alistair raised one well-shaped hand in a gesture of defeat. "Touché. You have made your point, my fiery friend. I shall endeavor to see what I can do to throw myself into the political fray. In the meantime, I have kept you here long enough. Your family will begin to wonder where you are."

"I very much doubt it. Papa, as usual, is buried in the library. Charlie is mounting guard duty, but he lives in the barracks anyway.

And Elizabeth and Aunt Almeria are closeted with the dressmaker. Besides, they are quite accustomed to my frequent comings and goings and pay them no heed."

"Yes. I should think that where you are concerned, expecting the unexpected is a very useful maxim," the marquess replied in a teasing tone. But for all his bantering air, he was reflecting quite seriously on how lonely her existence must be. An intelligent, energetic woman in a society that preferred decorative, passive ones—not that she was not decorative with the tendrils of flame-colored hair escaping from the severe coil she had wound at the nape of her neck to cluster around the animated face with its enormous dark blue eyes.

Alistair himself had often felt isolated and set apart from his fellows by his refusal to follow blindly the accepted views of his class, but at least in the army, with danger and privation breaking down many of the artificial barriers that existed among men in the fashionable world, he had been able to discover like-thinking men and enjoy their companionship.

Lady Harriet, he suspected, had never known such companionship, even with her brother. Charlie was well enough in his own way—Lord Chalfont had dealt with his type of officer often enough—eager, lively, courageous to a fault, and likely to have more bottom than sense. In short, Charlie was a man who preferred action to thought. Harriet was worth twice her brother for it was obvious even to the most casual observer that it was her serious reflections on things that led her to action rather than the other way around.

Oddly enough, Alistair found himself wishing that he could provide such companionship for Harriet. They were two of a kind, after all, but friendships like that simply did not exist in the world they inhabited. They might exist between brother and sister or cousins perhaps, but never between a man and a woman who were unrelated but happened to be of a like mind. As Alicia's image flashed before him. Lord Chalfont thought grimly that certainly such friendships did not often exist even between husband and wife. A delicate cough brought him back to the scene at hand. "I beg your pardon, I—"

"Was woolgathering again. I seem to have this soporific effect on you, my lord." Harriet's tone was apologetic, but her eyes were dancing.

"Not at all. Quite the opposite. In fact you cause me to reflect a great deal on things, which in my case, tends to inhibit conversation. I am rather slow-witted, you know, and must think carefully before I reply."

"What a bouncer!" Harriet laughed. "And what momentous considerations have caused such a thoughtful state? I wonder." Harriet, who had posed the question half in jest, was surprised to observe a grave, almost uneasy look cloud the marquess' customarily mocking expression. Whatever had he been thinking of? she wondered. It was most unlike the glib Lord Chalfont to be at a loss for words, much less hemming and hawing awkwardly as he was doing at the moment.

"Well," he paused and fixed her with a glance that was half rueful, half questioning, as though he were at a loss as how to proceed. Then, he seemed to decide something and plunged quickly ahead before he could change his mind. "You see, I was thinking that you must be rather lonely what with being so unlike the other vapid young ladies one finds frequenting the ton, and that you must find yourself wishing you had someone who shared your views, someone you would enjoy talking to. I find that I am often in the same position myself."

"You!" The idea of the dashing Marquess of Kidderham suffering from lack of companionship appeared ludicrous in the extreme. Why, if the reactions of the inhabitants of Mrs. Gerrard's were anything to go by, he was more likely to be afflicted with an excess of company rather than too little. "How can that be? Why wom—er, people, fall all over themselves to be with you."

Alistair grinned at her slip. "That is not the same thing as true friendship. Lady Harriet, and well you know it. But this discussion has gone far enough. I feel myself getting on dangerous ground. For all that you think your family pays little attention to your whereabouts, I am sure they will start to notice if you are gone too long, not to mention your long-suffering maid who, I observe, is hovering near the front door ready to rush in and protect you at a moment's notice." With a flourish the marquess closed the door to the schoolroom behind them and, offering her his arm, escorted her to the waiting hackney, then saw them off as they clattered toward Bond Street and Madame Celeste's.

Chapter 16

Determinedly avoiding the disapproving eye of the ever-watchful Rose, Harriet leaned back in the carriage and tried to collect her disordered thoughts. From Rose's pained expression, Harriet could clearly see what her maid thought of the licentious Marquess of Kidderham, but she herself was not so sure.

How could a man who was truly as debauched as his patronage of Mrs. Gerrard's would seem to indicate, be so disgusted at the thought of leading the comfortable and uneventful existence of a wealthy man of fashion? It did not fit somehow. And the last bit of their conversation gave her even more pause. How could a man who was apparently satisfied with the companionship of Mrs. Gerrard's ladies understand so well how alone and isolated Harriet often felt; and, furthermore, why would he care that she felt that way? It was all certainly most confusing, and not only to Harriet. The marquess, too, had seemed oddly ill at ease with his own observations and had hurriedly ended their conversation as though somehow he had revealed too much of himself to her.

However, there had been sympathy in his eyes and a warmth of understanding in his voice that had drawn her strangely to him. She, who preferred the quiet life of the country and her own intellectual pursuits, should have had little or nothing in common with a man who haunted the dens of iniquity—no matter how fashionable the dens were—in the metropolis, yet she felt closer to him than to most of the people she had yet encountered in London. How very odd.

Enough of such useless speculation, my girl, Harriet scolded herself. You have more important things to occupy your mind than a Bond Street beau, things such as discussing with Madame Celeste the possible employment of Fanny as a new assistant.

This was going to be no easy task as Harriet well knew, for she could see that Madame Celeste, a woman of the world who was wide awake on every suit, would not easily be deceived as to Fanny's previous credentials. Harriet racked her brain for a story convincing enough to pass off on the shrewd modiste, but with no particular success. Unlike many of her peers, she abhorred dissimulation, and therefore found it extremely difficult to concoct a likely background for one of Mrs. Gerrard's ladies.

It was imperative to rescue Fanny, and soon, from Mrs. Gerrard's. Despite the rage and frustration that had overcome Harriet as she had tackled Sir Neville, she had been clearheaded enough to read the man's character and she knew that despite Mrs. Gerrard's prohibition against his returning to her establishment, he would find some way to come back and punish Fanny for the trouble she had gotten him into. The only solution, therefore, was to make sure that Fanny was somewhere else when he decided to do so.

It was a problem. There was no denying that, and Harriet was no nearer concocting an acceptable story for Fanny when she entered Madame Celeste's exclusive establishment than she had been when she had first started thinking it over that morning as they had made their way to Mrs. Gerrard's. In the bandbox at her side was a stunning spencer that she had had Fanny make up to demonstrate her skills as a seamstress. Finally laying down a piece of Uriing's net that she had picked up to examine while composing her thoughts, Harriet begged a private word with Madame Celeste herself.

Dismissing her assistants, the proprietress led Harriet to a small room at the back of the shop and begged that her patroness be seated. It was not unusual in itself for a fair customer to request to be alone with Madame in order to broach some delicate business, but Harriet did not seem the type who would wish Madame to direct a bill to a wealthy protector or, as certain fashionable ladies did, to a gentleman other than their husband. No, Madame thought as she waited patiently for Harriet to speak, this particular customer's request was bound to be something quite out of the ordinary.

And it was. Madame's carefully painted face remained impassive as Harriet, swearing her to me strictest confidence, recounted Fanny's story, unembellished by any false details. After all, Madame Celeste was someone who had seen a great deal of the world and, though she assumed an air of strictest gentility, Harriet felt that a woman who had made her way in the metropolis successfully enough to have her own shop in Bond Street, must know something about life below the select portion of society with which she now dealt exclusively.

Harriet had been entirely correct in her judgment that the truth was likely to be far more persuasive than any fiction she could come up with. The former Sally Brimblecombehad been most fortunate in her seducer, for the marquess of Moresby had been a truly kind man and genuinely fond of the young housemaid who had been the object of his affections, and he had set her up to make her own way in the world when they had parted company. However, Madame Celeste was well acquainted with other girls who had fared far worse, girls who had been utterly ruined instead of being given funds to become their own mistresses. She listened sympathetically as Harriet spoke of Fanny's latest misfortune, nodding her head grimly as she replied, "Yes. Even here we have heard of Sir Neville's nasty reputation. No woman of any breeding would have anything to do with him. But much as I would like to help you, I do have my own reputation to consider and I must be assured of what she can do before I can consider taking on this unfortunate young person."

Harriet produced the spencer which was of canary gros de Naples richly ornamented with primrose satin.

Madame took it from her and walked over to a corner table where a small, grimy window allowed in a bit of daylight. Turning the garment over and over and inside and out, she examined the workmanship carefully and critically, frowning as she did so. Harriet held her breath as she tried to read the proprietress's expression.

At last Madame returned to her. "It is done neatly enough. Is the design her own?"

"Oh yes," Harriet replied, trying not to sound too eager. "And she made it up for me most expeditiously."

"I could use an extra pair of hands"—Madame began slowly—"but only as the most junior of my assistants, mind you, and only executing other people's designs. I will have no prima donnas here. I have the other girls to think of."

"Oh certainly. I understand perfectly and Fanny is well aware of that. She only wishes to escape her imminent danger and will be most grateful to have some way of earning her keep."

"Not that she cannot rise if she is a good girl and works hard."
Madame Celeste continued to examine the spencer which was truly
exquisitely done. "You must warn her that there will be none of the
socializing to which she is undoubtedly accustomed at Mrs. Gerrard's. Only the most senior of assistants is allowed any contact with
our distinguished customers. As to the question of lodging which
would undoubtedly arise, she could most likely find it with Mary,
one of my newest assistants. I believe her mother takes in lodgers."

Harriet's face lit up. "An excellent suggestion. Truly I do thank
you. You have been most generous and understanding."

And so have you, the modiste thought as she rose to usher out her
unusual customer. Lady Harriet was not a beauty by any standards,
but when she smiled she was an enchanting little thing, and something quite out of the ordinary. It was generally Madame's policy to
maintain the strictest distance from her customers, but all of a sudden she found herself wanting to do something for this particular
young woman, and she resolved to oversee personally the making
up of any garment that Lady Harriet might order. Wise in the ways
of the ton, the proprietress sensed that Harriet was far too concerned
about other more serious issues to spend much time on her appearance, and in the fashionable world, appearance was all. Well she,
Madame Celeste, would spend the time to insure that heads would
turn whenever Lady Harriet Fareham walked into a room.

After conducting her young customer to the door, Madame returned to her senior assistants to inform them of the latest addition
to her staff and to instruct them as to the preferential treatment that
was to be given Lady Harriet Fareham.

Meanwhile Harriet, well satisfied with her morning's work, was
remarking to the skeptical Rose as they made their way down Bond
Street, after having dismissed the hackney in the usual manner,
"There, you see. Rose, some good will come of our visiting Mrs. Gerrard's after all."

"Just so long as it is more good than bad that comes of it, my
lady," the maid responded darkly. "But I have my doubts. I do have
my doubts." Rose shook her head gloomily. "Born for trouble, you
were, my lady, born for trouble. Trouble in the country is one thing,
but trouble in the city is quite another."

"Oh, Rose, you are such a worrier. Don't be so hen-hearted. It will all come out all right for everyone, you will see," Harriet responded in a rallying tone, refusing to be drawn into such a gloomy picture of things.

But Harriet's optimism was to be dealt a severe blow some nights later as she accompanied her family to a production of The Recruiting Officer. She would have preferred attending La Clemenza di Tito that was being presented at King's Theatre, but Elizabeth insisted that the fashionable world in general, and Lord Rokeby and his friend Lord Aylward in particular, were more likely to be at the Theatre Royal. Besides, Charlie was all in favor of a play that featured such a military sounding tide.

Harriet, resigned to an evening of modest entertainment, was leaning on the edge of the box wishing she were listening to Mozart when her eye fell on Sir Neville who was in the pit ogling the boxes in the most disgustingly forward manner. With a gasp she drew herself back into the shadows of the box and then cursed herself for a fool because her involuntary reaction had naturally done quite the opposite of what she had intended and caught his attention.

Harriet remained frozen, hoping against hope that the distance was too great for her to be identified, but it was too late. With a sinking heart she watched the sinister smile steal slowly across the thin. cruel mouth as he raised his quizzing glass to get a better look. My wretched hair, she fumed silently. If only I were old enough to wear a cap.

She knew it was useless to wish for anonymity, for whatever else she might be. Lady Harriet Fareham was never inconspicuous. Sir Neville was not the only one whose attention had been attracted by the sight of candlelight gleaming on coppery curls. Lord Chalfont, raising a hand to stifle a yawn of purest boredom, had also caught a glimpse of them and found that his interest in the evening's outing had perked up considerably. He had listened politely to every possible on dit concerning the occupants of the adjacent boxes that Alicia and her mother could dredge up, and had just been wondering how he was to keep himself awake and amused during what promised to be an interminable evening when a hasty movement to his left made him look up just as Harriet retreated into her box. The sight of her brother Charles, resplendent in his regimentals, lounging back in a chair next to his sister, brought joy to the marquess's heart as he saw an opportunity to escape the stultifying atmosphere of his own box for the more congenial conversation in the Fareham's. On the pretext of greeting a long-lost comrade-in-arms, he excused himself to Alicia and her mother at the end of the second act and made his way to the Fareham's box where Charlie greeted him most cordially.

"Nice of you to stop in, Chalfont. Promised Harriet here I would join her at the theater but I tell you I find it to be deuced dull stuff. Can't hold a candle to Astley's. Now there's entertainment that a fellow can truly appreciate, if you ask me."

The marquess chuckled. "You have been soldiering too long, Fareham, and now nothing will satisfy your craving for excitement. Surely Lady Harriet here can offer a more rational criticism of tonight's offering." Alistair turned to Harriet, who had been unusually quiet thus far, and was surprised to find her looking unaccountably somber. Thinking quickly, he turned to Charlie and, nodding toward a box across from them, wondered aloud, "Is that not Colonel Dan Mackinnon? Now there is a soldier if there ever was one."

His attention completely diverted, Charlie leaned forward, trying to make out the identity of the man in question while Lord Chalfont whispered in Harriet's ear, "Is something amiss? You do not look to be at all the thing you know."

"Does it show? I am sorry, but Sir Neville is here and was looking up at our box. I am persuaded he recognized me." Harriet responded under her breath.

"Surely not. The man is not that clever. Do not alarm yourself." Alistair smiled reassuringly.

But Harriet remained unconvinced. "He may not be clever, but I do feel that he is vindictive and he is not the sort of person to forget an insult."

Seeing that she was genuinely upset, the marquess laid a comforting hand on hers. "Do not disturb yourself over this. I shall take care of it. Can you contrive to meet me in the park tomorrow?"

Harriet nodded silently.

"Good."

It was the exchange of a moment before Charlie, who was surveying the box opposite, turned back to say, "No, I do not think that it is MacKinnon. He is not likely to be caught at a place as tame as this." But in that brief interchange, Harriet experienced a sense of being watched over and cared for that she had not felt since her mother died. It was the most fleeting of sensations, but nonetheless intense for its brevity, and Harriet was left to marvel at it while her brother and Lord Chalfont, inspired by the topic of Colonel Mackinnon's exploits, soon became immersed in yet another discussion of the Peninsular Campaign.

Chapter 17

The bell sounding the beginning of the next act forced Lord Chalfont to return to his own box where his attention was not focused on its occupants or the action onstage, but on the disturbing news that Harriet had confided to him. He scanned the audience carefully and at last was able to single out Sir Neville among a noisy group of fellows in the pit. Alistair scowled. It was just like Fletcher to seek out the most vulgar of companions—not that he, Alistair, was such a stickler for the niceties that he did not occasionally escape the stiflingly genteel atmosphere in the boxes for the more congenial and riotous atmosphere below, but somehow Sir Neville always stepped beyond the bounds. At the moment, he was paying no heed to his companions, who truly did look to be ruffians of the worst sort. Instead, his eyes appeared to be fixed on the row of boxes above, and on one box in particular.

Damn! Alistair swore silently. Harriet was entirely correct. Even at this distance there was no mistaking the cunning smile twisting the swarthy features into a more sinister expression than usual. The marquess ground his teeth. Without question the man was a scoundrel of the worst sort, and there was nothing more that Alistair would rather do than deliver another stunning blow to that villainous countenance. But he could do no such thing. In fact, he had no right to do anything at all. To all intents and purposes, Harriet's welfare was her family's concern and no one else's, but Alistair could not help wanting to make it his. After all, he alone knew her situation and the danger she was in. Certainly her father was too absorbed in his own scholarly interests to care, and Charlie had not the slightest idea of the alarming nature of his sister's pursuits.

Alistair bit his lip. The well-being of Lady Harriet Fareham might not be his responsibility, but he was damn well going to look out for it, no matter what anyone might think. She needed his help and they both knew it. He could not have mistaken the desperate look in her eyes this evening when she had spoken of Sir Neville, nor could she misinterpret his reassurances. The sigh of relief that had escaped her when he laid his hand on hers had been proof of that. Without expressly articulating it, she had begged for his assistance and he had pledged it most willingly. Now he meant to stand by it, but first he needed to talk to her again.

They would meet in the park tomorrow. She had promised him that at least, though knowing her self-sufficient turn of mind and independent spirit, he was not sure how much else she would agree to as far as his assistance was concerned.

By the time she had reached the foot of the theater's magnificent double staircase and followed her sister and Lord Rokeby into the vestibule after the play, Harriet was ready to put her fate into the capable hands of the Marquess of Kidderham. As the Fareham's had exited their box. Sir Neville had appeared at her elbow and, looking directly at her, had murmured in the most threatening of tones, "My dear Lady Harriet, how delightful to see you. We must talk sometime, you and I."

Before she could even react, much less respond, he had vanished into the press of people on either side without anyone else's taking notice of him.

Harriet was not one given to nervous starts or alarmist fits of fancy, but even she, stalwart that she was, could not help glancing anxiously behind her as they climbed into the carriage.

All the way to Berkeley Square as she toyed with the lace scarf that was carelessly tossed over her shoulders, Harriet's mind raced. What was she to do? He was bound to expose her and then not only would she, but more importantly her family, be ruined. Not for the first time she wished that she were a man. If she had been she could have called him out and there would be an end to it, but as it was, he had her in his power and could toy with her as a cat did a mouse. She had been able to read that well enough in the sinister smile he had directed at her as he had slipped back into the crowd. Oh, it was intolerable to be in the power of such a despicable character. She would not stand for it! But what was she to do?

Harriet continued to fret as Rose helped her out of her white lace evening gown and gently brushed her hair. Sleep eluded her and Harriet tossed and turned, racking her brain for a clever solution that refused to come. At last the image of Lord Chalfont, cool, calm, and comforting, rose before her. He had not seemed to be the least bit alarmed by the fears she had confided to him. "Can you meet me in the park tomorrow?" was all he had said. He must have a plan. After all, if half of her brother's stories were true, the Marquess of Kidderham was a man of infinite resources. She would just have to possess herself of as much patience as she could until the next morning and see what he had to suggest.

The thought of Lord Chalfont was oddly comforting, and Harriet found that the expectation of meeting with him the next day was sufficient to calm her. She fell asleep with some hope that there was a solution to her dilemma, and that even if there was not, at least she was not alone.

Having slept far better than she would have believed possible, Harriet was up and out betimes the next morning. Her natural buoyancy of spirit had reasserted itself enough so that she was able to enjoy the fineness of the beautiful spring day, the soft air, the newly washed freshness of young leaves, and the golden promise of daffodils as she and Brutus trotted sedately through the park.

They had been there only a matter of minutes before Lord Chalfont appeared on Trajan. He greeted her unsmilingly, his face dark with concern. "I watched him last night. You are in the right of it; he did recognize you and watched your every move for the rest of the evening."

"I know. He spoke to me as we were leaving."

"Damnation! I beg your pardon, but the fellow's impudence passes all bounds. I cannot believe that he dared to address you in such a public place, surrounded as you were by your family."

"Oh, he dared well enough," Harriet muttered through clenched teeth. "But I will not let him intimidate me. He is a weak cowardly man who makes himself feel brave by picking on those who are weaker and more defenseless than he is. He must be stopped and I shall stop him."

"No. We shall stop him. You are not to do this alone, Harriet. I forbid you."

"You forbid me! What right have you—" Her blue eyes blazing, Harriet rounded on him furiously.

"I beg your pardon," the marquess apologized again. "I realize how arrogant that must sound—"

"Most arrogant, my lord." Fear was making Harriet's prickly independence even more pronounced than usual. Half rising in the saddle, she was poised for flight, ready to dig her heels into Brutus's flank.

"Harriet, Harriet, forgive me. In my concern for your safety I am putting this badly."

"You certainly are," she replied frostily. Somewhat mollified by his apologetic air she sank back into the saddle.

Lord Chalfont chuckled uneasily. "All I meant to say is that if half the stories one hears about him are true. Sir Neville is an out-and-out blackguard who will stop at nothing to get what he wants. You are a woman of infinite resource and indomitable courage, but I think even you will admit that alone you are no match for him."

A barely perceptible nod acknowledged this remark.

"Very well then. Since I am the only person who is privy to your secret I think it only fitting that I should help you deal with Sir Neville," Alistair concluded hastily, eyeing her carefully to judge her reaction.

She appeared to take it under consideration for some minutes and then, frowning thoughtfully, she agreed with a resigned sigh. "I suppose you are right, but I would so much rather call him out"

The marquess gave a crack of laughter. "I know you would, but you are in enough of a bumble broth as it is. No, the only solution is for you to let me help you."

"But how?"

"At the moment, I am not entirely certain," he admitted, "but rest assured, I shall think of something. I shall take care of him; I promise you that. Now let us enjoy the day by ceasing this discussion of such a vile person."

Harriet felt reassured, though she could not say why. After all, Lord Chalfont had not even come up with a rational plan to deal with the threat of Sir Neville, but even his promise to look into it made her feel safer, and she was able to relax and appreciate the beauty of the day as he had ordered her to.

This sense of security was short-lived, however, as the very next day, just as she was about to climb the steps to Mrs. Gerrard's, a man detached himself from the shadows of the doorway next to Mrs. Gerrard's. It was Sir Neville.

Too surprised to react, Harriet stood transfixed, hands clenched at her sides, an expression of rigid disdain hardening her ordinarily sunny countenance.

"You may look down on me all you like, my fine lady," the man sneered, "but you will soon change your tune. That haughty air of yours will do you little good when the whole world learns that you have been spending your days at a bawdy house." Harriet drew herself up to her full height. "As if I give a rap for the opinion of the world. Leave me, sirrah."

"Have care what you say to me, young lady. You may not care what the world thinks of you, but your sister does, and she will not thank you for ruining her chance of becoming the Countess of Sandford." He grinned evilly. "I see you had not thought of that. Do not underestimate me. I have made it my business to learn about you and your family, Lady Harriet, and there is very little I do not know."

"What is it? What do you want? I have money. It will take me some time to procure it, but—"

"Money! Ha! You underestimate me, my dear. I have all the money I could possibly want. What I need is a wife—a young attractive wife, a wife who is welcomed in the highest circles of the ton."

By now Sir Neville had moved so close to Harriet that she could smell the liquor on his breath. Oh why had she let Rose hurry into Mrs. Gerrard's ahead of her? If only the jarvey in the waiting hackney would come to investigate, but she dared not cry out for it would only make matters worse. What a truly disgusting man he was!

Harriet's fury overcame her surprise and fear at the man's bold accosting of her. "You are mistaken, sir," she replied coldly. "I would not even give you the time of day, much less entertain such a ridiculous notion. I bid you good morning." And turning on her heel, she marched up the steps and into Mrs. Gerrard's.

Chapter 18

Once the door had shut behind her, Harriet stopped and sagged against it, holding onto the knob for support until she could regain her composure. Her breath was coming in ragged gasps and she was trembling all over. She could not remember a time when she had been so completely shaken. The scoundrel! How dare he threaten her? Why she would—Harriet took a deep, steadying breath. What would she do? What could she do without revealing her secret? At the moment only Rose and Lord Chalfont were privy to it and she certainly intended to keep it that way at all costs. Lord Chalfont. In her distress, Harriet had completely forgotten his offer of assistance. Now the thought of him steadied her as she recalled the look of concern on his face. His vow to deal with Sir Neville had an oddly calming effect, enough so that she was able to enter the schoolroom and greet Kitty, Fanny, Violet, Bessie, and the others with a tolerable degree of equanimity.

It was not the best of lessons, but Harriet managed to get through it by sheer force of will, completely unaware of the covertly curious looks directed at her from time to time by her pupils. Their vivacious instructress was unwontedly quiet and serious this morning—a state of affairs that provoked considerable comment the minute the door closed behind her.

"Fairly blue-deviled, she was," Fanny remarked, shaking her head in puzzlement. "It is not like her in the least, her usually being so gay and all."

"Perhaps she misses the marquess," Violet, who had continued to insist that the Marquess of Kidderham and Miss Harriet would make a match of it, suggested slyly.

"Oh, Violet, do get off that silly hobbyhorse," Bessie snapped. "I have told you times out of mind that the marquess has been promised to Miss De Villiers since she was born."

"But he likes our Miss Harriet." Violet refused to be daunted.

"And where is his lordship?" Fanny wondered aloud. "It is not like him to be absent on a Tuesday. Something must be amiss."

"Whatever it is, it is none of our affair," Bessie concluded firmly. "Now let us go over the lesson before we forget everything we learned today."

The discussion was effectively silenced, but not forgotten. And while they did focus on their lessons, the girls devoted only half of their concentration to the matters at hand, allowing the other half to indulge in an orgy of speculation concerning Miss Harriet and the marquess.

Meanwhile the marquess, who had a very good reason for not being at Mrs. Gerrard's, had emerged from White's where he had spent Harriet's accustomed lesson time engaged in desultory conversation until the moment she was most likely to be climbing into her hackney when he sauntered down Saint James's. Keeping a weather eye out for anyone else who might be demonstrating an unusual interest in the carriage or its occupants, he strolled along with the air of a man absorbed entirely by his own thoughts.

Alistair disliked missing the opportunity to see Harriet at Mrs. Gerrard's, but his instincts, sharpened by years spent in a hostile countryside and coupled with his intense mistrust of Sir Neville, warned him to keep an eye on her. Difficult as it had been-for him to forgo the chance to see her, it was far more important that he discover whether or not she was being watched or threatened in any way. Fletcher was an unscrupulous knave with very little to lose. The veiled comments he had made to Harriet at the theater were likely to be followed by more concrete and unpleasant demands.

The more Alistair thought over the entire situation as Harriet had described it to him, the more convinced he had become that she needed looking after. He had resolved to take this task upon himself for the moment until he could find someone reliable enough to replace him. Unfortunately, as he had made his way toward Saint James's earlier that morning, he had been hailed by a long-lost acquaintance from the Peninsula and thus been detained long enough to miss Harriet's unpleasant encounter with Sir Neville.

As he observed the notable lack of interest being exhibited in the hackney's progress he was congratulating himself on his forethought while wondering if his concern for Harriet had not made him over-react. By the time the carriage had reached Bond Street, Alistair, on foot and thus unimpeded by traffic had caught up with them.

One look at Harriet's set white face as she emerged from the carriage convinced him that something was amiss and he hurried over, doffing his glossy beaver. "Good day. Lady Harriet." He greeted her politely, publicly, the social smile plastered to his face while he murmured urgently under his breath, "What on earth has occurred to upset you so?"

Harriet responded in an uncharacteristically bright voice, "Good day, my lord." And then, in hastily lowered tones she added, "I cannot tell you here. Tomorrow in the park." Pinning a brilliant smile on her own countenance, she nodded to him and disappeared into Madame Celeste's shop before Alistair could catch his breath, leaving him with nothing to do but proceed along Bond Street in the same direction in which he had been following her. He kept to an aimless course with the greatest of effort, for in truth, he wished to rush after her and demand to know what was going on. However, the self-discipline that came after years in the army paid off and he managed to present to passersby an image of utmost boredom and unconcern.

He was obliged to maintain this facade with as much patience as he could muster until the next morning when he saw Harriet galloping across Hyde Park at her customary breakneck speed.

"You look as though all the demons of hell are at your heels," he remarked as he caught up with her.

"No, just one—Sir Neville Fletcher." Harriet's voice dripped with disdain, but Alistair, attuned as he was to her every gesture, detected a note of panic underneath.

His eyes narrowed as he leaned forward to scan her face. "What? Has he annoyed you further?"

. "He, he ..." With a shaking hand, Harriet brushed back a few copper wisps that were escaping from underneath her bonnet. Doing her best to rid her voice of all emotion and in the fewest words possible, she related the incident that had occurred in front of Mrs. Gerrard's the day before.

Lord Chalfont sat silent, his eyes never wavering from her face as she spoke. He made no comment until she had completely finished, then burst out, "That scoundrel! He should be hung for this, at the very least."

"Oh, no," Harriet protested. The marquess' angry frown was so thunderous that for a moment she could not help thinking he might do just that. "You must not. Think of the scandal."

"I am thinking of it, or believe me, I would have done something like that long ago. But things have gone far enough; I do believe it is time you told your family. They are the ones to put an end to this villainy. I have no right to threaten him with prosecution, but they do."

"No." Harriet leaned over to lay a pleading hand on his sleeve. "Papa has not the least notion of how to deal with anything and Charlie will work himself into such a tearing passion that he would very likely do himself a mischief. I could not sacrifice him to save myself. With your help I shall think of something." She pressed her hand to a forehead already aching from a sleepless night spent racking her brain for a solution.

"So I am to be the sacrifice, am I?" Lord Chalfont spoke in a rallying tone as he strove to divert her mind to less dire thoughts.

Harriet looked up in dismay. "Oh, I do not... I would never... I mean, I just need you to help me to think best what to do. I would never—"

"Do not fly into the boughs. I was merely funning. Of course I intend to do more than offer you advice, and I would consider it a great honor if you were to allow me to sacrifice myself for you, Lady Harriet."

The rallying note was gone now and there was no mistaking the depth of sincerity in his voice. Harriet stared at him. Gone too was the teasing glint in the eyes that gazed down into hers, with a wealth of sympathy and understanding that quite took her breath away. This was no idle response of the well brought up gentleman, Harriet realized with a shock. Lord Chalfont was actually prepared to back up his words with actions.

No one that Harriet had ever met had offered such a thing. Certainly none of the ineffectual young men of the ton or her preoccupied father, and not even Charlie who, though he paid more attention to her welfare than most people did, was easily distracted.

Unaccountable tears stung Harriet's eyes as she smiled mistily at Alistair. "Why—why, thank you. Of course it will not come to that, but I am grateful for your offer just the same." Then, unable to bear the intensity of his gaze any longer, she laughed uncomfortably, "But I must be going. Absentminded as my Aunt Almeria is, she would notice it if I were not to appear at the breakfast table."

With that she prepared to dig her heels into Brutus, but was stopped in mid-flight by Lord Chalfont who leaned over and grabbed her reins. "You must promise to let me do what I can to take care of you."

"But what can you do?"

"A man with a reputation as unsavory as Sir Neville's must have secrets he does not wish known. At the moment he is able to cling to the edges of society because the only whisperings against him are the merest innuendos. Given hard cold examples of his nefarious ways, society would disown him in an instant. I mean to discover those examples and threaten him with exposure, or worse, if he does not promise to leave you alone."

Judging from Alistair's murderous expression Harriet thought that the or worse seemed far more likely to overcome Sir Neville than exposure and social ruin. "I should be—I mean I wish I ... oh, do be careful," she pleaded. Then glancing around her at the growing number of riders who had entered the park by now, she concluded, "I truly must be going."

Thankful that he had let go of the reins, she again dug in her heels and moved toward home, leaving Alistair to wish that he had been able to offer her more than a vague plan to neutralize the threats of Sir Neville Fletcher. Looking down into her eyes, bright with unshed tears, he had longed for nothing more than to wrap her in his arms and cover her face with kisses, promising her safety, security, and protection from anything that might threaten her happiness even for an instant.

But much as he might wish to hold her and comfort her, Alistair knew that it was action Harriet needed. There was no time like the present to confront her persecutor. A man of debauched tendencies. Sir Neville Fletcher was very likely in bed at this hour sleeping off a night of excess. He would therefore be at his most vulnerable. As someone who had enjoyed similar evenings himself, the marquess knew that a person was not at his best the morning after.

Thus resolved, he turned Trajan in the direction of Grosvenor Gate and thence to Fletcher's lodgings in Curzon Street where he tossed half a crown to a likely looking lad, asking him to walk his horse while he conducted his business inside.

Chapter 19

Just as the marquess had suspected, Sir Neville had not yet arisen. It took some doing, but when at last Lord Chalfont had convinced the surly manservant that he was not about to quit the premises until he had spoken with his master, he was asked, none too graciously, to wait while the man went to rouse his master.

Left alone, Alistair glanced about the room, but there was nothing about it, beyond a general untidiness and lack of distinguishing taste, to give any clue as to the character of its occupant. Other than a half a bottle of port, an empty glass, and a mound of what looked to be crumpled up vowels hastily flung down on the table next to them, there was little else of interest in the sparsely furnished chambers.

The door opened and Sir Neville, in a hastily tied dressing gown of rich brocade, marched out. "I would like to know what is so damned important that I am imposed upon at this ungodly hour." Recognizing his visitor he came to an abrupt halt, the expression of annoyance turning into one of anger. "Oh, it is you, is it? Come to stick your nose into something that is none of your affair?"

"Ah, but all despicable behavior is my affair"—Lord Chalfont responded blandly as he brushed a nonexistent speck of lint off the lapel of his dark blue coat of Bath superfine—"particularly when it threatens a person whose boots you are not fit to lick. I have merely come to inform you that you are to have no further communication with the person in question; and, if I discover that you have not heeded my friendly warning, you will find yourself utterly and thoroughly ruined, at the very least. I trust I make myself clear. Good day."

And, without giving Sir Neville a moment to reply, the marquess turned on his heel and strolled out, leaving his outraged host to clench his fist and splutter furiously before sinking into the chair by a dark and cold fireplace. "Well, what are you looking at, imbecile?" Sir

Neville snarled at the ghoulish-looking servant who hovered anxiously nearby. "Get me another bottle of port and be quick about it." He tossed down the remains of the open bottle and stared unseeingly into the empty grate.

Slowly a wolfish smile spread over his swarthy features and he chortled gleefully to no one in particular. "So, Lady Harriet, you think you can fight me. We shall see, my pretty little spitfire. You should have taken my offer of marriage when you had the chance. Now you shall not be so lucky. What need have I for a wife of good standing in the ton if I am to be ruined anyway? No, Lady Harriet, I shall take you simply for the pleasure of taming someone who has caused me far too much trouble as it is. We shall see who wins this battle yet, you or I. And when I make my move, there will be no chivalrous gentleman to rush to your aid: of that you can be sure." And rubbing his hands together in an ecstasy of spiteful merriment, Sir Neville began to plot furiously.

Striding purposefully back to Mount Street, Lord Chalfont was also cudgeling his brain. He did not delude himself for a moment into believing that he had intimidated Sir Neville into leaving Harriet alone. In all probability this confrontation with the man was more likely to precipitate some action rather than forestall it. Alistair would have to move quickly if he wanted to be ahead of the game.

Upon reaching his chambers, he instructed Richards to keep an eye on Lady Harriet at all times. The valet, who had been a seasoned soldier long before the marquess had made him his batman, offered only the faintest of protest for he, like his master, had been missing the excitement of their previous existence. "But, my lord, who will do for you if I am to take upon myself this surveillance?" he asked.

"Why, no one. I shall do for myself," Alistair responded with considerable surprise. Then, catching sight of his henchman's worried expression, he laughed. "Relax, Richards. I am only asking you to do this for me because I can trust no one else to do it so well or to be as loyal to me as you are. Tonight I shall be attending Lady Morecambe's ball, which undoubtedly will be honored by the presence of the young lady in question so you need not begin your watch just yet. However, I would appreciate it if you would learn all you can about the affairs of Sir Neville Fletcher, a man of dubious reputation who is no better than he should be. I need facts to back up the unpleasant hearsay that follows him wherever he goes."

Richards grinned, as much in relief as at the prospect of adventure. "Yes, sir. Very good, sir. When shall I begin? Now, sir?"

"Immediately."

"Thank you, sir. Rest assured, I shall find out something."

"I have complete faith in you, Richards. Anyone who could continually produce a roast chicken with vegetables in the godforsaken places we have been together should have no trouble uncovering damaging information about a thoroughly unsavory character. I await your report."

With a wink and a nod, the servant was gone, only to appear a few hours later with the information that it was universally believed that Sir Neville had acquired his considerable fortune by cheating at cards. Furthermore, it was rumored that upon one occasion he had actually been accused of it, but since his accuser was the notoriously unsteady Lord Harry Markham, younger son of the Duke of Silchester, who was also in his cups at the time, it had been quickly forgotten. Richards had inveigled this information from a servant at a fashionable gaming hell who had witnessed the entire episode.

Upon receiving this report, Lord Chalfont leaned back in his chair, smiling through half-closed eyes. "Very good, Richards. You have outdone yourself. I trust you paid the man handsomely for the revelation and gained his assurance that he would back up Lord Harry's story if necessary."

"But of course, my lord." Richards looked wounded at the very thought of his failing to insure the man's compliance.

"Now it is up to me. And I fancy I shall meet with everyone I need to at Lady Morecambe's, except, of course, Sir Neville."

Lord Chalfont had not been mistaken. Among the first people he saw when, with Alicia and her mother on each arm, he finally escaped from the press of people in the imposing entrance hall into the brilliantly lit ballroom were Lady Elizabeth and her fiancé, Lady Harriet and Lord Aylward, with Aunt Almeria and Harriet's father deep in conversation behind them. At the sight of Lord Aylward, the marquess's eyebrows drew together in the faintest of frowns. He had seen that fellow more than once in Lady Harriet's company.

Surely she was not interested in that dullard? Aylward was a pleasant enough sort, but no match for the scintillating Harriet.

"Chalfont, you are not attending." Alicia's silvery voice broke into his thoughts. She continued to nod to acquaintances, smiling brilliantly, but there was an edge to her tone that hinted at her severe displeasure in not being the focus of his attention. Not for the first time Alistair wondered if she even cared about who the person was behind the Marquess of Kidderham.

Just then Harriet turned and, catching sight of him, smiled. It was nothing more than a friendly smile of recognition, but it was completely spontaneous and genuine, as though she was truly glad to see him. Alistair found himself grinning foolishly back at her as his pulses quickened in a most uncharacteristic manner. What was wrong with him? Thousands of women had cast far more alluring looks in his direction without eliciting such a reaction. He must be entering his dotage if he was now responding that way to a pretty girl's smile.

Guiltily he turned back to Alicia, trying to concentrate as she related one little tidbit of gossip after another. Did he know that the Favells were quite done up and were leaving immediately without waiting for the end of the Season? And Letty Harleton had finally caught poor Lord Dorling, though it was really the handsome income and snug little manor house that her father had settled on her that had done the trick.

Nodding automatically, Alistair let it all flow by him as he thought about how he was going to procure a dance with Harriet. He had been so preoccupied with ending Sir Neville's pursuit of her that he had totally neglected to tell her he had followed her suggestion and called on some of the most influential men in the government whose political views coincided with his. The prospects they had offered him were quite exciting and he wanted Harriet to be the first person to share it with him.

At long last, he was able to break away from Alicia and her mother just as Lord Aylward was returning Harriet to her family after standing up with her in the quadrille. Good. It was now his turn for surely the man was too discreet to ask her to stand up with him again.

"May I have this dance?"

The deep voice at her elbow startled Harriet who had been gazing abstractedly over the multicolored throng and wondering how she was to endure another suffocating evening of aimless dances and even more desultory conversation. She whirled around. "Oh, it is you, my lord." Then, realizing that this sounded as though she had been waiting all evening for him to approach her, she broke into a flood of inanities: the weather, the sad crush of people, her dance with Lord Aylward.

Alistair grinned and held up an admonitory hand. "Enough, enough. You have convinced me that you were not hoping to talk to me in the least." A vivid blush rose to her cheeks and, taking pity on her, he held out his hand and led her to the dance floor, remarking, "I have been waiting to have a moment alone with you even if you have not been waiting to talk to me." He lowered his voice until Harriet could barely make out his words. "I have spoken with Sir Neville and warned him in no uncertain terms that should he have any contact with you again it will go very badly for him. That should stop him for a time; however, I shall continue in my efforts to discourage him from remaining in London."

Harriet smiled shyly up at him. "I am forever in your debt, my lord, and I wish ... I wish there were some way I could thank you."

"Think nothing of it; you already have."

She raised her eyebrows in surprise. "I have?"

"Yes. By encouraging me to sit up and take stock of the world around me. You are entirely in the right of it; there is a great deal to be done. I have already met with Brougham, Lansdowne, and Grey—even Burdett, Cochrane, and Romilly—in an effort to learn more about the problems besetting us and the solutions being proposed. I am now pledged to take my seat and devote my energies to the questions at hand as you suggested I do. I cannot thank you enough for provoking me into action. For the first time in months I feel as though I can still accomplish something with my life even though I am no longer in the army."

The light in his eyes and the energetic tone of his voice were abundant proof of the truth of this statement. Harriet could not help feeling gratified at her role in this transformation. "It is very kind of you to give me such credit, but I am persuaded that in time you yourself would have come to such an inevitable conclusion."

Involuntarily Alistair glanced in Alicia's direction. How very different her cool, patrician beauty was from the vivid face turned up to his. He wondered if his betrothed would even countenance his entering into politics to improve the lives of the poor soldiers and desperate laborers looking for work. Certainly she never would have suggested such a thing, and she would have laughed at the absurd notion that he was searching for something to do that would give meaning to his life and interest to his days. How little she knew him, his exquisite fiancée; and would she even care that she did not? Alistair resolved to put this question to the test as soon as he returned Harriet to her family.

These were the reflections of a moment, but Harriet, intensely aware of her partner's every move, was able to come up with her own reasonably accurate interpretation of the sudden change in his expression from one of vitality and enthusiasm to something close to resignation. She herself considered Alicia to be as dull as a stick what with her airs and graces and her slavish devotion to the rigid dictates of the ton. But Harriet had always been uncomfortably aware that men were not so nice in their judgments where great beauty was also involved. However, here was one gentleman, at least, who did not appear to be awestruck by the sight of the Honorable Alicia De Villiers. Harriet was unusually silent for the rest of the dance, a thoughtful frown wrinkling her brow, but her partner was now too preoccupied with his own unsettling reflections to notice.

Having restored Harriet to the Farehams and paid his respects to the rest of the family, Alistair strolled in a leisurely manner back to his own group to lead Alicia on to the floor for a second dance. She hesitated for a fraction of a moment as he offered her his arm. "I am not accustomed to dancing more than once with a gentleman, but now, as we are betrothed, I suppose I need not worry about any gossip," she explained.

Lord Chalfont raised his eyebrows in faint surprise. "And what if we were not betrothed, Alicia? Might you not stand up with me a second time simply because you enjoyed it?"

Alicia stared at her fiancé, or at least she looked at him as long and hard as it was possible for a young lady who had been taught since infancy that it was rude to stare. "Of course not. You would not want me so lost to all sense of propriety as to do that."

One corner of Lord Chalfont's mouth twisted into an ironic smile. "Believe me, I should never expect such a thing, Alicia."

Even Alicia, literal-minded as she was, was not quite certain of how to take his last remark and she hastily changed the subject. "We have seen very little of you these past few days, my lord. I trust you have been happily occupied."

Alistair, refusing to take this as any reflection on his lack of attentiveness, replied equably, "Why yes. I have decided to make myself useful by going into politics, and to that end I have been calling upon various people."

"Politics," Alicia echoed blankly, looking for all the world as though he had proposed a journey to India or something equally as absurd.

"Yes. Now that the war is over, there is a great deal of unrest and something must be done."

Alicia wrinkled her nose delicately as though she had just caught a whiff of something most unpleasant. "Yes. Papa was saying not long ago that things were getting quite out of hand, what with the demands of the lower classes, but he is hopeful that the efforts of his friend Lord Sidmouth will go a long way toward keeping these unruly elements in order." She paused to shudder delicately and then continued. "I suppose if you must involve yourself in such things. Papa could speak to Lord Sidmouth and Lord Liverpool on your behalf."

"That is kind of you, Alicia, but you need not trouble your father on my behalf," Alistair responded quickly, forbearing to add that it was precisely the narrow vision and repressive actions of Lord Sidmouth and his cronies that were prompting him to go into politics in the first place. He could immediately see that Alicia did not look favorably upon his new interest and it behooved him to tread carefully—not that she could prohibit him from following the course he had set for himself, but she could certainly make his life uncomfortable. The less she knew the better.

It was a great pity for he would have liked to share his ideas with someone, but Alicia was certainly not that person. She never had wanted to know anything about his life except when it had to do with her. Otherwise she preferred to remain ignorant of everything, from his experiences during the war to his opinions on just about any subject. In fact, she would quickly change the topic if they happened to stray into a discussion that was not somehow connected to the world of the Upper Ten Thousand or her position in it.

Alistair stifled a sigh as he pasted an expression of polite interest on his face and finished out the set in silence. Alicia was not, and never would be, a kindred spirit, but at least she was well-bred enough not to meddle in his affairs. About the best he could hope for was that they could coexist peacefully, going their separate ways. It was a bleak enough picture, but a supportable one, and he could have been much worse off, married to a wealthy shrew as was poor Lord Wharton, or continually embarrassed by his wife's vulgar antics as was Sir Roland Foxworth. No, Alicia would never be a companion, but she would always be a credit to him.

Fortifying himself with this cold comfort, Lord Chalfont spent the rest of the evening smiling mechanically and nodding at his betrothed's observations on the various members of the ton present at the ball who were worthy of comment He waited with as much patience as he could muster until he could deposit Alicia and her mother at home before going in search of the erratic Lord Harry Markham who, absent from Lady Morecambe's, must have sought amusement at a place more congenial to his jaded tastes.

Chapter 20

At last Alicia declared the evening to be a dreadful squeeze. Lord Chalfont had escorted the De Villiers' women back to Hanover Square and, after bidding them good night, had gone in search of his quarry whom he quickly tracked down in Jermyn Street at the gaming hell mentioned by Richards. His lordship was pretty well to live by the time Alistair managed to drag him away from the hazard table, but not so far gone as to look about uneasily at the mention of Sir Neville's name. "Relax, man, he is nowhere in sight." The marquess laid a reassuring hand on the young lord's shoulder. "I am not asking you to do anything at the moment beyond signing your name to this paper here, but should it become necessary I shall make it worth your while to repeat your story. You can rest assured that I can produce witnesses who will support you."

Lord Harry continued to look distinctly uncomfortable and Alistair, making a quick, but accurate assessment of the state of affairs continued blandly. "I have no small experience with this sort of thing as a number of young men under my command in the Peninsula found themselves in, er, similarly unfortunate circumstances. I can be extremely persuasive and I have no doubt that I can convince the person in question to give up what ever hold he has upon you. If you but sign your name to the description I have written out of what occurred, you need trouble yourself no more and I shall advance you a sum to win back what you lost; however, I suggest you do it somewhere else as the play here is notoriously unfair."

Lord Harry opened his mouth to protest. He was not a bad young man, only a very weak one who had been largely ignored by his parents and his tutors and had thus grown up without restraint of any kind. He quickly gave in to the look of steely determination in Lord Chalfont's eyes, not to mention the wad of notes he thrust into his lordship's limp hand. "Very well," he replied sulkily, "but it will do you no good. No one ever bests Fletcher."

"Perhaps not," the marquess calmly conceded, "but then, you see, he has never dealt with me before. No one ever bests me either, and I fancy that far more dangerous opponents have challenged me than have challenged Sir Neville."

Glancing sullenly at the marquess' implacable countenance and powerful build. Lord Harry had no difficulty in believing this and he was not eager to continue a conversation that had such unpleasant overtones. With an effort, he shrugged in as careless a manner as he could muster, scrawled his name at the bottom of the paper and, stuffing the notes in his pockets, replied with a nonchalance he was far from feeling, "That is your affair. Well, I am off to greener pastures." Doing his best not to stagger, he made it to the door without a backward glance, leaving the marquess to smile ironically as he folded the paper containing the evidence against Sir Neville and thrust it in his pocket.

Well satisfied with his evening's work, he returned home to dash off a quick note to Sir Neville informing him that if he had made the mistake of believing Lord Chalfont's threats to be groundless, he had best reconsider as that gentleman now had in his possession a sworn affidavit of Sir Neville's villainy from Lord Harry Markham himself, who was also enjoying the Marquess of Kidderham's protection. "That should stop him, for the moment," Alistair muttered as he gulped down a final glass of brandy and prepared himself for bed.

Unfortunately, Lord Chalfont had laid his plans without taking into account the state of mind of a desperate man. Born into a family of dubious reputation that had been slowly eroded by generations of wastrels who had barely avoided open censure. Sir Neville had pledged himself to restore not only his family's finances, but its former social standing. Fate, however, was against him. The last of the Fletchers was blessed with neither wit nor grace; he had no personal charms and such was his upbringing that he only knew how to advance himself at the expense of others, through guile and cunning rather than openly, honestly, and in a manner destined to win him true friends and admirers instead of mere hangers-on in search of the money he could lend them. As Sir Neville's winnings had increased, so had his list of enemies—men whose lives he had ruined in order to advance himself. The more his fortune grew, the more he longed to establish himself among the society that continued to shun him. The more his goal receded, the more determined he became to win it until acceptance in the ton had become an obsession with him.

The discovery of Lady Harriet's identity as being one and the same with Fanny's rescuer had been heaven-sent and Sir Neville, though not a believer in anything but his own grim determination, had taken this singular coincidence as a sign that he was to succeed after all in his quest for respectability. Never doubting that Lady Harriet would sacrifice herself to save her family's honor, he had not even been daunted by her furious rejection of him on the steps of Mrs. Gerrard's. Sir Neville had broken women far more worldly and experienced and with a good deal less to lose than Lady Harriet Fareham stood to. He had no doubt of winning in the end.

But now this infernal meddler Chalfont insisted on sticking his damned officious nose into affairs that were none of his business. Sir Neville was not a coward, though he preferred to beat his enemies by foul means rather than fair, but he knew he was no match for the Marquess of Kidderham in whatever arena. The marquess had the enviable reputation of being top-of-the-trees, a true Corinthian who distinguished himself wherever he went. From Jackson's rooms to Manton's shooting gallery to the ballrooms of society's starchiest matrons, he was welcomed with enthusiasm as being exceedingly adept at whatever he did. Such a man would inevitably triumph no matter how clever Sir Neville was. And now that the marquess had taken it upon himself to protect Lady Harriet, he would always stand in the way of Sir Neville's hopes for advancement, if he did not out-and-out ruin him.

Sir Neville scowled darkly as he read Chalfont's note. No, there was no way he was going to attain his goal now, but he was not going to let that stop him. The Marquess of Kidderham might keep him out of polite society, but he was not adroit enough to keep him from Lady Harriet. Lord Chalfont might have the ton behind him, but he did not hold all the cards. Sir Neville would act swiftly and catch him unawares. He would give it out that he had left town and then, when the marquess, his fears allayed, relaxed his vigilance. Sir Neville would strike. He chuckled grimly. He might not succeed in repairing his reputation, but at least he could utterly destroy someone else's. After this, Lady Harriet would be beseeching him to marry her. How he would enjoy seeing that little spitfire humbled and begging him. Sir Neville licked his lips in anticipation. The picture of it alone was almost worth the loss of his dreams.

Meanwhile Harriet, unaware of the plots being laid against her, or of Richards's surveillance, went about her business as usual. Fanny was now working for Madame Celeste, and Harriet congratulated herself that she had been able to help at least one of Mrs. Gerrard's ladies move closer to her dream.

Encouraged by Fanny's successful relocation, Harriet was impatient to do the same for the rest of them and could hardly contain herself in between her weekly lessons at Mrs. Gerrard's. She had gone shopping, occasionally joining Elizabeth and Aunt Almeria in their calls, and took in a visit to the Egyptian Hall with the protesting Charlie in tow to see the mosaics from Nero's baths, blithely unaware that Lord Chalfont's Richards was following her to all these things at a discreet distance.

Richards had communicated to the marquess that a stable lad generously paid for keeping an eye on Sir Neville's movements had reported that Sir Neville had departed for his estate in Hertfordshire, but the marquess was too old a campaigner to relax his vigilance. "Mark my words, Richards," he had responded to this news, "the man is a thoroughgoing villain. Scoundrels such as he do not give up so easily. No, I think it behooves us to remain on our guard."

"Very good, sir." The batman's face remained impassive, but his brain was working furiously. There was more to this than a disinterestedly chivalrous concern for a lady's reputation or the marquess' natural distaste for low characters such as Sir Neville. No, there was a note of concern in Lord Chalfont's voice that Richards had never heard before as well as an uncharacteristic air of worried preoccupation.

Richards had been with the Marquess of Kidderham through bad times and good, had seen him charge the French single-handedly and comfort dying friends, but he had never seen him this way before. To Richards who knew that under the devil-may-care exterior was a man of deep feeling and great honor, it meant that there was a conflict now raging in his lordship, and it was tearing him apart. Richards was certain that Lord Chalfont would stand by his engagement to Alicia, but he was also aware that the marquess did not give a rap for that self-centered young woman, while he was beginning to care a great deal for the lady whose welfare was now such a matter of concern. The servant wished there were something he could do to help his master, but at the moment all that came to mind was to do as instructed and keep as close an eye as possible on Lady Harriet Fareham.

Thus it was that Richards was standing in the shadow of a flight of steps leading to a building a few doors away from Mrs. Gerrard's several days later when Rose emerged from the establishment all alone and headed off in the direction of Bond Street. Richards was instantly on the alert. He had not been keeping an eye on Lady Harriet long enough to be absolutely certain of her routine at Mrs. Gerrard's, but he knew that this pattern differed from the last time he had followed her there, and he thought it highly unlikely that Harriet would dispense with the protection of her maid when that would mean she was all by herself in a place of questionable repute.

Suspiciously Richards sidled closer to Mrs. Gerrard's doorway and waited. He carefully scrutinized the hackney that drew up to the door a few minutes later, but could see nothing amiss there. However he was watching closely enough to observe Harriet, who had hurried down the steps soon after its arrival, hesitate as she began to enter me carriage and then appear to lose her footing as she disappeared inside as though someone had jerked her in roughly. The door was slammed shut more violently than was customary, and the jarvey whipped up the horses and drove off at an uncharacteristic clip.

Thoroughly alarmed by these disturbing events, Richards only stayed long enough to note the direction of the carriage and then hastened back to Mount Street to relate his misgivings to the marquess. "Of course I could be mistaken, by lord, but it looks havey-cavey to me," he concluded, still panting from his mad dash back to Lord Chalfont's chambers.

Alistair, who had risen immediately from a desk awash in correspondence, grabbed his jacket and began pulling on his boots before the first few words were out of his batman's mouth, did not stop to discuss it beyond ordering that his horse be saddled and brought around. Hastily scribbling a note to Harriet's brother Charlie, he handed it to Richards instructing him to deliver it to the captain at his barracks in an hour's time. "And do not let that young hothead try to follow me whatever happens," he tossed over his shoulder as he headed out the door. "Do what you must to stop him. I know that things are in good hands with you, Richards. You've done excellently thus far. Fletcher is no match for the pair of us."

The old soldier's weatherbeaten countenance broke into a rare grin. "That he is not, my lord. Now off with you, sir, and Godspeed." And may you find the young lady safe and sound, he muttered to himself as the door slammed behind Lord Chalfont.

Chapter 21

In the meantime, the young lady in question was struggling violently to free herself from her captor's iron grip. Harriet had been puzzled when the new serving girl at Mrs. Gerrard's had greeted her at the door of the schoolroom with the information that Rose, feeling faint, had gone outside for fresh air and was waiting for her in the carriage. It was most unlike Rose who was proud of saying that she had never had a sick day in her life, but Harriet had been too preoccupied with the lesson she had just taught to give it much further consideration until, climbing into the carriage she had spied a pantalooned leg in the doorway instead of Rose's skirts. She had hesitated, trying to see into the murky depths of the carriage, but by then it had been too late. One hand had grabbed her wrist and pulled her in while another had stuffed what she presumed to be a handkerchief into her mouth.

Almost before she had realized what was happening, the door slammed behind her and the carriage clattered off down the street. Harriet fought furiously, kicking and wriggling with all her might, but it was worse than useless, for the hands only gripped her more tightly and her abductor chuckled heartily at her efforts.

"Squirm all you like, missy, but you are in my power now and you will dance to whatever tune I choose. If you become any more unmanageable, I shall not hesitate to bind your hands and feet."

Recognizing that for the moment she was at a severe disadvantage, Harriet ceased resisting and, stiffening her back, mustered what dignity she could in such a humiliating situation. The hands that had gripped her were now forcing hers together behind her back, binding them tightly. Though this meant the hands were no longer covering her mouth, the handkerchief had been stuffed in so far that it was all she could do not to gag, much less spit it out. Her eyes stung as the cords cut into her wrists, but Harriet refused to blink lest her captor think she was shedding tears of weakness.

I will not give way, I will not give way, she repeated to herself over and over again as she tried to collect her scattered wits. Even now when she was free to turn her head, she refused to look her abductor in the face. There was no doubt that it was Sir Neville. She recognized the disgusting hands with their short stubby fingers covered in black hair from her last struggle with him.

No, there was no doubt at all in Harriet's mind as to who it was or what he was going to do with her. The only question that remained was when, and how long could she forestall him, for, in spite of her confidence in her own resourcefulness, Harriet could not foresee that she would ever be clever enough to escape such a thoroughgoing villain. Why he must have enacted such scenes dozens of times if half the stories she had heard at Mrs. Gerrard's were true.

She was safe for the moment at least for surely he was not going to have his way with her in the carriage. Either he was taking her to some den of iniquity within the metropolis or he was carrying her to his estate in the country. Either way it would not be long before they arrived at their destination or changed horses, and perhaps she would have a chance to escape or at least call for help. Think, Harriet, think. She closed her eyes, trying to focus her energies on freeing herself from such a dreadful situation.

"You think to feign sleep, my little spitfire. Go ahead, sleep then. That will only make you all the more wide awake later and I like my women to be lively." He chuckled again in an exulting way that made Harriet long to wipe off the gloating smile she knew was on his face with a punishing blow. Never in her life had she yearned to be a man as much as she did at this moment.

At last they slowed and pulled into what must have been the yard of an inn. Harriet could hear horses stomping, the rattle of harnesses, and the shouts of ostlers, but before she could formulate a plan for escape or for enlisting the aid of a sympathetic bystander, she felt something hard thrust into her side.

"Do not think to call for help, my fine young lady, or you will be a dead young lady," an unpleasant voice growled in her ear. A voluminous cloak was thrown over her head, and she was hauled out of the hackney and into another carriage so quickly that she had no time to put up a struggle even if she had dared.

The carriage in which she now sat was more luxurious than the hackney, well cushioned and well sprung. With a sinking heart Harriet realized that it must be Sir Neville's own traveling carriage. There was nothing to do but close her eyes and lean back against the cushions, awaiting further developments with as much composure as she could muster. Though outwardly calm, Harriet was having some difficulty fighting the rising panic within her.

She had been hoping that they would remain in London where she at least had some hope of prevailing upon a sympathetic or curious person. In the crowded metropolis there were many more opportunities for attracting attention. Imprisoned in the country, she was likely to be surrounded by retainers whose livelihood depended on Sir Neville's favor and would therefore be unlikely to be at all disposed toward helping her. Harriet wondered how long it would be before Rose raised the alarm. Even then, would they be able to guess what had happened to her?

For some strange reason the image of Lord Chalfont rose before her, causing her to swallow to get rid of the aching lump in her throat. He had saved her from Sir Neville once before, but he could not save her now. Even if he knew she had disappeared, which was highly improbable, he could not forever be rescuing a young woman who was the merest acquaintance. But oh she did wish for him to come and rid her of the odious beast sitting next to her with the same dispatch as he had done before.

Harriet squared her shoulders against the seat. Buck up, my girl, she admonished herself severely. There is no use repining. The only person who can rescue you is you, so you had better start thinking, and quickly, about what you are going to do to save yourself. However, when they stopped to change horses some time later, she was no closer to a solution than she had been at the outset. Her captor pulled down the shades and kept her well away from the windows so there was not the least hope of attracting any notice.

At last, they appeared to slow their slapping pace and turn onto what sounded like a gravel drive. The journey had seemed endless, but Harriet supposed that in reality it had not been much more than two hours, if that. Where was she then? She racked her brain trying to think if she knew where Sir Neville had his estate—Surrey, Buckinghamshire, Sussex? She had been too upset at the beginning to listen for any telltale clues as to which way they were leaving the city. In fact, she could not even say whether or not they had crossed over the river—not that any of this speculation did her the least bit of good; she was well and truly caught, for the moment that was.

At last the carriage halted and the door was opened. "We have arrived, my pretty one," the hateful voice whispered in her ear.

Refusing to give any sign of acknowledgment or recognition to her abductor, Harriet allowed herself to be helped down and led into the house. She made no attempt to struggle or break free. Sir Neville seemed to expect it, to hope for it even, and he watched her as a cat watches its prey, ready to pounce at the least sign of movement. But Harriet was not about to give him the satisfaction of overcoming her. Resistance only seemed to excite him, and the last thing she wished to do was gratify his brutish impulses.

The only servants she saw as he led her into a cavernous dark entry and then down dimly lit corridors were a sour-looking butler and the half-witted boy who came to hold the horses. There was no help here, no chance of prevailing on the sympathies of a housekeeper or maid, some woman who might be made to see the misery of her situation.

Finally they came to a bedchamber as uninviting as the rest of the house. Dust lay thick on the chest of drawers and the escritoire, while the hangings on the enormous bed were moth-eaten and dangling in shreds.

Sir Neville freed her hands and untied the gag that had been choking her. "And now my little fire-eater, and now ..." He glided toward her, rubbing his hands together.

At last Harriet was able to take a gulp of fresh air. "Stand back, sirrah," she gasped.

"Oh no, I am coming a good deal closer, my dear." He chuckled ominously as Harriet shrank involuntarily. "Oh yes, a very good deal closer."

Harriet clapped a hand to her mouth and muttered through her fingers, "I warn you. I am about to be quite unwell." It was the truth. The close air, the motion of the carriage, the handkerchief jammed in her mouth, coupled with the natural tension of finding oneself in such a dire situation had made her head ache dreadfully and her stomach lurch queasily. Undoubtedly she could have overcome these unpleasant symptoms if she had wished to, but it occurred to her that it was better to suffer these than something far worse.

Sir Neville hesitated. His captive did look rather green about the gills and while overcoming the struggles of an unwilling victim had its charms, forcing himself on a sick one did not.

Seeing his indecision, Harriet took advantage of it by gagging most convincingly and glancing desperately around the room for a chamber pot.

The would-be ravisher had had enough. Hastily he retreated from the room slamming the door behind him and turning the key in the lock.

Continuing to make retching noises and banging about as though she were indeed searching for the chamber pot, Harriet sank into a chair by the window. A cloud of dust rose around her, but she could have cared less. At least she was alone for the moment. Freed from her captor's oppressive presence she could at last marshal her scattered thoughts and plot her escape.

Trying to keep herself from being seen by anyone set to watch her, she peered cautiously around the curtains at the window to the park below. The window catch looked easy enough to undo and the window large enough to climb out of, but it was a twenty-foot drop to the ground below and there was no convenient tree or vine to cling to. Furthermore, this part of park appeared to be surrounded by a high stone wall with no gate in sight nor any tree or shrub she could use to scale it.

Harriet sighed. She was in the very devil of a coil and with no obvious means of escape. For the moment she could fob off Sir Neville by feigning illness, but this would only serve as the most temporary of excuses and then she would have to think of something else.

If escape was impossible, then outright assault appeared to be the only solution. She had already had proof of his brutal strength and knew that unless she had a most superior weapon she was destined to be beaten in any physical contest. In fact, she could deduce from his remarks that such a contest would only serve to heighten his enjoyment of the situation. No, there could be no struggle. She would have to eliminate him with the first attack, whatever form that was to take.

Desperately Harriet crept soundlessly around the room in search of a weapon, but could lay her hands on nothing more threatening than the poker leaning up against a fireplace that looked as though it had not been used during the past twenty years. It was not possible to conceal it while waiting for a propitious moment; therefore, she would have to strike the minute he appeared. Carefully she hefted it, testing its weight and envisioning how she would have to position herself in order to bring it down with all her force upon his head. Or course, immobilizing Sir Neville would only be her first challenge. After that, she would have to deal with the servants, though judging from the condition the place was in, there were not many of them.

Holding the curtain up to hide her, Harriet craned her neck around the corner of the window trying to get a better view of the place in order to establish the location of the stables and determine the possibility of finding a horse there on which she could flee. It was a desperate situation, but she was resolved not to be conquered by it. Having concocted as much of a plan as was possible, she took up her position to one side of the door, her hands firmly wrapped around the poker, and she waited.

Chapter 22

While Harriet was biding her time with as much patience as she could muster, Alistair was galloping north toward Hertfordshire at breakneck speed. Discreet inquiries had revealed that Sir Neville Fletcher's family estate, now fallen into as much disrepair as its owner's reputation, lay not far from St. Albans outside the little village of Smallford. He figured that Sir Neville had only an hour to an hour and a half's head start on him at most and that he would have had to change from the hackney to a traveling carriage at some point. At any rate, a man on a horse could travel faster than a carriage, cutting across country to save time and distance if need be, while a carriage was obliged to stick to the main roads. Given these circumstances, the marquess hoped to arrive at Fletcher's estate not too long after Sir Neville himself, and thus come to Harriet's aid before too much damage had been done.

Lord Chalfont had seen enough of Lady Harriet Fareham to know that her own resourcefulness would keep her captor at bay for a little while. She was a clever and courageous young lady, already angered by Fletcher's brutish treatment of Fanny. This anger would fuel her resistance at the outset, but eventually she would be no match for the bigger, stronger Sir Neville and whatever servants he managed to command. Once again the picture of Harriet struggling in Sir Neville's grasp at Mrs. Gerrard's rose before him and Alistair gnawed his lip in frustration as he leaned forward over Trajan's neck, urging him to even greater speed.

The marquess was banking on the premise that an estate let fall to rack and ruin would have few servants about, servants who would be no match for the man who had once given an entire regiment of French cavalry pause.

Skirting St. Albans and its crowded streets, he turned off the main road and headed toward Smallford on a less traveled road until he found a likely looking farmer whom he stopped to ask directions. Inclined to be conversational at first, the man became a good deal less friendly when he learned of the marquess's destination. Apparently Sir Neville's reputation was as unsavory in the country as it was in town.

At last a park with its crumbling gate came into view. Alistair rode boldly up the gravel drive, scanning the countryside on either side of him for any signs of activity, but there was none. Only some fresh looking tracks made by the wheels of a carriage in the gravel gave any indication that the estate had been visited recently. A deserted air hung about the place as though no one, not even servants, lived there. Passing through gates that hung awry on rusty hinges, he trotted up to the door and dismounted, noting with satisfaction that there were still no signs of activity: no stable boy came to hold his horse, no butler stood in the doorway. If it had not been for the scuffed-up gravel indicating that a carriage and its occupants had arrived not long ago, the marquess might have thought that even Sir Neville and his captive had not been there.

Alistair banged the heavy brass knocker repeatedly until at last the door swung open and a cadaverous looking face peered around it. "There is no one at home," a sepulchral voice intoned as the door began to close again.

The marquess leaned one broad shoulder against the door, effectively forcing it open as he replied in the friendliest of tones, "Of course there is, my good man, and I suggest you take me to him immediately or it will be the worse for you."

The servant looked anxiously around him. Though he had been well paid by Sir Neville, he had not been paid well enough to deal with this sudden and totally unexpected change in events. The master had assured him that nothing more would be required of him than making sure that there was food in the house, a few fires lit, and that the girl did not escape. No mention had been made of a large, determined, and dangerous looking man coming in pursuit of her. He wavered. Sir Neville was a vicious man to cross, but he was no more threatening than the person who now stood glowering at him as though he were about to tear him limb from limb.

"Loyalty, or whatever it is that binds you to your master, will do you little good, for when I am finished with him he will be ruined and therefore no longer in need of your services. Now, where is the young lady?"

"No—I mean, I cannot say—" the man stammered.

Alistair gripped him by the throat until his eyes bulged. "Cannot say, or will not say. I shall find him anyway, but your telling me will save me time and you a good deal of discomfort."

"She's—she's up there," the man gasped, clawing ineffectively at the hands gripping his throat and nodding over his right shoulder. "The first bedchamber in the east wing."

The marquess relaxed his grip. "Very good. Now, if I were you, I would make haste to clear out of here for things are bound to. become very unpleasant."

"Yes, sir, very good, sir." The man scuttled off into the gloom as Alistair turned and ran up the marble staircase two steps at a time. Reaching the top, he stopped, listening for any signs that either Harriet or her kidnapper was near. At first he heard nothing, then a cry, hastily muffled, and a crash.

"Harriet! Harriet!" he shouted. "I am here." He tried the knob of the first door on the right with no success. Stopping to look around and make sure that he had followed the servant's directions correctly, he put his ear to the door and listened. Unmistakable sounds of a struggle issued from the other side. Alistair threw his weight against the door, but though it rattled, it did not give. Forcing himself to stop and examine the lock, he observed that it was not all that strong and, gritting his teeth, he stepped back and threw himself against it once more with all his might.

There was a tremendous crash as the door suddenly gave way and slammed back against the wall, causing a painting to tumble to the floor. For a moment Lord Chalfont paused, fighting to master the surge of rage threatening to overcome him at the sight of Harriet, her face tense and white, struggling in Sir Neville's arms. Then Alistair's head cleared and a colder, more implacable anger took over. "I shall give you precisely ten seconds to unhand this woman and leave the room or I shall kill you," he announced calmly, pulling a deadly looking pistol from his pocket.

Sir Neville looked up, his face contorted with fury. "You! How dare you draw on an unarmed man in his own home! At least put down your weapon and fight like a gentleman instead of a coward."

"I would if I had a gentleman to fight, but at the moment, I am hunting vermin and I find that this"—the marquess waved his pistol—"is the most effective means of eliminating them. Now, I really have no more time to discuss it as I must restore this young lady to her family. If you wish to remain intact, I suggest you leave. In fact, I suggest you leave the country entirely for awhile unless you want to have it bruited about that your fortune is built upon cheating at cards." Alistair held up his hand as Sir Neville opened his mouth to protest. "Do not bother to argue. As you know, I have a sworn statement from a reliable witness that will destroy your credibility even in the lowest gaming hell and I have also uncovered other witnesses. I shall see to it that those who have been swindled will be clamoring for reimbursement until you have not a feather to fly with."

"I refuse to be bullied, you bastard. You are bluffing." Sir Neville shouted, even as he released Harriet and backed toward the door. "You shall not get away with this, I tell you, I—" Standing in the doorway, he shook his fist at Lord Chalfont who, by now thoroughly bored by his opponent, had turned his back on him and was giving all his attention to the lady.

"Harriet, Harriet, my poor girl, are you all right?" He demanded frantically as he pulled her into his arms.

At first Harriet did not move or respond in any way, for she was too overwhelmed by the horror and the swiftness of events to react at all.

After Sir Neville had locked her in, she had stood watch by the door, poker in hand, for what had seemed ages, though it had in fact been little more than an hour. At last she had heard heavy footsteps in the hall outside the door and knew her moment had come. Raising the poker high over her head, she had listened to the key grating in the lock and watched the turning of the doorknob in horrified fascination, her heart thumping so hard against her ribs that she was sure Sir Neville would also have been able to hear it.

As the door had swung open, Harriet had brought the poker down with all her might, but unfortunately her captor knew her all too well. The moment he entered the room he glanced to his right and, seeing her there, sprang, twisting the poker from her hands as it arched toward his head. "Not so fast, my pretty lady," he said with a laugh as the poker clattered to the floor. Still clutching the hand that had held the poker, he had dragged her toward him, wrapping his other arm around her waist.

"You are a hotheaded little wench—just as I suspected you would be. I like 'em that way—all the better to tame." He leered at her lasciviously and Harriet, nearly gagging at the stale scent of spirits on his hot breath, shut her eyes.

Suddenly he was kissing her furiously, shoving his thick tongue between her clenched teeth and gripping the back of her head, forcing her to look up at him, but Harriet refused to open her eyes or acknowledge any contact with him.

A tremor of disgust began to sweep over her, but with a tremendous effort, she willed herself steady, rigidly maintaining an unresponsive posture as he pulled her closer to him. Struggling was of no use. She was already well aware of how easily he could overpower her and resistance only excited him all the more. All she could hope was that his passion would overcome his sense of self-preservation at some point and then, when his guard was down, she could break free and grab the poker. Emptying her mind of everything else, she tried to visualize where the poker had fallen in relation to her and to the door.

His hands roved over her body, sending a wave of revulsion through her so strong that Harriet feared she might faint. This was how poor Fanny had felt, how all of Mrs. Gerrard's ladies must have felt time and time again. Harriet vowed to break free and revenge herself on this man for what he had done to her and to so many others.

She tried not to wince as one hairy hand tore at the lacy fichu around her neck. He was breathing harder now and his hold on her was loosening. Soon, she sensed, he would be in the grip of passion and too preoccupied to think of anything but gratifying his own lust, and then perhaps she could take advantage of his relaxed vigilance to save herself.

The lace came away, revealing the flesh beneath it and Sir Neville stopped to savor the moment. He licked his lips in anticipation. It was in that instant that Harriet twisted and fought in his grasp, just as she heard her name being called. So frantic was she that for a moment she thought it was her own disordered brain supplying her with the comforting sound of Lord Chalfont's voice, but then came the thundering crash and, miracle of miracles, the rescue she had never let herself dare hope for.

He was here to save her. Sobbing with relief she had broken free as he had forced Sir Neville from the room. Now she turned to him without even stopping to wonder how such an incredible thing had occurred, how he had known what had happened to her in the first place, and then known where to find her. She had needed him desperately and he had appeared. It was as simple as that; so simple that it seemed as natural as breathing, and she had sought the comfort and reassurance of his arms as though she had always belonged there.

Chapter 23

For several moments Harriet remained in the marquess's embrace. Gulping in great gasping breaths of fresh air, she tried to regain her composure while she reveled in the strength of his arms around her and the warmth of his breath in her hair as he whispered, "There, there, my brave girl, everything is all right; I'm here and nothing shall harm you. Hush now." Harriet could not recall ever having felt so safe or so protected in her life as she did now, resting her head on the marquess' broad shoulder, feeling the hardness and the strength of his body against hers.

At last she raised her head. "How ever did you know what had happened to me and where to find me?"

Alistair smiled down at her, the tawny eyes warm and comforting. "Believe me, once I knew that villain had discovered your identity I never let you out of my sight. If I was not with you, then my man Richards was keeping a watchful eye on you. I suspected that the blackguard might try something, and I made certain I found out the place he might take you should he slip through my guard which, I am ashamed to admit, he did."

Harriet gazed at him in wonderment, the dark blue eyes wide and questioning. Alistair longed to pull her close again and kiss the worried look from her face, caress the parted lips with his own, but wisely he held back, sensing that the horror of Sir Neville's unwelcome attentions was still with her.

"But had we not better escape before, sir"—Harriet shuddered at the very thought of the man—"before he comes back? and what if he does not heed your threat and decides to return to London after all? He swore he would destroy me, you know."

"I know." The marquess' face was more grave than she had ever seen it as he took her hands in his. "But believe me, little one, he will not harm you now, and on that I pledge you my word. I have known

many men of his type—brutes and bullies where the weak are concerned, but cowards when faced with determined resistance. And he
knows well enough that should he ever so much as look at you again,
I shall not only ruin him, I shall kill him."

Lord Chalfont spoke in the most conversational of tones, but the
very casualness of it lent a deadly seriousness to his words. To the
marquess, Sir Neville was of as little concern as any fox that had gotten among the chickens or a rat in the corner—a pest, that if it continued to harm, would be eliminated without a second thought.

Harriet shivered and once again was pulled into his arms. This
was an entirely different Lord Chalfont and this new vision gave her
pause. She had been introduced to the irreverent man about town.
Gradually she had come to recognize that there was more to him
than the wild libertine bent on his own amusement, and she had
come to see that he was a man of principle, of ideals even; a man
who reflected seriously on life and its purpose. Of course after all her
brother's tales of Lord Chalfont's wartime exploits she should have
known that the soldier existed underneath it all, but it still came as
something of a shock to see the lips that were usually curled into an
ironic smile set in an unyielding line and the eyes that had been so
warm moments ago glinting as bright and hard as agate. The marquess seemed more like a grim stranger than the man who was forever teasing her, challenging her, trying to make her lose her countenance and her temper, or both.

"Relax, my poor girl. It shall not come to bloodshed, I promise
you that. Undoubtedly the man is well on his way to the Channel by
now." Just as quickly as the grim stranger had appeared, he was gone,
and the marquess was tilting her chin to look deep into her eyes.
"Promise me you will think no more of it?"

There was no avoiding the penetrating gaze. "I promise." "Good.
That's settled. And now I very much fear you are about to experience
the most uncomfortable part of this entire adventure, which is to
ride pillion until I can discover an inn where I may hire a carriage.
I rather think we shall be forced to return to St. Albans before we
find something because between here and the London road there is
nothing but a wild stretch of heath. Now come along." The marquess
helped her on with her pelisse and, still holding her with one protec-

tive arm, led her from the bedchamber, down the long dim halls, and out into the sunlight.

They met with no resistance; in fact, the entire place appeared to be so completely deserted that Harriet could almost believe the whole adventure had been a horrible nightmare except for the very real presence of Lord Chalfont. He held her so close that she could feel the comforting warmth of his hand and the strength of his fingers through her sarcenet pelisse and the thin muslin of her gown.

Alistair's horse, trained to obedience by years in the Peninsula with his master, was waiting patiently for them in the gravel drive. "Now comes the difficult part." The marquess shot a teasing smile at Harriet. "You shall be forced to sit quietly in front of me while I guide us tamely to the nearest inn. It is far more comfortable than riding pillion, but still a trial for someone who is accustomed to riding her own horse, and at breakneck speed."

His attempt at humor won only the faintest answering smile from Harriet who was still far too shaken by the morning's events to think of anything else.

"What? No stinging retort? My dear Lady Harriet, you are more seriously discomposed than I had realized."

A distinctly watery smile was her only reply and it wrung his heart to see the delicate mouth droop and the sprinkling of freckles across the pert little nose stand out in dark contrast against her still pale skin. Alistair looked deep into the eyes which were dark and troubled. "Come now; what's amiss? All's well that ends well."

"I know," Harriet sighed. "And I thank you for rescuing me, only ... only I should have been able to save myself. I should never have fallen for his stratagem. I should have looked first in the carriage before I got in. Oh, I have been wretchedly stupid."

Alistair longed to hold her close and kiss all her doubts away, to smooth her hair and comfort her, but he sensed that at the moment, she needed to have her confidence restored more than she needed to be consoled. He had seen the same thing often enough among his men after a particularly horrific battle and knew that a bracing tone was the most effective. "Nonsense. You appeared to be defending yourself quite creditably when I arrived. As so often happens in war, reinforcements only hasten the inevitable. My presence did not save you as much as insure that you will arrive home soon enough that no one will be the wiser. Now up with you, and we shall be on our way." He tossed her up in the saddle as easily as if she were a small child, swung up behind her, and they trotted off down the drive without further incident.

They rode in silence for some time along a road that appeared to be little used. Obviously Sir Neville was a most infrequent visitor to these parts, and the house lay far enough off the main roads that there was little through traffic.

In spite of Lord Chalfont's reassuring words, Harriet could not help thinking as they rode along that it was most fortunate he had arrived when he did, for given the deserted location of the estate, it would have been a matter of considerable luck if, having managed to escape on her own, she could have made her way far enough to discover someone to render her assistance. In fact it was not until the tower of the abbey in St. Albans came into view that they saw anything much in the way of habitation.

Finally they drew up in a spinney not far from the abbey and a group of houses, at what looked to be the main crossroads. Alistair jumped down and helped Harriet to dismount. Setting her carefully on the ground he held her for longer than was customary, searching her face for signs of distress. Having satisfied himself that she seemed to have thoroughly recovered from her unpleasant escapade, he began to set forth his plans for her.

"On my way here I noted a posting inn not far ahead and observed that they had stables sufficient to supply us with a suitable conveyance. Loathe as I am to leave you here alone, I am even more unwilling to subject you to the possibility of scandal by having you appear at a posting inn in somewhat dubious circumstances. Even were I to claim that I am your brother, there is bound to be comment surrounding two people and one horse who appear out of nowhere. Now"—he turned to pull a pistol from his saddle—"I know both you and Charlie well enough to feel certain he has taught you to use one of these."

At last, an answering sparkle appeared in Harriet's eyes as she nodded.

"Very good. I leave this with you then, and I trust that you can remain hidden enough so that no one will be the wiser should they pass by."

Harriet nodded again.

"Good girl." Alistair dropped a light kiss on her forehead before swinging himself into the saddle and trotting in the direction of the crossroads.

Left alone, Harriet sank gratefully on a nearby log, the pistol slipping from her nerveless fingers. For some minutes she did not bother to retrieve it, but sat bemused, staring off in the direction Lord Chalfont had disappeared. Utterly worn out from the fear and anger that had kept her tensely alert from the moment she had been abducted, she could barely assimilate all that had happened to her. Once the marquess had arrived, she had allowed herself to follow his orders passively, trusting in his air of authority and command. What had come over her? It was not at all like her to give up control of a situation so easily. In fact, she could not remember one instance when she had not been directing others—doing all the thinking and acting for them.

I must be slipping into my dotage at a very young age to turn into such a weak, biddable thing. I shall have to be careful that I do not turn into a milk-and-water miss like Alicia, Harriet scolded herself. But deep in her heart she knew that it was not her courage and resolution that were slipping so much as that the marquess's superior capabilities had come to the fore. After all, he must have become accustomed to this sort of adventure on a regular basis when he was in the army. I should be foolish not to allow him to offer assistance in an area where he is so accomplished, she comforted herself.

However, even the chagrin at being rescued by Lord Chalfont instead of saving herself was not the true issue upsetting her; it was something far more fundamental and disturbing than that, something that had been brought to light by that last butterfly kiss.

Except for wishing that she had been born a boy so she could enjoy the same adventurous life that Charlie enjoyed, Harriet had never given much thought to men and women and the relationships between them. At school she had scoffed at the girls who had sighed over the dancing master as fools who were swept away by a handsome face and a gallant manner. Equally silly, in her view, were the girls such as Alicia who viewed men as nothing more than a means of social advancement or escape from their families and the confining rules that governed the behavior of unmarried women. It was not until recently, when she encountered Lord Chalfont, that Harriet had begun to realize there was something else, another reason for the relationship between a man and a woman that had nothing to do with social conventions.

Of course being a country-bred girl who had seen animals mating every spring, she knew the facts of life. She even knew that men, in the grip of their passions, sought out such places as Mrs. Gerrard's. What Harriet had not been so aware of was that women enjoyed these passions too, not, that is, until she had heard Mrs. Gerrard's ladies commenting so favorably on the attractions of Lord Chalfont.

Once she had heard them talking, she had found herself beginning to think of nothing else. There was something quite compelling about his dashing irreverence. His quick wit and his ready smile had exerted a dangerously seductive power over her even before he had come to her defense the first time against Sir Neville. It was then that she had become quite uncomfortably aware of his physical presence, the strength and agility of his well-muscled body. This had only become more apparent as he had held her in his arms on the dance floor and ridden with her in the park. In fact, she was unable to put those thoughts of him out of her head no matter how deep their intellectual conversations might be.

Oddly enough, her visceral revulsion toward Sir Neville and the underlying implications of her abduction only served to throw her reactions to Lord Chalfont into stronger relief. The strength of his arms around her, the reassuring hardness of his body against hers, and the caress of his lips on her brow were all the more potent to a body whose senses had already been heightened by their violent reaction to Sir Neville.

Harriet did not care to contemplate the implications of these revelations or to admit that she longed for more such moments with the marquess. For the time being all she wished to do was to close her eyes and recapture the amazing sensation of being held by him. The thought of his kiss quite took her breath away, making her feel oddly giddy, yet intensely alive.

Soon he would return, and having at last faced these feelings, she would then need to suppress them until later in the privacy of her bedchamber. But for now she could indulge herself to her heart's content.

Chapter 24

Harriet sank back against the meagerly padded seat cushions with a sigh of relief as though it were the most luxurious of traveling carriages. Lord Chalfont had reappeared in a very short time after he had left, helped her into the carriage, tied Trajan behind, climbed in beside her, and waved to the postboys who set them off at a slapping pace.

There was silence for some time as both of them sat back and recovered from the stress of the last few hours. Finally laying a re-assuring hand on hers. Lord Chalfont spoke. "I hope that you will not think it too interfering of me, but I took the liberty of sending a note to Charlie asking him to send word to Berkeley Square that he had taken you to the Egyptian Hall to see the paintings there. Yes"—he directed a wry grin at her— "I realize that it is highly un-likely that your brother would care about such things, but from what you have said, I gather that most of the members of your household are too preoccupied with their own affairs to question it. I have also instructed my man Richards to find your maid and convince her that all is well. I should not worry. He is most resourceful and should be able to reassure her as to your safety."

It was such a well-conceived plan that Harriet did not have the heart to mention to the marquess that Charlie, who had already tak-en her to the Egyptian Hall and pronounced it to be sadly overrated, would be unlikely to take her there again, so she merely nodded in approval.

Rose had been more than reassured by Lord Chalfont's batman who had finally caught up with her as she was emerging from Mad-ame Celeste's, a puzzled frown on her face. Rose had considered it rather odd that Harriet had sent Mrs. Gerrard's new maid to ask Rose to wait for her at the modiste's, but Rose, the most dependable of servants, had not thought to question her mistress's instructions until she had waited at the shop a good deal later than the time she and Harriet customarily arrived from Mrs. Gerrard's. Wondering at her mistress's tardiness. Rose began to review the events of the past hour in her mind and was not at all reassured by these reflections.

The more she considered it, the more she became aware that the young maid was completely unfamiliar to her. Naturally Rose had kept her dignity and her distance as far as the members of Mrs. Gerrard's unusual household were concerned, but the establishment was not a large one, and Harriet's maid was reasonably certain that she could at least recognize everyone who worked there. The person in question had been a complete stranger to her, however, and this realization filled Rose with a vague sense of unease.

Deciding that the only way to set her mind at rest was to return to Mrs. Gerrard's and inquire after this particular person. Rose was just closing the glossy yellow door of Madame Celeste's behind her when a wiry little man with a leathery face and the bearing of a soldier cautiously approached her. Lifting her nose with some hauteur and twitching her skirts. Rose was about to sweep by him when the man addressed her.

"Excuse me, Miss Rose, but I am come to you at the instructions of my master, the Marquess of Kidderham, who most earnestly begs your assistance."

Though it pained her to acknowledge such a low person, Rose stopped, looking him up and down without uttering a word. Certainly his accent and address indicated the proper respect, but Rose was not accustomed to associating with anything but the most rigidly proper of gentlemen's gentlemen and this person, though appropriately enough attired, had none of the fine obsequiousness that distinguished such persons. But the mention of the Marquess of Kidderham's name did go a long way. "Yes? What is it?" she demanded impatiently.

Richards had not become Lord Chalfont's batman for nothing. It was as much for his diplomacy as his resourcefulness and courage that he had been appointed to his present position and granted his lordship's trust and reliance. Maintaining his attitude of deepest respect for Rose's exalted position as maid to Lady Harriet, he gestured in a most deferential way for her to walk on. "Believe me. Miss Rose,

I should never "approach you in such a manner if it was not of the utmost importance," he began in such a confidential tone that she was forced to lean quite close to him in order to hear, "but, as you no doubt know, Lord Chalfont has been quite concerned about Lady Harriet's safety for some time."

Rose had not known this, but she was definitely not going to let on such ignorance to this person, no matter how gentlemanly his manners might turn out to be. He certainly conducted himself more properly than one might first expect from his rather rugged appearance. Unbending a little, she nodded graciously, inviting him to continue with his story.

"Well, the long and short of it is that he asked me to keep an eye on her."

"What? Follow my lady? Why I never heard of such impertinence!" The frostiness had returned to Rose's voice and her chin rose just a fraction of a degree.

"Lord Chalfont begs that you and your lady forgive him for his presumption, but he felt it was best for both of you that you remain unaware of this plan so that you would continue to behave as naturally as possible." In truth, Richards thought, the maid seemed to possess the same prickly independence that characterized the mistress and that had made Lord Chalfont's task so difficult. Naturally, the marquess had not confided in him on this point, but the batman, ever sensitive to his master's needs, had most certainly been aware of it.

"Oh." Rose was at a loss as to a reply.

Richards pressed his advantage. "Yes, and all has worked according to plan." That was not precisely true for Lord Chalfont had not counted on Lady Harriet's abduction, but it would never do to admit such a thing to this haughty young woman. "Even now, my lord is rescuing her from Sir Neville and will be restoring her to her family with the utmost expedience."

"What!" Completely forgetting the dignified air that was due her position. Rose clapped one hand to her mouth while with the other she gripped her companion's arm in a most agitated manner.

"Naturally, being aware of Sir Neville's villainous reputation and his vengeful nature, you have been as concerned as his lordship that something like this might occur. You may now rest easy that the scoundrel will not bother her again." Richards lowered his voice to a conspiratorial whisper. "Now, you who know the lady's brother far better than my master does, must realize that Lord Chalfont thought it far more likely that the entire affair could be successfully hushed up if the captain were kept in the dark as long as possible."

Well aware of Harriet's brother's propensity to act first and think later, Rose nodded slowly, wondering what further astonishments this man had in store for her. His countenance might be rather vulgar, but he did appear to have a good head on his shoulders, and certainly the marquess who was, according to Captain Fareham, a man well accustomed to difficult and dangerous situations, would not have an idiot in his employ.

"But what are we to do?" Rose wondered aloud.

Richards quickly suppressed the smile of satisfaction that rose to his lips. Good. He had won her confidence and now he could proceed with the rest of Lord Chalfont's plan. "I have been charged to deliver a letter to Lady Harriet's brother instructing him to give you a message to take to Berkeley Square, informing the family that encountering his sister in Bond Street, he decided to escort her to the Egyptian Hall and then for a stroll in the park. His lordship knew he could rely on you to keep all of them in Berkeley Square in ignorance of the entire episode, and I can quite see from your manner that his trust in you was well founded."

Here Richards allowed himself an approving nod in Rose's direction. Except for her brief exclamation, she had behaved most creditably, with no screams or fainting fits. Like mistress, like maid, he remarked to himself. No wonder the marquess was so taken with Lady Harriet. If she exhibited half as much self-possession and quickness of understanding as her servant did, then she was a rare woman indeed.

Richards decided that once this escapade was over, it would behoove him to pay more attention to Lady Harriet Fareham, for it was obvious that whatever the present impediments were, she was the lady for his master. At the moment the batman was not sure how he was going to do so, but he vowed to see that his master was freed from the self-centered clutches of the Honorable Alicia De Villiers and happily allied with someone who could bring vitality and happiness to his lordship's life and share his interests.

"Very well, I shall do as you say," Rose agreed, surprised that she should feel so gratified by this stranger's obvious trust in her capabilities.

"Thank you. And now I must hasten to Portman Street to speak to the captain." With a quick bow, he turned and was gone leaving Rose less puzzled, but no less thoughtful. Like her mistress, the maid had at first had her doubts about a gentleman who was so often encountered at Mrs. Gerrard's, but unlike Harriet, Rose, who had been blessed with the more objective point of view of an observer, had quickly arrived at the conclusion that the chief attraction for the marquess at Mrs. Gerrard's establishment was Lady Harriet and no one else. Of course, Rose would have died rather than discuss such a thing with the inhabitants of Mrs. Gerrard's, but she was not above eavesdropping where her mistress's welfare was at stake, and she had soon learned that Mrs. Gerrard's ladies shared her opinion.

Rose was also aware of his lordship's betrothal to Miss De Villiers, but she was equally aware of the warmth in his eyes whenever they rested on her mistress and the animation in his voice whenever he spoke with her. One would have to be very dull indeed not to recognize how strongly the two of them were drawn to each other. Underneath Rose's rigidly proper exterior, there beat the heart of a true romantic and the maid, though she freely acknowledged the difficulties raised by the marquess's prior engagement, was steadfast in her belief that somehow all would come out right where true love was concerned. Of course, it was not true love at the moment, but the recent turn of events seemed likely to encourage its development.

And certainly there was no woman who deserved true love more than her own dear mistress. To be sure, Lady Harriet was less biddable than her elder sister and far more likely to tumble into scrapes, but she was nonetheless a sweet-tempered young woman. If at times she hid this under a mischievous facade, it was only to protect herself from her all-too-ready sympathy for her fellow creatures. As far back as Rose could remember, Harriet had sprung to the defense of anyone in distress, animal or human, and many of her misadventures as well as her reputation for being something of a scamp, had resulted directly from this incurable desire to help others. At last it seemed that she was being repaid for this and being rescued herself.

In spite of her concern for her mistress. Rose returned to Berkeley Square in a most optimistic frame of mind. The man, Richards, seemed thoroughly assured of his master's ability to effect a rescue without anyone being the wiser and, from the little she had seen of the Marquess of Kidderham, Rose was inclined to agree with him. To be sure, his lordship had a teasing, irreverent way about him, but she had watched the expression in his eyes change in an instant from laughter to an intensity of interest and purpose not commonly observed among men of his class. There was no doubt that Lord Chalfont's commanding figure and masterful air had even caused the little maid's heart to beat faster, no matter how loyal she was to dear Jem, her childhood sweetheart and the son of a prosperous farmer back in Thornby.

While Rose was busy with these speculations, Richards was at the Portman Street barracks inquiring after Harriet's brother who, it appeared, had just returned from guard duty at St. James. The captain was on his way to his quarters when one of his fellow officers pointed to Richards waiting for him, note in hand.

Charlie cocked a questioning eyebrow at the batman before taking the note and scanning it quickly. "The. damned—"

"Gently, sir, gently," Richards admonished, leading him off to a corner. "Now the marquess is as capable a gentleman as ever drew breath. He'll put things to rights, sir, never fear. Your going after him will only upset his plans. Furthermore, I believe he would consider it insubordination on your part were you to interfere," he remonstrated sternly at the sight of young Fareham's flushed face and clenched fists.

The severity of his tone had its desired effect. The captain sank into a nearby chair and frowned ferociously at the floor.

"Besides, there is the rest of the note in which his lordship asks you to take care of things on this end, things that are equally important for helping the, er, young lady in question. You know ladies, sir, their reputations are as precious to them as their lives."

Charlie snorted, "Not my—"

"Shhh. No names, please." Richards held a warning finger to his lips. "Discretion is all. His lordship needs you for this task because it is one that only you can accomplish. Now, let me explain it further."

Quickly and quietly the batman outlined Lord Chalfont's plan and supervised the writing of the note that would inform the household of Charlie escorting his sister to the Egyptian Hall.

"And now if you'll just wait here, sir, all right and tight, I shall come find you when they have returned and you can conduct her to Berkeley Square with no one the wiser." After faithfully promising Charlie that he would be included in any further punishment exacted from Sir Neville, should the man have the temerity to return to London, Richards bid him a cheery good day and made his way back to Mount Street, secure in the knowledge that he had done a respectable day's work.

Chapter 25

The carriage bowled along at a slapping pace and for some time Harriet gazed unseeingly out the window, comparing this trip with the one she had taken only a few hours earlier. How desperate she had felt then, and how secure now. Thinking this, she could not help turning to the man who had effected this miraculous transformation and smiling at him gratefully.

Harriet struggled for a way to convey her thanks and to let him know how indebted she felt, but the words would not come. How did a person thank someone for saving one's life—for that was most certainly what Lord Chalfont had done. Harriet knew she could not have borne to live if Sir Neville had accomplished all that he had set out to do. Even now, her repugnance for him made it difficult to accept the fact that he had touched her. She wanted nothing so much as to get home where Rose would pour her a bath and she could wash every trace of contact with him from her.

"I cannot tell you how—" Harriet began and then stopped. She had been going to say that she was grateful, but grateful was a pale expression of her true feelings and thank you was no better, but it was all she could come up with. "I cannot think why you went to such trouble to save me, but—"

"Shh." Alistair gently laid a finger on her lips. "I want you to forget that such an unfortunate incident ever occurred. If I had been more watchful, you never would have had to suffer such indignities, and for that I heartily apologize."

"Oh no." Her lips moved softly against his finger. "I fully accept responsibility for what happened. If I had not insisted on going to Mrs. Gerrard's, I never would have met Sir ..." Harriet shuddered. She could not even bring herself to say his name.

That shudder tore at his heart. The marquess pulled Harriet into his arms, cradling her protectively. "Hush. It is all over."

"Thanks to you." Harriet smiled up at him.

He had only meant to hold her, to comfort and reassure her, but when she gazed up at him with a tremulous smile on her soft lips and unshed tears glistening in her eyes, it was too much. He gathered her closer to him and bent his lips to hers.

Alistair had kissed countless women in his life, from innocent but eager country wenches to the most sophisticated flirts of the ton, not to mention several of Mrs. Gerrard's most sought-after ladies, but he had never experienced the curious breathlessness that came over him now as his lips met Harriet's. She felt so tiny, so vulnerable, and her lips felt so smooth and gentle under his. He had hungered for this so long that he was almost dizzy now that he was finally experiencing it.

How long had he been dreaming of it? Until now, it had not been a conscious wish, but as his lips moved against hers gently and long-ingly, Alistair realized that he had wanted it for a very long time, almost from the first moment he had seen her that day in the school-room. She had been so very angry at him, spitting at him like a fright-ened kitten, and he had loved her all the more for it. He groaned and buried his hands in the red curls. It was love. He had been too afraid to admit it, had been avoiding acknowledging his attraction to her—an attraction that went far beyond physical desire—but now there was no denying it. He could not have helped himself even if he had tried. But for this one precious moment at least, he did not want to try.

Lord Chalfont now knew that he had not been acting on chival-rous impulses alone when he had chased after her into Hertfordshire and rescued Harriet from Sir Neville. He had also done it because he was half out of his mind with worry over her and because he could not bear the thought of her in another man's arms, especially Sir Neville's. But he had no right to feel this way.

Alistair sighed and pressed his lips more firmly against hers. He was Alicia's affianced husband and she would never give him up. Of course she did not love him, nor he her, but she was enamored of her role as the future Marchioness of Kidderham and she was not going to allow anything to stand in the way of that goal.

Harriet's lips parted gently under his and Alistair thought he had never known such sweetness. She seemed to melt in his arms and meld with him in a closeness, an intimacy that he had never before experienced with another human being. To Alistair it felt as though she had been made for him, that somehow they had been meant for each other, to be partners throughout life, experiencing and sharing it together.

Harriet had come along at the moment when his life was losing all meaning and she had restored his waning faith and enthusiasm. But was that to be all there was? Surely not. Surely he would not feel this way about someone who was to leave his life as quickly as she had come into it. The thought was intolerable. Yet how could he stand to be near her, to see her impish smile and her quick, light way of moving, or the little frown that wrinkled her forehead when she was puzzling over something, if he could not have her? Would he be able to bear being near her any better than he could bear being without her? Alistair thought he had never known such agony. The years of hardship in the Peninsula watching his men die was nothing compared to what he was experiencing now as he realized that he had found what he had been searching for most of his adult life and now he could never have it. "Oh, Harriet, Harriet, whatever shall I do?" he whispered against her hair.

Surprised by the anguish in his voice, Harriet pulled away and regarded him curiously. His face was drawn, his eyes full of pain. She had caught only the briefest glimpse of this pain before, but now it was so strong it was almost palpable. Longing to comfort him, but not knowing what to say or do, she reached up and gently stroked his cheek.

Alistair caught her hand with both of his and held it, kissing it slowly and caressing it with his lips as, lost in thought, he stared at nothing in particular. At last he looked at her, gazing deep into her eyes. "It's no use, my love. I know I should not say it, but I cannot lie to you. I love you, Harriet. I always have." A bitter laugh escaped him. "And I think I always will."

Harriet stared at him in astonishment. Truly this had been a most remarkable day. She had gone from the depths of loathing to ... she did not know precisely what. She had emerged breathless and shaken from a kiss that had sent strange quivers of longing through her entire body, but at the same time had felt so perfectly natural, so right somehow, that she was thoroughly confused by it all.

The only thing that Harriet was sure of was that she had not wanted the kissing to stop. Then he had whispered words of love and that had brought her up short. She was Harriet Fareham, known as the scapegrace of her family and something of an oddity. Men, especially men such as the Marquess of Kidderham, did not whisper pretty nothings in her ear, rather they steered clear of a woman who was more likely to laugh at such protestations than believe them. However, Lord Chalfont appeared to be deadly serious.

"You stare. Is it so impossible that such a thing should happen, that I should love a gallant, beautiful woman who devotes herself to the welfare of others. Is that so improbable?"

"But—but what about Kitty and the rest of Mrs. Ge—"

Alistair gave a crack of cynical laughter. "Love has nothing to do with that, my darling girl. I only visited Mrs. Gerrard's in the first place because I was so damn bored." And, he thought, because I could not bear the idea of a future tied to Alicia. But Alicia was something he did not wish to discuss at the moment. She was too painful a reminder of the impossibility of the situation. "The rest of my visits were only to see you."

"To see me?" Harriet responded wonderingly. Then her mouth quirked into a skeptical little smile. "I am not such a green girl that you can make me believe that for a minute. You enjoyed yourself far too much."

"Ha! And that is where you are fair and far out Miss Know-it-all. Ask anyone at Mrs. Gerrard's if I was there any other time except Tuesday mornings. Ask any one of Mrs. Gerrard's ladies why I was there. They knew even if you did not."

"Oh." Harriet was too nonplussed to say anything more. The whole situation was too incredible for words. That a man of the world such as Lord Chalfont, should ever fall truly in love, much less admit to it, was surprising enough, but that he should do so with someone such as Harriet was nothing short of astounding. She shook her head in amazement.

It was not that she disliked the idea, far from it. In all honesty, Harriet had to admit to herself that the prospect of encountering

Lord Chalfont had added a great deal to her own enjoyment of the sessions at Mrs. Gerrard's. Even though she had deplored the reasons for his presence there, she had, nevertheless, looked forward to it more than she had allowed herself to acknowledge. Now it seemed that his being there had not been to satisfy his appetites after all, and her last defense against him—her disgust at such licentious behavior—crumbled as easily as a castle in the sand before the incoming tide, leaving her helpless to resist the warmth of his eyes and the persuasiveness of the lips that came down again on hers.

Unable to think or to act, Harriet gave herself up to his kiss, opening her mouth under his as he tasted her hungrily. She was intensely aware of the muscles rippling in his arms as he pulled her to him, and the warmth and strength in his hand as he slowly slid it up the back of her neck to entwine his fingers in her hair and pull her closer to him.

A strange fluttery sensation began in the pit of Harriet's stomach and spread slowly and languorously throughout her entire body until she was breathless and tingling all over, until she could think of nothing but how delicious it was to give herself up to the amazing sensations he was evoking within her.

So this was what had brought that sly, secret smile to Kitty's face when she had referred to Lord Chalfont. Harriet sighed dreamily. She could well understand it now and she wanted it to go on forever. But all too soon, the carriage hit a stone in the road and lurched crazily, bringing both of them back to their senses.

Alistair was the first to recover. Raising his head, he shook it in a dazed sort of way and sighing, he set her gently, but firmly back on her side of the carriage. "Forgive me. Lady Harriet. I had no right. I cannot say what came over me. It was the relief of finding you safe and unharmed after all that worry that made me speak out of turn. But there is no excuse. I—I beg your pardon." His voice was hoarse with emotion and he was breathing oddly in a manner that was totally unlike the self-assured Lord Chalfont she was accustomed to.

"It's quite all right. Think nothing of it," Harriet replied in a small voice. For a moment she had almost believed what he said, that he truly cared about her. But now her heart, which had been soaring just seconds ago, plummeted.

Upset as he was by his own conflicted feelings, Alistair could still recognize the pain in her voice and see her anguish in the way she straightened herself and stared purposefully out the window. "Harriet, Harriet, I am making the most dreadful mull of all this. What I mean is that having gone from concern for your welfare, to rage at Sir Neville, to relief at discovering you, I was overwhelmed by my feelings and not thinking clearly. I only knew what I wanted to say and do, not what I should say and do, but my momentary lapse does not make any of it less true. It is just that now my judgment has reasserted itself, I know how impossible a dream loving you is. I am betrothed to Alicia, and honor forbids me from saying to you any of the things I might wish to." It was the marquess's turn to bite off his words and stare unseeingly out the window.

Harriet stole a glance at the stern profile, and her heart was torn by the lines of unhappiness etched in his face and the grim set to his mouth. She knew as well as he did what a penance life with the exacting and proper Alicia would be for someone who possessed the reckless nature and lively mind of Lord Chalfont. But she also knew that for Alicia there was no other choice in life but to marry the man who had been chosen for her, no matter how little she had in common with him.

From childhood, Harriet had sensed the limited choices open to girls. After her experiences at Mrs. Gerrard's she was all the more aware of these limitations, and the unhappy fates of those who did not abide by them. It was a hopeless situation. There was nothing to do but make the best of it and do what little she could to make it easier for the man to whom she owed her escape from the clutches of Sir Neville. Summoning up a watery smile, Harriet laid a hand on Alistair's sleeve. "I quite understand, believe me."

"Do you?" The amber eyes searched hers for answers and found them in their steady, trusting gaze. "Yes, I believe you do. You understand a great deal more of the world than do most people. You are a wise little thing despite your impetuosity and youth." Alistair took her hand in his, murmuring to himself as he turned it over, "So small, yet so strong, like its owner." He looked up, examining her face intently for a moment before continuing, "I do hope that we can continue our friendship despite what has occurred, for I value your advice and your point of view on things too highly to give that up."

"Why—why, thank you," Harriet stammered. In some ways, this declaration was as surprising and gratifying as his words of love, not to mention rather unexpected, from a man who heretofore had seemed to indulge in only one sort of conversation with women—flirtation. The rest of the journey was accomplished in virtual silence, both of them wrapped up in their separate sobering reflections.

Chapter 26

There was just the faintest hint of pink in the western sky as they pulled up in front of the Portman Street barracks. Leaving Harriet in the carriage, Alistair dispatched one of the postboys in search of a hackney while he went to look for the lady's brother.

Charlie was seated with his brother officers finishing off a bottle of port and trading stories of the Peninsula when Lord Chalfont walked in, but Alistair could see that his heart was not in it. A preoccupied frown clouded his usually sunny countenance, and he leaped up the minute he heard the door open.

The captain was at the marquess's side in a moment. "Chalfont!" He gave Alistair a hearty buffet on the shoulder as he led him out into the deserted entrance hall where he lowered his voice to demand anxiously, "Harriet, how is she? If that blackguard has hurt her, by God—"

"Relax, Fareham, she's as right as a trivet. I fancy we shan't be seeing Sir Neville around here again," the marquess reassured him. "In fact, the most difficult task of the day is that which lies before us, or before you, I should say, and that is to act convincing enough so that everyone in Berkeley Square believes Harriet to have been in your company the entire time that she was not with Rose. I happened to have visited the exhibit at the Egyptian Hall myself so that I can coach you on the particulars should someone question. But come, see your sister. I have ordered a hackney to conduct her home as soon as I pay off the postboys."

Charlie followed Lord Chalfont outside where he assured himself that his sister was not the worse for wear after her harrowing experience and helped her out of the post chaise and into the hackney, then climbed in beside her. As they pulled out he leaned out of the window to address the marquess, "I can't thank you enough, Chalfont. You can rest assured I shall do my part and no one will be the wiser."

Alistair nodded. "I count on you to take it from here." Then smiling at Harriet, he gave a sign to the jarvey and they were off down the street, leaving him standing there to feel strangely bereft when he should have felt elated. For the first time since the Peninsula, he felt as though he had actually done something. He had outwitted the enemy, pitting himself mentally and physically against Sir Neville in a way that had gotten his blood flowing again, and had proven to his own satisfaction that he had not lost all the skills he had spent so many years perfecting. In fact, it had been a most invigorating day, but now it was over and he had just bid farewell to the most invigorating part of it.

"Damn and blast!" Alistair cursed as he vaulted into the saddle. "You are a proper fool, Chalfont, blurting out your feelings like a schoolboy still wet behind the ears. You have gone and ruined it. At least before this you could talk to her as a friend, but now—" Realizing that he was speaking aloud like some poor creature from Bedlam, the marquess closed his mouth with a snap, but he could not close his mind, which kept picturing Harriet again and again in one scene after another: Harriet struggling furiously against Fletcher, Harriet smiling that special smile of hers as she realized that he had come to save her, Harriet with her eyes closed opening her lips beneath his, and Harriet, her eyes large and bright with unshed tears whispering, "I quite understand."

And that was the damnable thing of it all—she did understand. It was her understanding and compassion for Mrs. Gerrard's ladies that had drawn him to her in the first place. And it was her understanding of so many things—world affairs, the political problems facing England, his own corroding sense of boredom and uselessness—that continued to draw him to her.

But now he had to forget all that. Having declared himself, he could not seek her out now, pretending that it had all never happened, disguising his need for her company with teasing banter. Unlike so many other females he knew, Harriet was too honest to laugh and flirt when she had more serious concerns on her mind. She was very different from his first love who had been able to win a duke as her protector, swearing all the while that her heart was Alistair's alone; and she was definitely not like his own betrothed who never let a serious thought threaten her perfect equanimity. Being unable to ignore what had occurred between them or, to be more exact, what he had precipitated like the cursed fool that he was, both he and Harriet would now be forced to avoid one another instead of enjoying one another's companionship as they had before—a companionship that had come to mean more to Alistair than he liked to think. To be sure, they had promised to remain friends, but that blessed state of indifference was unlikely to occur for a long time, for him at least. His memories of her were too powerful, his feelings too raw for him to be able to hide them.

Wrapped in these gloomy thoughts, Alistair made his way slowly home, paying so little attention to his direction that he was forced to backtrack when he discovered that in his preoccupation he had completely missed the turn into Mount Street His wretched state of mind was not improved as, dismounting, he caught sight of an elegant barouche sweeping by and he suddenly remembered that he had entirely forgotten his promise to drive Alicia and her mother in the park that afternoon. "Hell and damnation!" He clapped a hand to his head. "I am in the basket now. I shall never hear the end of it."

Arriving at his lodgings, he handed Trajan over to one of the stable boys and raced up the stairs to his chambers two at a time. After giving Richards a hasty recapitulation of the day's events, he asked his batman to lay out fresh clothes while he did his best to wash up and refresh himself after the day's adventures. In short order he was on his way again, resplendent in a superbly cut bottle-green coat, elegantly tied cravat, and biscuit-colored pantaloons, looking as though he had involved himself in nothing more arduous all day than strolling along Bond Street and enjoying a hand of whist at White's.

Framing various excuses in his mind he had almost made it to Hanover Square when he suddenly stopped dead on the pavement. Chalfont, your wits have gone begging, he muttered to himself. To appear abjectly on her doorstep full of apology is only to invite an uncomfortable session while she makes you feel as though you have failed utterly in your position as her fiancé. It is far better to settle this by sending an explanatory note than to endure the pained expressions.

That decided, he executed an about-face and retraced his steps, shaking his head at his own stupidity. It was unlike him to be so obtuse. Ordinarily he was awake on all suits, easily capable of outthinking his fellow creatures, and he could only blame his lapse in good sense to his obsession with a certain red-haired sprite.

"Do not say a word, Richards," Lord Chalfont growled as his startled servant opened the door for him. Striding over to his desk, Alistair pulled out a heavy sheet of crested stationery, grabbed a pen, thrust it in the ink, scrawled a few words, sealed it, and handed it to his hovering batman. "And you can wipe that silly grin off your face. My attics are not completely to let, you know. Now take this around to Miss De Villiers in Hanover Square, would you."

Richards was able to contain his mirth, but it was not without a struggle. He found it truly amusing that his lordship had been too concerned about a certain young lady to spare a passing thought for his betrothed. And when he had finally come to his senses and remembered Miss De Villiers, he had hurried off to beg forgiveness with an alacrity that spoke volumes about how guilty he felt. Lord Chalfont was not one to live under the cat's paw; in fact, he often frustrated his betrothed by refusing to play the role of her abject servant, a role she quite obviously expected him to fulfill. Only one thing could make him act in such an apologetic manner and that was a feeling of guilt for ignoring the claims of one woman in his overriding concern for another.

However, the closer Richards got to Hanover Square, the more sober he became. In truth, it was a grave situation and one that even the resourceful batman was forced to admit looked hopeless. It had been humorous to see his lordship's guilty haste and his equally guilty realization that he was not up to facing the wrath of his betrothed, but it was not the least humorous to think of him in that woman's toils. Richards had known women like Miss De Villiers, women who were not satisfied until everyone danced to their tunes. Oh, they could be sweet enough about having everything their own way—all smiles and charm—but the fact still remained that they always had things exactly as they wanted them regardless of the wishes of others. Richards knew that such a life would be a living hell for his lordship after all those years of freedom and independence—not that the marquess would ever allow himself to be twisted around the lady's little finger—but it would be a never-ending struggle of wills.

Now with the other one. Lady Harriet, there would be battles of course, for both the marquess and she were proud, strong-willed, and hot-tempered, but the battles would be the kind that would flare up and be over with no rancor on either side. Both of them were too free-spirited in their own rights to want to bend the other to their will and too warm-hearted to bear a grudge.

The batman shook his head. It was definitely a predicament, but he was determined to sort it out for it was as plain as the nose on his face that Lord Chalfont belonged with Lady Harriet. After he had spent time with her he returned refreshed and full of energy and enthusiasm for life, while any time spent with his betrothed left him quietly cynical and bored to death by all he surveyed. Such a future did not bear thinking of.

Richards would have been astounded to know that at least one other person in London was in full agreement with him. While not so convinced of the necessity of her own presence in Lord Chalfont's life, Harriet was as convinced as the marquess's batman of the deleterious effect of Alicia's influence on her betrothed. Harriet had returned from her adventure more certain than ever that the Marquess of Kidderham and the Honorable Alicia De Villiers were completely unsuited to each other and that their marriage would be a constant source of irritation, if not worse, for both of them.

One look at Lord Chalfont as he had faced Sir Neville, hands clenched into purposeful fists, nostrils flaring, and eyes blazing had proven to Harriet beyond all doubt that he was thoroughly invigorated by the confrontation. To be sure he had been infuriated by Sir Neville's dastardly behavior and worried about her, but beyond that, he had reveled in the opportunity to pit his wits and skills against another's, to take on a challenge and win. How well she understood this feeling and sympathized with it. Alicia, on the other hand, would have considered the entire episode to be excessively bad ton and been made miserable by it, no matter how happy the outcome.

There was no doubt about it, the two of them would be wretched with one another and since no one else appeared to have recognized this obvious state of affairs, Harriet decided it was up to her to do something about it. After all, she owed the marquess a great deal—

possibly even her life—for had he not rescued her she would certainly have done either herself or Sir Neville a mischief.

But what was she to do about the situation, now that she was aware of it? Propping her chin in her hand, Harriet gazed absently out the window of the hackney as they made their way to Berkeley Square and struggled to come up with a solution as all the while Charlie blathered on about what a Trojan Chalfont was—not, of course, that he could not have done the same thing for his sister had he but known about the episode, but being on guard duty, he had been entirely in the dark until he had received the marquess's note. Clever fellow, that Chalfont, had a plan for everything and a solution to every possible problem.

"Owe Chalfont a great deal. Harry, you know," the captain commented, handing her down from the carriage when they had arrived in Berkeley Square. "Must make it up to him."

"I shall, Charlie. I shall," his sister responded abstractedly as she climbed the front steps, her mind working feverishly. Then, suddenly remembering her role, she turned, speaking loudly enough to be overhead, "And thank you, Charlie, for escorting me to the Egyptian Hall. Of course Napoleon's carriage was interesting, but I found the animal exhibits more amusing." With a quick wave she disappeared behind the door being held open for her by one of the Fareham's long-suffering footmen.

"Thank you, Wibberly." Sighing with relief that no family members were around to observe her, Harriet raced upstairs to the peace and quiet of her own bedchamber.

There, curled up in a chair by the window, she began to hatch her plan. Ordinarily, Harriet would have scorned such machinations for she deplored, scheming females, but this was all for a good cause, and though her major objective was to free the marquess from Alicia's confining society, she sympathized enough with women whose livelihood depended on men not to leave her former schoolmate high and dry without a replacement for Lord Chalfont.

Harriet smiled slyly as a devilish thought struck her. No, she would not ignore Alicia; in fact if all worked according to plan, she would supply her with a partner equally as eligible as the Marquess of Kidderham and far more malleable. That it would help out Lady

Harriet herself, who was finding Lord Aylward's attentions just the tiniest bit embarrassing, hardly entered into it at all.

Harriet hugged herself in delight at her own cleverness. The Earl of Woodbridge and Alicia were perfect for one another. Both of them were attractive enough in a conventional sort of way and neither of them possessed an original bone in his or her body. At the moment they were both paired with people who made them distinctly uncomfortable. For his part, Lord Aylward was far too well-bred to do anything but follow politely any conversational topic Harriet might introduce. Yet more than once she had seen an involuntary spasm of unease convulse his pleasant features when she waxed too enthusiastic on some particular issue. No, the Earl of Woodbridge, like his friend Rokeby, deserved a biddable young woman as his wife. Alicia was not necessarily biddable, having grown accustomed, as beauties often did, to having her own way, but she was far too concerned with the good opinion of the ton to cause Lord Aylward a moment of discomfort.

Harriet sighed with satisfaction. She had arrived at a practicable solution to everyone's problems. Now all that was left to do was to set things in motion, which she planned to do the very next evening.

She had at last prevailed on her family to attend La Clemenza di Tito where she could only hope the De Villiers and Lord Chalfont would put in an appearance. Lord Aylward and Lord Rokeby had already agreed to accompany the Farehams, so with a little luck, Harriet could begin her campaign to free Chalfont and bring Lord Aylward and Alicia together tomorrow at the opera.

That settled, she could now free her thoughts to concentrate on her next course of action as far as Mrs. Gerrard's ladies were concerned. Having found a position for Fanny, she could turn her attention to Lucy or Violet, though she had far fewer connections of use to a potential tavern serving girl or nurserymaid than she did for a seamstress.

Harriet wrinkled her brow in thought. It was a considerable challenge, but one she looked forward to. The challenge she was not equal to, however, was one she could not even bring herself to admit to avoiding—which she most definitely was. She must eventually deal with her own reactions to the events of the day, the loathing and disgust she had felt at the touch of Sir Neville and her equally disturbing reactions to the marquess. Harriet shook her head. No, she would not, she could not entertain the dangerously seductive memories of a strong male body pressing close to hers, evoking responses in her that she had never known existed until now. Resolutely putting such alluring thoughts from her head, Harriet picked up a discarded copy of The Times she had left lying on the floor and did her best to divert herself by reading the deadly dull account of Parliament's debate over the income tax.

Chapter 27

Though his note to Alicia had put off a confrontation for the moment, Alistair knew there was no avoiding it forever; therefore, the very next day he offered to escort his betrothed and her mother to the exhibition at the Royal Academy by way of apology. Alicia was far too well-bred to mount a direct attack on her fiancé for his blatant dereliction of duty, but she could not refrain from commenting sweetly as the carriage made its way through the press of traffic in the Strand, "We were sorry you were unable to accompany us to the park yesterday, my lord. Undoubtedly there was some urgent problem requiring your attention?"

There was no mistaking the question in her voice, nor was there any ignoring it. "Yes. An old friend was in desperate need of help and I was fortunate enough to be able to render assistance."

"I should say, rather, that your friend was the fortunate one. It was a close friend, and a matter of some severity, I trust?"

With an effort. Lord Chalfont kept his temper in check. He had never answered to anyone for his actions before, and he was certainly not about to begin to do so now. "It was a most private affair. I am sure you can understand my not wishing to discuss it with anyone," Alistair replied in a level tone. But anyone who cared to observe would have noticed the muscle twitching in his cheek that gave ample evidence of the tight rein he was keeping on his annoyance.

A prudent person would have left well enough alone, but Alicia, serenely unconscious of anything but her own claims on his attention, persisted. "Not even with your affianced wife?"

"Not even with her." Alistair responded tersely.

It was as close as the marquess had ever come to snapping at her, and though the edge in his voice was nothing compared to what he was feeling, and his tone was more restrained than it would have been with anyone else, Alicia took instant exception to it. "I am not accustomed to being addressed in such a manner, Chalfont," she responded frostily. "As your future wife, I expect more courtesy."

Alistair controlled himself with an effort. He did not ask much of Alicia in terms of intelligence—certainly she was no Lady Harriet—but he did expect her to be clever enough and well enough versed in the ways of gentlemen to know that where affairs of honor were concerned there was a strict code of silence to be maintained. Without question Harriet would have grasped such a thing instinctively and would have immediately dropped any discussion the moment she detected any reluctance on his part. Alicia was not Harriet, however, more was the pity. "Then there is an end to it." There was a note of finality in his voice that was obvious enough to warn even Alicia that there was to be no further debate on this particular topic.

She sniffed audibly, but ventured no response, turning instead to her mother. "I wonder if the Willinghams will dare show their faces in the park this afternoon now that it is generally known that Evelina has run off with her half-pay officer. How she could be so dead to all sense of family feeling, much less propriety, I cannot fathom."

Lady De Villiers smiled weakly at her daughter and nodded in agreement. Dear Alicia was so firm in her opinions and such a high stickler herself, but her latest interchange with Lord Chalfont had given her mother pause.

After years of marriage. Lady De Villiers knew that it was unwise to provoke a gentleman the way Alicia had provoked the marquess. Men had their own peculiar notions of conduct and were notoriously stubborn about sticking to them; take her own husband, for example. His concept of honor was very rigid indeed which was perhaps where Alicia had gotten her own iron will. Lady De Villiers had seen the irritated expression on Lord Chalfont's face, even if her daughter had not, and she knew it behooved Alicia to tread carefully. In part she was to blame for she had indulged her beautiful daughter to such a degree that Alicia could not conceive that anyone might find fault with her conduct, though she always felt completely justified in voicing her own criticisms wherever she saw fit.

The marquess was far too honorable a man, and the relationship too longstanding for him to do anything as drastic as crying off, but he certainly could seek solace elsewhere, and he very likely would.

Everyone knew that gentlemen had other interests and it was almost expected that they would court an opera dancer here and there, but Alicia's obdurate behavior might very well force him into a dalliance with one of the ton's more sprightly matrons, such as Sally Jersey, and that would never do. Alicia's pride would never withstand such a blow.

Making a mental note to discuss this with her daughter, Lady De Villiers allowed herself to be helped down from the carriage and led through the magnificent vestibule of Somerset house to the doorway that led to the Royal Academy's exhibition.

The gallery was so thronged with the ton that to all intents and purposes it might have been another squeeze held by one of society's more fashionable hostesses, Alistair thought cynically as he gazed around. In fact he appeared to be the only one at all interested in the paintings on display. Lady De Villiers being too concerned over the impression her daughter was making, and Alicia far too interested in nodding and smiling at the appropriate people to have much time or effort to waste on the pictures themselves. Alicia, however, did pronounce several landscapes to be rather pretty and one or two portraits to be a most remarkable likeness.

In less than an hour. Lord Chalfont found himself thoroughly bored and longing for some excuse to escape. It was not that he failed to appreciate the display for he enjoyed paintings as much, if not more, than the next man. To him, appreciating a work of art required such an emotional and intellectual investment on the part of the viewer that it was not something to be entered into lightly, certainly not like this with so many pictures and so many people jammed together that observation and discrimination were utterly impossible. He found himself wondering what Harriet would say about it all and whether she liked the dramatic canvasses of Turner or preferred the more meticulous representational style of Constable. Though he felt reasonably certain he could guess which she would choose, he longed to debate their merits with her and then tease her about her opinions, for undoubtedly she would be most passionate in defense of her taste.

Alistair glowered at the sweeping landscape before him. He must stop these accursed thoughts and comparisons, forget that Harriet gave energy and meaning to every aspect of life while Alicia rendered everything, even art itself, trivial. He squared his shoulders, admonishing himself severely for this lapse. He was a soldier, after all, trained to endure hardship whether it was the physical challenge of a forced march across unforgiving terrain or the emotional one of endless hours on watch or waiting for the orders to engage the enemy. He comforted himself with the thought that dull as Alicia's world was, it could never surpass the numbing boredom of a night watch.

Smiling grimly at his own ironic humor, Alistair nodded and responded mechanically to Alicia's chatter as he escorted her and her mother back to the carriage. Yes, he could do it, he could bear this just as he had borne the privations of army life; and in time it would become just as familiar and easily dealt with as they had been.

With the army still on his mind, Lord Chalfont was quick to notice the green uniform, dusty and tattered though it was, of the beggar who approached them just as Alicia was settling into her seat. The marquess had always held the men of the Ninety-fifth Rifles in high regard after having shared action with them at Salamanca, Vitoria, and it grieved him now to see one of the proud regiment rendered so destitute that he was reduced to asking help from the passersby.

"A penny for a poor soldier, if it please you, sir." The halting, diffident voice told Alistair that the poor fellow was unaccustomed and ill suited to an existence that depended on the bounty of others. He hung back, almost as though he wished not to be heard, but one glance at the gaunt cheeks and sunken eyes was enough to show the marquess that the soldier's need was all too real. The beggar had already begun to turn away when Alistair pulled out his purse and handed it to him.

"Bless you, sir, but I have no need of all that." The soldier drew himself up proudly. "All I wish is just enough for a bit of grub until I am back on my feet again."

Alistair smiled. He had known that this was no ordinary beggar and it pleased him to have his good opinion of the Ninety-fifth borne out. "Very well. But I can do better than that. Perhaps I can find a place for you in my household. If you take this"—Alistair, who after years in the field was never without the means to send a message, pulled pencil and paper from his pocket and scrawled a few words—

"to my lodgings in Mount Street, you will find that my batman will be happy to make you comfortable and you will also find that Richards holds the Ninety-fifth in as high esteem as I do."

The man's eyes filled with tears that he hurriedly blinked away. "Bless you, sir. I thought there was something of the military in your bearing or I never would have approached you. I will do anything. I can—"

But Alistair, laying a hand on his shoulder, cut him off. "Think nothing of it. You go along and fill your stomach and then we shall talk."

Recognizing the voice of command, the soldier touched his forehead and with another, "Bless you, sir," hurried off down the Strand in the direction of Mount Street, his gait almost jaunty at the prospect of a good meal and a sympathetic reception.

Lord Chalfont gazed after him, frowning thoughtfully until an audible sniff from Alicia brought him back to his senses. "Really, Chalfont, it is too bad of you to keep all of us waiting for it is decidedly chilly today. Surely you do not plan to stop and offer assistance to every beggar who accosts you. At that rate we shall never get home."

It was with great difficulty that Alistair held his temper in check as he climbed into the carriage and took his seat across from her. Her supercilious air so infuriated him that it was some minutes before he could trust himself to reply civilly as she sat there smugly, gazing disdainfully over the sea of humanity thronging the Strand. For the briefest of instants, he longed to wrap his lean brown hands around the slender throat and squeeze it until she knew, however momentarily, what it was like to face death as he and thousands of other soldiers had done in the Peninsula. Even that would give her no sense of the years of danger and hardship they had all suffered together. Even if he were to shock her out of her complacency, she would never understand anything but the world as it revolved around Alicia De Villiers, and certainly she would never have a particle of sympathy for anyone but Alicia De Villiers.

Again the image of a vivid face, the blue eyes shining with interest and compassion, rose before him and he found himself having to swallow a lump in his throat before replying firmly, "I shall endeavor to give aid to anyone who truly needs it, particularly fellows such as he who devoted their lives to their country, so you might as well resign yourself to it."

Alicia had never before had her wishes so completely disregarded. Her eyes sparkled with anger as she opened her mouth to reply, but turning to speak to her betrothed, she observed the grim look of determination on his face and thought better of it. Alicia had occasionally suspected that Lord Chalfont, unlike the rest of her admirers, did not live in fear of her slightest frown. In fact, lately she had become uncomfortably aware that her future husband had a great many other interests in his life besides herself and though he was willing enough to act as her escort when the situation demanded it, he did not live to indulge her every whim. It was a sobering thought, and an entirely new one for a beauty who had been deferred to her entire life. Of course Alicia was determined to change all this, but though she was confident of eventually reducing Lord Chalfont to the slavish devotion demonstrated by the rest of her cicisbei, she realized that it might take her longer than she had expected and that at the moment, it behooved her not to press.

They rode in silence until they reached Bond Street when Alicia, unable to bear the lack of conversation any longer, decided to try a new approach. "You shall soon need a much larger establishment, my lord, if you are to give employment to every old soldier who requests your aid." She tapped him playfully with the ivory handle of her parasol, smiling coyly up at him and peeping out under her lashes in a manner she knew to be utterly bewitching.

Alistair remained unmoved by this display. "Perhaps, but there are too many such cases for me to aid them all personally. I can only effect a material change in their welfare by acting politically."

"Politically?" Alicia echoed in dismay. "Surely you are not going to become one of those ridiculous people who is forever agitating for reform?"

"Agitating for reform." The marquess nodded. "I like the sound of that. Yes, Alicia, I thoroughly intend to agitate for reform. There is so much in this country that needs to be changed, and the need is most urgent. It will take a great deal of agitation, as you call it, to fix all that is wrong."

"But, Chalfont, you have a position in society to maintain," his betrothed moaned in horror as she saw her dreams of being hostess to the most brilliant members of the ton fading rapidly away to be replaced by the unpleasant picture of her as a neglected wife of one of those dedicated politicians who were frequently too busy promoting their dreadfully unfashionable views to escort their wives to the proper social functions.

"That is precisely the point. And my position in society demands that I exert all my rank and influence, not to mention wealth and intelligence, to help people who are unable to help themselves."

It was hopeless. Alicia fought the tears of disappointment and betrayal that welled up in her eyes. She knew Chalfont well enough to recognize when his mind was made up. And once his mind had settled on something, his iron will drove him until he had accomplished it, whether it was riding his father's hunter when he was not allowed on anything more spirited than his pony, or going off to fight the French in spite of everyone's objections.

Alicia stifled a sob. She did not deserve this. An incomparable as exquisite and charming as Alicia De Villiers should grace the ballrooms and salons of the most exclusive members of the Upper Ten Thousand, not be forced to consort with politicians who had not the slightest notion of style or elegance, or their equally dull wives who were, more often than not, the most ferocious bluestockings.

She gulped again and then raised her chin defiantly. No. She would not endure such a fate. Chalfont would just have to relinquish these ridiculous notions. Somehow she would convince him to leave such things to men with ugly wives. At the moment, Alicia was not precisely certain as to how she was going to accomplish this, but she felt confident of succeeding in the end. After all, she had never met a person, especially a member of the male sex, who could resist her when she truly wanted something. It was merely a matter of persuading someone to give her what she wanted, and Alicia De Villiers was mistress of the art of getting what she wanted.

Chapter 28

But Alicia had reckoned without the interference of another equally determined young woman. Lady Harriet Fareham was not one to let the grass grow under her feet once she had reached a conclusion and, having decided that Lord Aylward and Alicia were as perfect for each other as Lord Chalfont and Alicia were disastrous, she began her campaign to enlighten them all that very evening at the opera when in response to Lord Aylward's simple inquiry after her enjoyment of the entertainment she allowed herself to wax more eloquent than usual on the beauties and complexities of Mozart's operatic form. Harriet noted with a good deal of satisfaction the bewildered expression on the Earl of Woodbridge's face as she expounded on some of the more technical aspects of the composer's works.

Lord Aylward did his best to nod politely as though he completely followed her line of reasoning, but she could see that her superior knowledge and the intensity of her enthusiasm were making her companion distinctly uncomfortable. "I beg your pardon," Harriet apologized contritely. "I see I am boring you. You must forgive me, but I am someone who likes to delve deeply into whatever strikes my fancy. This superficial acquaintance with things that satisfies the rest of the world is entirely too insufficient for my taste." She could have hugged herself as she saw his eyes widen with alarm. However, Lord Aylward's beautiful manners quickly reasserted themselves as, recovering from his dismay, he responded politely, "A most commendable sentiment, I am sure."

Having thus alluded to her bluestocking tendencies, Harriet moved rapidly on to the next part of her scheme, which was to provide his lordship with a charming antidote to her eccentric views. She allowed her gaze to travel around the room and light casually on the De Villiers' box where Alicia was doing her best to engage Lord Chalfont in conversation. "Oh, I vow that is Alicia De Villiers. I have not seen her this age. We were in school together and it would be most remiss of me not to speak to her."

If her artless tone rang thoroughly false to Harriet's ears, it did not appear to do so to Lord Aylward's. Always happy to oblige a lady, he leaped up from his chair. "Pray, allow me to escort you to her box."

It had been too easy, Harriet thought as they made their way through the glittering throng promenading outside the boxes between acts. No wonder Alicia was so bent on making men dance to her tune: it did give one a dangerously heady sense of power. Harriet quickly squelched her misgivings. She was doing this for the benefit of others, and not for herself. And she was immediately rewarded when she saw the salutary effect their visit had on both gentlemen concerned. Lord Chalfont's smile of welcome would have been more than enough to ease her conscience, but Lord Aylward's audible gasp of admiration was most gratifying.

Indeed, Alicia was in her best looks this evening in a white lace dress over a white satin slip. The only ornamentation was a bow of white satin in the center of her bodice which drew attention to the creamy white skin and gentle curves revealed by her décolletage. This was matched by smaller bows on the short puffed sleeves. The very simplicity of it all called attention to the divine complexion of its wearer and provided a contrast to the dark glossy curls and the brilliant blue eyes set under delicately arched brows. The rosy lips that had drooped somewhat petulantly at Lord Chalfont's obvious lack of interest now parted in a delicious smile of welcome that revealed pearly teeth and two bewitching dimples at either corner of her mouth.

It took less than an instant for Alicia to see that she had completely captivated Lord Aylward. That the Earl of Woodbridge had been a noticeably regular escort of another woman, even if that woman was only her former schoolmate Harriet Fareham, added to the piquancy of the moment.

Darting a quick glance out of the corner of her eye at the marquess, who appeared to remain totally unaware of the profound effect she was having on such an eligible man, Alicia greeted the earl with charming enthusiasm. "Harriet, I am so delighted you have made Lord Aylward known to me"—she responded graciously to

Harriet's introduction—"for I know he is much admired wherever he goes and I have long wished to make his acquaintance."

For her part, Harriet, who was well aware of Alicia's propensity for putting herself in the situation to meet every possible admirer, was hard put not to laugh at such a bouncer. As it was, she was forced to turn what threatened to be a serious giggle into a cough. Worse yet, she happened to catch the marquess's eye as she did so, and his skeptically raised eyebrows and wicked grin very nearly overset her. Lord Chalfont had been trying to make her lose her countenance from the very instant they had met and by now she was more than a match for him. Besides, Harriet had her own plans to put forward, which involved asking him if he had had the opportunity to peruse Mr. Robert Wilson's article in The Edinburgh Review addressing the high price of corn and labor and their effects on the farming interests.

"No, I have not read the article, though I have not been as idle as you might think. I spent a good deal of time this morning with Brougham himself who is preparing a speech to deliver to Parliament on that very subject. Of course he had a great deal to say to the purpose, but it strikes me that the best way for me to understand the problem is to visit my own estates in Oxfordshire and find out for myself. I have an excellent agent in Tomlinson, but he does his best to keep problems from me rather than burden me with them so I am unlikely to learn anything from that corner. I fear I have been remiss in not doing this long ago."

"But you were away fighting so much of the time, how could you concern yourself with such things? And now, though it is most commendable for you to seek firsthand knowledge of the state of affairs, it is far more important for you to exert yourself in London where you can influence those who are making the laws." Harriet came to his defense.

Alicia, who could not bear being without the undivided attention of both the men in the party and therefore had been listening in on the conversation, now seized the opportunity to direct it along more appropriate lines and broke in to the discussion. "I agree with Harriet, Chalfont. You really have no need of a visit to the country, especially at the height of the Season. People will think it most odd.

"But we should not be talking politics at the theater," Alicia chided her fiancé gently. "It is excessively tedious, do you not find it so, my lord?" She smiled most beguilingly at Lord Aylward.

Put on the spot by such a beautiful lady, his lordship could do nothing but agree before deftly turning the conversation to the far less inflammatory topic of the Countess of Margrave's upcoming rout.

Alicia seized on the subject gratefully. "I do look forward to it. They say she always offers the most unusual entertainment to be found anywhere. It is rumored that she has even convinced Catalani to come over from Paris to favor the guests with an appearance, though I do not see how that could be, for Catalani has become so sought after of late that she can command whatever sum she wishes." Having thoroughly recaptured everyone's attention, Alicia then proceeded to discuss the various performers most admired by the ton and those who had fallen from favor.

With almost all eyes focused on Alicia, Harriet took advantage of the opportunity to murmur to the marquess, "I did not mean to criticize you, only to absolve you of any self-recrimination. I think it an excellent idea for you to return to the country and reacquaint yourself with all those whose livelihood depends on you. There is nothing like a personal appearance to elicit true opinions and to reassure everyone of your continuing concern, especially when times are as difficult as these."

"Thank you. I had hoped you would feel that way." It was a most prosaic response, but Alistair was not successful in hiding the longing in his eyes or his voice and Harriet, acutely aware of him as she was—of his every movement, every gesture, every glance—sensed it immediately. A delicate flush tinged her cheeks making her look even more adorable, and Alistair wanted nothing so much as to have her back in his arms again, to hold her close enough to feel the beating of her heart. As it was, he could only imagine it as he watched the quick rise and fall of her breasts under the delicate net of her corsage.

Taking a deep steadying breath, he clenched his hands at his sides. What was wrong with him? He had lusted after scores of women and eyed hundreds of well-shaped bosoms, but none of them had made his breath catch in his throat as it did now. Perhaps it was because he knew that the heart beating under Harriet's décolletage was a heart in the best sense of the word, one that noticed the sorrows of others, one that felt for them and did its best to alleviate them. There was something infinitely compelling and totally endearing, not to mention unique, about a woman who cared about her fellows as Harriet cared. Alistair had never encountered such a phenomenon before and he found himself totally captivated by it.

They could have sat there forever, each one silently, burningly aware of the other, had not the bell rung for the next act. Harriet jumped as though she had been shot and looked about her guiltily only to discover the marquess's gaze fixed upon her with an intensity that quite took her breath away. He was not even touching her, yet she felt as close to him as if he were holding her and kissing her the way he had done in the carriage. For a moment she could do nothing but stare back into those compelling amber eyes. Then, with a supreme effort she turned back to Lord Aylward and Alicia, still deep in discussion of the latest on dits, both of them completely oblivious to Harriet and Lord Chalfont.

Harriet was astonished. She felt as though the whole world must have seen what had passed between her and the marquess as clearly as if they had flung themselves into one another's arms, but apparently such was not the case, for everyone acted very much as though nothing out of the ordinary had occurred.

Certainly Alicia had not been aware of anything beyond the blatant admiration in the Earl of Woodbridge's eyes, an admiration that was balm to a pride that had suffered a great deal in the last few days. Except for his title and fortune, Lord Chalfont had never been the most satisfactory of fiancés and recently he had been downright disappointing. In fact, now that Alicia considered it, he had very little to recommend him beyond wealth, rank, and the hero's status that secured him an illustrious place in the ton. However, he had never taken advantage of this status and now was actually threatening it with his ridiculous notion of helping the nation politically. While it was true that they had been promised to one another practically from the cradle, he could at least demonstrate some gratitude for having the good fortune to marry someone as admired and sought after as Alicia De Villiers. But there was nothing in his lordship's attentions toward her that betrayed the least awareness of her position as an incomparable, a woman whose very presence set the pulses of men like the Earl of Woodbridge racing.

Alicia had stolen a quick look to see if Lord Chalfont was observing the besotted expression on Lord Aylward's face, but much to her disgust, he had been immersed in a discussion of musty old politics with Harriet, who was an eccentric if there ever was one. It was only to be expected that a girl who had exhibited such odd, studious tendencies in school would turn into such a raving bluestocking. Why it was a wonder Lord Aylward saw anything in her at all, poor man. Undoubtedly he was being kind to the sadly awkward thing. Alicia resolved to rescue him from his own good intentions by offering him the opportunity to devote some time to a female worthy of it. "How nice of you to stop by, Harriet, but I do not wish to keep you from the next act. And thank you for introducing your delightful companion." Alicia bestowed another dazzling smile on Lord Aylward. "I do hope you ride in the park, my lord. Mama and I drive out every day. We have very little of interest to share with each other, but you are a fount of information and we would welcome your conversation."

Lord Aylward flushed with pleasure. "Yes, I do ride and I hope, er—I mean, you are too kind." Recollecting Harriet at his elbow, he flushed an even deeper shade of red and turned in some confusion to offer her his arm.

Well pleased with her evening's work, Harriet did her best to immerse herself in the action onstage for the rest of the evening, but even Mozart's divine music failed to erase the vision of a pair of tawny eyes, looking deep into hers.

Chapter 29

No matter how firmly Harriet tried to put the Marquess of Kidderham out of her mind, he would keep intruding in the most unsettling way, such as each night when she lay in bed staring at the blue damask canopy over her head. Then, with all the distractions of the day put aside she was left alone to remember in far too tantalizing detail every moment, every word, every touch of their time together in the carriage from Hertfordshire.

Fortunately Lord Chalfont had gone to visit his estates in Oxfordshire so that during the day, at least, she ran no risk of encountering him in the park, at Mrs. Gerrard's, or on Bond Street. In the evenings she could look forward to entering a box or a ballroom without fear of seeing his tall, powerful frame towering over the assembled multitude. Harriet was supremely grateful for this peace of mind, but at the same time, life seemed decidedly flat. In fact, it had never been so dull, and Harriet, who had never endured a minute of boredom in her life now suffered from hours of it.

The only thing that did hold her interest, aside from the welfare of Mrs. Gerrard's ladies, was her project to bring together Lord Aylward and Alicia, and that was progressing very well indeed. It entailed Harriet's being seen in Lord Aylward's company so often that Lady Elizabeth began to hope that Harriet was going to settle down at last, though of course she would never have mentioned such a thing to Harriet. What Elizabeth neglected to notice was that upon each occasion when the Earl of Woodbridge escorted Harriet, whether it was to the Countess of Nayland's ridotto or Mrs. Drouet's benefit concert in the Argyll Rooms, she made certain that they invariably stopped to exchange a few words with Alicia and her mother.

Though Elizabeth was unaware of such a pattern, Harriet did explain it to Lord Aylward one evening after they had left the De Villiers' box to return to their seats for the celebrated Kean's performance in A New Way to Pay Old Debts. "I feel quite sorry for poor Alicia, what with Chalfont in Oxfordshire, you know."

"Sorry for Miss De Villiers?" Lord Aylward echoed in surprise. That anyone should feel anything but breathless admiration for the lovely young lady in question seemed to be beyond his comprehension.

"Yes." Harriet nodded emphatically. "For though naturally enough she is not madly in love with someone to whom she has been betrothed all her life, it is hard for her to be without his escort. One can see that it is exceedingly awkward for one accustomed to being the cynosure of all eyes to be forced to attend these things with only her mother as a companion. Of course she would never let on to such a thing, but naturally she must feel his lack of attention keenly."

"Naturally," his lordship agreed, much struck by the wisdom of her observations. This conversation inspired Lord Aylward, a most kindhearted young man who was moved by sympathy for the neglected Miss De Villiers, to ride out several days in a row at precisely the hour he knew the De Villiers' barouche would be appearing in the park. There, he discovered the truth of Harriet's remarks, for Alicia was almost pathetically delighted to see him, or so it appeared.

Each time she bade him farewell she asked after his plans for the next day with such particular interest that the earl began to take it as a point of honor to ride at her side every day. Since Lady Harriet had made it perfectly clear that one early-morning ride in the park with her brother was more than sufficient exercise. Lord Aylward felt no qualms about deserting her to accompany the De Villiers' ladies as they made their stately circuit every afternoon.

Certainly Alicia herself felt no misgivings about such an arrangement. It pleased her immensely to have such an eligible and devoted gallant attending her so assiduously and showering her with the praise and adoration so notably lacking where her fiancé was concerned. To be quite truthful about the matter, she was happy to dispense with Lord Chalfont as long as there was someone of equal rank and éclat to take his place. That this person also showed a far more proper appreciation for the affairs of the ton than did the marquess only added to her satisfaction, and she had gone from being quite put out by Lord Chalfont's absence to quite enjoying it.

For her part, Harriet watched this growing intimacy with increasing satisfaction. She did her best to fan the flames of Lord Aylward's interest in the neglected belle by concentrating as much as possible on the lovely Alicia as a topic of conversation whenever he and Harriet happened to share a moment of private conversation waltzing at Almack's or between acts at the theater. Through Miss De Villiers's former schoolmate, the earl soon learned that Alicia and the Marquess of Kidderham, though united by years of acquaintance and a common background, really shared very little else, their interests being so widely divergent and their characters so dissimilar as to render them almost opposites of one another.

"It is truly quite gothic in this day and age to find such different people bound together by a marriage of convenience, especially one that was contracted when they were little more than children," Harriet observed as she and the earl were performing the figures in the quadrille one evening in Lady Haslehurst's opulent ballroom.

"Surely she is not being forced against her will?" Lord Aylward was aghast.

"Not as such, but then, she is so very well brought up that it would never occur to her to question such a thing no matter how unhappy it might make her."

"Yes, she appears to be all of that and possesses a proper, dutiful nature that is extremely rare in a young woman these days." The earl agreed so readily that Harriet felt quite on the defensive. She did not think that she was so badly brought up, after all, merely less slavishly devoted to appearance than the young lady in question. But she quelled the retort that rose to her lips and enumerated instead Alicia's manifold feminine charms, which consisted chiefly of always looking exquisite and never putting a foot wrong.

Lord Aylward seemed to be much struck by these revelations. Indeed, he remained in a thoughtful mood for the rest of the evening and bade Harriet adieu in an unusually abstracted manner as though his thoughts were concentrated elsewhere.

And that should take care of that, Harriet crowed to herself triumphantly as she prepared for bed later that night. Now all that remains is to convince Alicia that she is truly as unhappy as I have led Aylward to believe she is.

This part of the scheme was not so easily accomplished, for Harriet had spent more of her life avoiding Alicia and people like her than courting them. Thus it was difficult to seek out her former schoolmate without seeming quite out of character and arousing suspicion. Fortunately for Harriet, who had been racking her brain for some reasonable excuse to encounter Alicia in a way that would appear perfectly natural, she happened to run into her in Bond Street just as Harriet was emerging from Madame Celeste's, having done her best to insure Madame's continued employment of Fanny by purchasing not one, but two fetching bonnets.

Expecting to make several purchases, Harriet had requested the use of the carriage that morning and was thus able to offer Alicia a place in it which, after dispensing with her maid, she accepted gratefully as the De Villiers' equipage had been commandeered by her mother who was visiting a sick friend.

As they rolled down Bond Street Harriet turned to Alicia. "I had no idea that Lord Chalfont was the one to whom you have been promised all these years. You are indeed fortunate in being betrothed to a man who takes such a serious interest in the affairs of the nation."

Alicia raised delicately arched brows. "I do not concern myself with politics." She sniffed. "I think it is so unladylike for a woman to put herself forward in things better left to the male sex."

"But you will take an interest now that it is clear his lordship plans to devote so much of his time to it. And when you are married you will be able to accompany him in making the rounds of the countryside as he is now doing, which I must say I find most admirable. Not many of his rank and property show such an active concern for those less fortunate. Why, my brother Charlie says that in the army Lord Chalfont was known for being equally as solicitous of the troops in his command as he was for his brother officers."

It was a lucky shot, for Harriet could not have known the picture that this offhand remark conjured up in Alicia's discontented mind. Once again she saw the soldier begging in front of Somerset House and her fiancé, not content with giving the man money, going so far as to offer him the hospitality of his own quarters in Mount Street. She shuddered at the thought.

The unhappy pout to her lips was not lost on Harriet who could barely refrain from hugging herself with glee. "And when are you to be wed?" She inquired politely.

The pout became more pronounced. "I have not the least— we have not yet set a date," Alicia replied in a tone of finality that brooked no further questions. But Harriet could see that the seed had been planted and Alicia's visions, painted so glowingly in their school days, of herself as a leader of the ton were being replaced by the far less rosy picture of Alicia immured in some drafty country house forced to play hostess to highly unfashionable and radical political leaders bent on reform.

By now, much to Alicia's relief, they had reached Hanover Square and she bade Harriet adieu and, in a most serious frame of mind, climbed slowly up the steps to the modest house the De Villiers had rented for the Season.

It had never occurred to Alicia, until recently, that life with a wealthy peer would be anything less than perfect or that her husband would wish to devote himself to anything but lavishing her with the luxurious surroundings and expensive folderols she deserved. Of late, however, she had begun to have slight misgivings which her conversation with Harriet had only exacerbated.

Until this moment, Alicia had never really stopped to consider the character of the man she was marrying. It sufficed that he was of a rank and fortune a good deal superior to hers and that his lineage, though less ancient than hers, was respectable enough to make others envious. His personal characteristics, though far less important, were also such as to recommend him. His tall frame and aristocratic bearing insured that he looked the part of leader of the ton. Beyond that, Alicia had never stopped to consider anything else. Other than wishing that he had stayed at home and courted her more assiduously rather than going off to fight the Corsican monster, she had not wasted a second thought on his years in the Peninsula outside of assuring herself that he was attached to a sufficiently fashionable regiment. And while it had done her a great deal of good to be the fiancé of one of the heroes of the Peninsula in the euphoria following Napoleon's defeat, she had been too interested in seeing that he settled down and took his place in society to take much notice of that. In fact, it had irritated her when brother officers approached Lord Chalfont to share reminiscences with him or to extol his daring and courage, because these discussions had only served to draw attention away from her.

Alicia had been rather annoyed at the marquess's aversion to fashionable events and his preference for the congenial male atmosphere of the clubs along St. James, but she consoled herself with her confidence in the alluring power of her own beauty and charm. After all, had she not been able to bring even the most aloof of bachelors hurrying to her side with the flutter of an eyelash? She would do the same with the marquess. As the days had worn on, however, Chalfont had remained alarmingly indifferent to her moods and desires, failing utterly to be jolted into action by her frowns or to be dissuaded from something by the hint of her displeasure. Where other men had quaked, he was impervious, taking it all in stride and leaving her with nothing to do but seethe inwardly.

It was a most upsetting state of affairs not to be able to exert the same control over her betrothed that she had always exerted over everyone else, and as if that were not bad enough, he now appeared to be taking an unhealthy interest in things that had nothing to do with her or the life she had planned for herself. In truth, Alicia was feeling quite desperate as she climbed the stairs to her bedchamber after her conversation with Harriet. Fortunately her maid was there with soothing lavender water for her temples and several lavish bouquets of hothouse flowers from her usual admirers. That was one consolation; at least Chalfont did not object to the throng of fawning young men who hung on her every word. Alicia frowned as the thought occurred to her that perhaps he did not even notice or, worse yet, was not even jealous of them.

As she continued to think of her admirers, Alicia brightened as she remembered Lord Aylward. Now there was a man who appreciated her properly. Unlike so many of the young men who flocked around her simply because their friends did, the earl was entirely capable of recognizing her superiority to the other women of the ton. Furthermore, he showed it. Lord Aylward made Alicia feel as though she were some precious work of art to be cherished and treasured, which indeed she was. He would never put her off with desultory replies to her charming conversation while his mind was obviously elsewhere, as Chalfont so often did. No, he focused his entire attention on everything she had to say, and whenever they were together he was completely absorbed in catering to her comfort, whether it was being ready to catch her shawl should it slip from her shoulders, retrieve a dropped glove, or shift his position so she did not have to crane her neck to talk to him. He not only did all these things, but he obviously delighted in doing so. He was desolated when they parted and was patently eager for their next meeting. Now why could not Chalfont be like that instead of being given to such queer starts as offering assistance to an old soldier or jauntering around the countryside talking to poor people in a manner most unbecoming to a titled gentleman of property?

Chapter 30

At the moment the titled gentleman of property was asking himself much the same thing as he rode around the tenants' farms on his estate in Oxfordshire. Alistair knew very well why he had left London, however, and it had less to do with ascertaining the true condition of agricultural laborers than with a wish to avoid a certain lively and endearing redhead who exerted a powerful attraction for him.

Much to his dismay, Lord Chalfont was fast discovering that the absence of this particular redhead only made him think about her all the more. Away from both Alicia and Harriet, he was at liberty to reflect on the situation endlessly. The more he concentrated on Harriet, the bleaker his future with the frivolous, self-centered beauty appeared, and the more he thought about Alicia, the more precious every laughter-shared moment with Harriet became.

Harriet, Alicia. Alicia, Harriet. Both of them offered an existence entirely different from the one he had hitherto experienced: Alicia, closing off every opportunity for adventure, and the passionate immersion in affairs that had been his life until now; Harriet, opening up new vistas, new challenges and ways of making himself useful, and fulfilling his dreams in ways he had never imagined.

Harriet, Alicia. Alicia, Harriet. Why did he torture himself by comparing them? It was not as though there were any contest.. Harriet offered vitality and life, and Alicia only a mockery of it. And, it was not as though there was even any choice. Alicia was his duty while Harriet had never been anything but a brief glimpse of what happiness could be, a dream and nothing more. It would be better for all of them if he were to put that dream firmly from his mind, but try as he would, Alistair could not. Formerly he had been able to forget his mistresses, no matter how beautiful or how charming, and move on without undue regret. Now he could hardly think of anything else but Harriet and the way she lighted up a room for him with her enchanting presence. From there he progressed to the memory of their brief delicious moments together in the carriage, and his longing for her became so intense that it was physical. He literally ached to hold her in his arms again, to feel that wonderful sense of oneness, of peace and security, of the very rightness of it all.

At last, by sheer grim determination, Alistair was able to concentrate on the problems of his farmers who, crippled by the falling prices of corn, were groaning under the double burden of the income tax and the poor rates. He sympathized mightily with them, yet, having seen the poor in the city, and having listened to the sorry tale of the poverty-stricken soldier he had rescued, he knew that simply passing a law to increase the price of corn would not improve the situation. At the moment he could only offer his compassion, promise to do what he could in Parliament to make things better, and instruct his agent to set up a kitchen in an unused outbuilding where soup and bread could be made in large enough quantities to be distributed to all who needed it.

The evenings the marquess spent reading The Edinburgh Review, The Gentleman's Magazine, Cobbett's Political Register, and anything he could get his hands on that might give him some insight into the economic woes besetting the nation. Inevitably, as he perused these articles, questions arose in his mind and he longed to ask Harriet her opinion of them, to debate the pros and cons with her in order to gain another perspective. So intensely did he wish this that he could almost picture her sitting on the other side of the fireplace, her red hair glinting in the firelight, her forehead wrinkled in a thoughtful frown as she discussed the issues with him.

For the better part of the marquess's life, the idea of settling down with a woman had been anathema to him. He had chased after adventure and excitement, changing women as easily and as often as he changed locale. Now, settling down with one particular woman was all that he could think about. Even the idea of having children with Harriet was appealing. I must be touched in the upper works, Alistair muttered to himself as he shifted in his chair, took another sip of brandy, and tried for the hundredth time to focus on The Times in front of him.

Finally he gave up trying to read and concentrated on the problem at hand. Think about it, Chalfont, he admonished himself, with Alicia you will never have a moment's worry. She will look and act the part of the Marchioness of Kidderham to perfection, leaving you to pursue whatever course you wish, so long as you escort her to the requisite number of ton functions. Since she cares only about your title, property, and position, she will never be jealous should you have other interests, and she is far too well-bred ever to comment on such a thing. Life will be comfortable.

Unfortunately, this line of reasoning turned out to be as disastrous as every other because Alistair soon found himself wondering if Harriet would be jealous and if he would want her to be. It was most disconcerting to reflect that he was not at all certain whether she cared enough to be jealous. Did she feel about him the way he did about her? He had thought so in the carriage, but the more he considered it, the less sure he became. Such doubts were unique for a man who was far more accustomed to raising them in the minds and hearts of others than he was to experiencing them himself. Worse yet, would he be jealous of Harriet? The answer, a resounding yes, sent him flying from his chair in search of his long-suffering batman.

"Richards, Richards," he bellowed most uncharacteristically as he headed toward his bedchamber.

"Yes, my lord?" Richards emerged from the dressing room where he had been sorting cravats.

"I wish you to pack at once. We are returning to London tomorrow."

"Yes, my lord, very good, my lord." Richards's face remained impassive, but his mind was working furiously. What could have caused this sudden change in plans? There had been nothing in the post this morning that would have occasioned such a decision and while it was true that Lord Chalfont did have a penchant for travel and changing of locale, the man was not quixotic by any means. He usually gave his servant several days warning before decamping.

No, this was decidedly uncharacteristic for the marquess, Richards mused as he set about packing. In fact, it was so unlike his lordship that the batman did not have far to look for an explanation. "It is that Lady Harriet," he muttered beneath his breath as he closed the lid on one of the valises. "She is the only person who has affected him enough to be the cause of such a queer start."

Lord Chalfont's air of abstraction during their sojourn in Oxfordshire had not been lost on his servant, and Richards had a fair idea of the agony his master was suffering. The marquess had been unusually taciturn and, though he was never one to abstain from the bottle, he had consumed far greater quantities of brandy and port than Richards could ever remember. For a man of action, his lordship had wasted an inordinate number of hours staring out across the vast lawns of Chalfont or gazing into the fire, and it was obvious to even the most casual of observers that he was wrestling with thoughts of a most disturbing nature.

With all his heart Richards wished he could help his master. It did not seem fair that a Trojan like his lordship should be condemned to spend the rest of his life with a cold fish like the De Villiers' girl, especially when Lady Harriet was such a right one. The batman shook his head as he opened another valise. Even he, resourceful as he was, could not see a way out of this one.

Come to think of it, Richards reflected glumly, his own existence was also bound to become less comfortable, for undoubtedly his new mistress would insist that her husband hire a proper gentleman's gentleman to see to him. Was there ever such a coil? Richards doubted it. Well, there was no use repining. They would just have to make the best of it, and he would do his utmost to support his master while keeping his eyes, ears, and mind open. At least they were returning to London where Lord Chalfont was bound to encounter Lady Harriet. Richards had been of the mind that distance would ease the situation, but he had quickly changed it when he saw how much Lord Chalfont missed Lady Harriet. Although the marquess could not hope for anything more than friendship from her ladyship, he could still enjoy that, and Richards had been a witness to the happiness that friendship had brought his master. It was not difficult for the batman to know when Lord Chalfont had been spending time with the lady in question for he always returned to their quarters full of energy and brimming with ideas to put into action. There was always a light in his eyes and a secret smile hovering on his lips that told as plainly as if he were wearing a placard that he had been with Lady Harriet Fareham. Richards could not remember anyone, certainly no previous mistress, or even a brother officer, who had brought such companionship into the marquess's life. Any contact with a person such as Lady Harriet, no matter how little, was better than none at all. Why even just seeing her from afar; as Richards had occasionally witnessed, seemed to put Lord Chalfont in a happier frame of mind. Surely returning to London along with the possibility of seeing Lady Harriet would restore some of the vitality so notably lacking in the marquess during their trip into the country. The batman devoutly hoped so, but only time would tell.

Chapter 31

Lord Chalfont was not the only one suffering from his absence from the metropolis. Much to her dismay, Harriet was also discovering that life without the Marquess of Kidderham was decidedly flat. She continued her lessons at Mrs. Gerrard's and had the distinct pleasure of seeing Lucy moved by her new protector, a wealthy brewer, to a snug little house of her own in Marylebone. To Harriet it did not seem much of an escape from her former life, but Lucy was ecstatic. "I know it is not a tavern of my own, but all I have ever really wanted was a house of my own and a gentleman to take care of me. I know that the connection will not last, but at least I am established now and I know I can continue that way. You have taught me to act like a lady, which is what first captivated Mr. Ruggles's fancy, that and my knowledge of brewing. But what with the house and knowing how to read and do sums, I expect I shall do well for myself."

But somehow, despite her pleasure in Lucy's good fortune, Harriet was not as thrilled as she expected to be, partly because she had no one with whom to share the news. She longed to be able to tell it to the only person who could truly appreciate the significance of it all. Lord Chalfont.

But it was not only Harriet's visits to Mrs. Gerrard's that lacked their usual interest, so did her rides in the park, not to mention her appearance in the various ballrooms of the ton's fashionable hostesses. With something of a shock, Harriet realized, as she was joining in a country dance at Lady Milford's, that, when the Marquess of Kidderham was present, she had almost come to enjoy such affairs. Then she knew she could expect intelligent conversation for at least one dance.

What Harriet did not acknowledge was that she missed waltzing with Lord Chalfont, not so much because of the conversation as because of the way he made her feel. She had tried most assiduously to put aside all thoughts of the warmth of his hand on her waist and the closeness of the tall lean body to hers. Such memories brought back the even more aching one of his arms around her in the carriage and the feel of his lips on hers evoking longings and desires in her that she could barely identify, but which now, try as she might, she could not put out of her mind.

Harriet kept telling herself that over time these feelings would disappear, leaving her with the peace of mind and the enthusiasm for the pursuits she had enjoyed before meeting the Marquess of Kidderham, but they did not. In fact, the longer Lord Chalfont was away from town, the stronger these longings became and the only thing that truly seemed to distract her thoughts from such dangerous channels was her continuing campaign to bring the Earl of Woodbridge and Alicia De Villiers together. It was extremely lowering to be involved in such machinations at all, much less to take such an interest in them, but even this connection with the marquess, tenuous as it was, was better than none at all, though of course, Harriet could not admit such a thing even to herself. She saw it rather as helping an absent friend who was trapped in an unpleasant situation.

At any rate, her plan to bring Alicia and the earl together was highly successful. Naturally the Earl of Woodbridge did not enjoy the free and easy access to the De Villiers' household that the Marquess of Kidderham did, but he appeared at so many of the functions honored by Alicia's presence, and was such a habitual visitor to the park that in truth he spent a good deal more time in her company than her fiancé ever had. This assiduous attention was quite driving all thoughts of her betrothed from Alicia's mind, so much so that it was rather a shock when he suddenly materialized at her elbow as she was catching her breath between dances at Lady Margrave's rout.

"Chalfont!" She exclaimed in some surprise. "This is quite sudden. I had not expected you back so soon."

Though Alicia was never particularly warm, this was cool even for her. Alistair raised a quizzical eyebrow. "And here I thought you would be pleased to see me."

"Naturally I am always pleased to see you, my lord, but one expects some sort of communications, some sort of intimation when one's betrothed is returning to town."

The ironic look became even more pronounced. "Warning. Alicia?"

If the marquess had hoped to discomfit her, he was not successful. Never doubting the rightness of her own views on any subject, Alicia was not easily flustered. "Yes, warning. It is excessively unnerving, not to mention ill-bred, for someone to drop in and out of people's lives without so much as a by-your-leave."

"I see."

This time the satiric note in his voice was too pronounced even for Alicia to ignore. "It is common courtesy, my lord. You would certainly not approve if I did not keep you apprised of my whereabouts, and I should never just pop up by your side like some jack-in-the-box without some sort of notice."

"No, Alicia, I believe you would never do anything so impulsive."

"Impulsive? Heavens no." Alicia was genuinely horrified by such a notion, but she was clever enough to see that for some odd reason this was not necessarily a recommendation in his lordship's eyes. "I pride myself on always being where people expect me to be, when they expect me. Unreliability is excessively worrisome, not to mention impolite. I would have thought you knew that."

"Perhaps I did not understand it so fully as I do now," Alistair responded grimly.

The significance of this rather enigmatic reply was completely lost on Alicia. "I am glad, then, that we have had a chance to clarify this. I should not want you to be anything but perfectly confident in the behavior of the future Marchioness of Kidderham."

"You are all kindness," Alistair murmured sardonically.

"Did you have a pleasant journey, my lord?" Alicia inquired brightly, completely ignoring this last remark.

Lord Chalfont could not help but stare at her for a long moment before answering. He had been off immersing himself in economic affairs so grave that some discussion of them had even filtered into the drawing rooms and ballrooms of the ton, yet she inquired after his trip as though he had enjoyed a pleasant sojourn at a friend's hunting box. "Yes." What else was there to say? How could he explain the poor cottagers who worried about their next meal to someone whose most pressing concern was whether or not she would receive invitations to society's most select gatherings?

"Good. Having done that you have no further need to waste your time in the country." It was more of a command than an observation.

"On the contrary, in the future I plan to spend a good deal of time in the country for that is where one finds out the truth of things." At the moment, Alistair did not even know if he planned to do such a thing, but there was something in the calm way she disposed of his life that infuriated him and he could not help striking back.

Alicia paled and shut her mouth with a snap.

Alistair wanted to leave. A wave of revulsion for the whole super-ficial way of life that Alicia represented washed over him and he felt more trapped than ever before. However, there was nothing to do but ask her to stand up with him and then make his escape as quickly as possible, but as he led her onto the floor he caught a glimpse of gleaming red curls over in a corner by one of the ballroom's marble columns. Lord Chalfont heaved a sigh of relief. She had come after all.

Suddenly things did not seem so hopeless. The ballroom and the crowd that had been closing in on him just moments ago now ap-peared to be a gay and glittering scene, and his jaded senses felt re-vived. Alistair was quite surprised to feel his heart pumping and his breath coming in quick bursts as though he had just engaged in a bout of fisticuffs. Not since his salad days when he had fancied him-self in love with a girl in the village had he been so affected by the sight of a woman.

Somehow he got through the quadrille with Alicia, nodding me-chanically every time she made a remark, but her words were only a buzz in his ear, so intent was he on keeping an eye on the gleam of red at the other side of the ballroom. He restored Alicia to her mother and went off in search of Lady Harriet.

Lord Chalfont's patent desertion left Alicia seething with indig-nation. Spend her life in the country! Chalfont was mad if he thought he could bury his beautiful and charming wife in the depths of the country with no one for company except for a few greasy farmers' wives. It was insupportable! A lump rose in her throat. She could not, no, she would not bear it. Chalfont would just have to revise his ideas of their future life together.

Alicia drew herself up proudly. She would not give in to despair; after all, she had always gotten her way before. It might take more time and be a bit more difficult now that he had his mind made up, but she would win in the end. A vision of her betrothed's implacable countenance rose before her and some of her courage deserted her. While it was true she had been able to cozen her doting parents and other besotted admirers, she knew that the Marquess of Kidderham was made of sterner stuff. Suddenly the future, which had always seemed so bright, began to appear very bleak indeed. Unaccustomed tears stung her eyes. It was dreadfully unfair. She, who had been the model of all that was perfect in a woman, did not deserve this fate.

"May I have this dance?"

Alicia had been too wrapped up in her gloomy thoughts to be aware of Lord Aylward's approach and therefore she only caught the last word of his invitation. She regarded him in vague astonishment.

The Earl of Woodbridge smiled tentatively as he reiterated his offer. "I have come to claim the waltz you promised me, but perhaps you have thought better of it." Lord Aylward had never seen her look so agitated. His heart was touched by the drooping shoulders and the trembling lower lip that she was incapable of hiding. "Is something amiss?" he asked with gentle concern. "I am at your service. If I can do anything to spare you a moment's pain, I—"

"No, no ..." Alicia interrupted hurriedly. She stole a quick glance at her mother who appeared to be entirely absorbed in surveying the ballroom. "I shall be delighted to have this waltz."

They glided around the floor in silence for some moments before the earl, unable to stand the look of misery in her eyes, questioned her gently, "Is something amiss? I cannot bear that someone as exquisite and charming as you should be anything but happy."

His words were balm to Alicia's wounded spirit. This was the way she should be treated, with sympathy and reverence, not with the callous indifference displayed by Lord Chalfont.

A sob escaped her and her partner, sensing that she was about to break down entirely, waltzed her slowly and imperceptibly toward the open French doors leading from the ballroom onto a terrace. Once there, he released her and, taking one hand, led her into the privacy of the shadows. "Now, I beg of you, tell me how I can help."

It was too much for Alicia whose sense of ill usage had been steadily increasing. Tears rolled down her cheeks. "I can not, I mean it is unthinkable that I should be expected ..." She gulped and tried to regain her composure.

"Who is causing you such unhappiness? Just name the person and I shall—"

"No, no!" Alicia gasped. She had never heard Lord Aylward sound so fierce, and while it thrilled her to her very soul that he should be so ardent on her behalf, it alarmed her for she was well aware of her fiancé's reputation as a man of action. "There is nothing to be done. I must bear it as best I can." But this thought was so upsetting that covering her face with her hands, she began to sob in earnest.

The sight of Alicia crying was more than the earl could endure. Forgetting everything but her anguish, he pulled her gently into his arms. "There, there. Do not upset yourself. I shall do whatever is in my power to make you happy again."

The sobbing ceased and Alicia gazed up at him with flowing eyes. "Oh, if only you could, but it is impossible."

Her tearstained countenance was more lovely, more moving than anything he had ever seen. "I cannot believe that. There must be something I can do. I will do anything. I adore you, Alicia."

"Oh," she breathed, her eyes shining up at him. This was the way her life should be. This was what she deserved. Unconsciously she leaned toward him, willing him to worship her, to take care of her.

Overwhelmed by her beauty and the piteous expression on her face. Lord Aylward leaned down and kissed her gently, reverently.

It was at this moment that Lord Chalfont, frustrated by an unsuccessful attempt to talk to Harriet who had been led onto the dance floor minutes before he reached her side, strode out onto the terrace in search of peace, quiet, and fresh air.

Seeing the couple in the shadows locked in an embrace, he halted, unwilling to intrude, but as he turned to leave them in privacy, he heard Alicia's voice whispering, "Oh, Aylward." Alistair stopped dead in his tracks and turned to peer incredulously into the gloom.

"Alicia?"

The couple fell apart as the marquess approached.

"What is the meaning of this?"

For once, Alicia was bereft of speech. She could do nothing but cling to Lord Aylward and gasp in dismay. The earl, however, was made of sterner stuff. Gently disengaging himself from her clutching hands, he strode forward to look Lord Chalfont straight in the eye. "The lady was overcome with distress and, thinking to avoid comment while she recovered, I brought her out here."

"Undoubtedly." Alistair laughed cynically, but then, thinking better of it, he stopped. This situation, if managed properly, offered the perfect opportunity to make everyone happy. From the besotted expression on Aylward's face, the man was more than half in love with Alicia, and she with him, though Alistair doubted she would ever care for anyone as much as she cared for herself.

The marquess drew a deep breath. "I understand, and I thank you very much for your concern." Now, how was he to proceed? Lord Chalfont thought frantically for a moment. There was nothing for it but to take the bull by the horns. "It appears to me that you are devoted to Miss De Villiers's welfare and—"

"No, Chalfont. It was not what you think." Alicia, who had recovered her wits enough to consider the implications that her betrothed must be reading into the tender scene, hastened to defend herself.

"I do not think anything, Alicia. I know you too well to believe you are anything but the soul of discretion, as is Aylward here." He nodded in the earl's direction. "But it strikes me that I would be doing you a great disservice in keeping you from one who is obviously a person far more worthy of your regard than I am, a man who fully appreciates the particular qualities you have to offer, qualities that are lost on a rough soldier such as I." Careful, my man, careful, Alistair chided himself. You are doing it much too brown.

However, both the earl and Alicia seemed to be much struck by this idea.

Alistair continued. "The admiration offered to you by Aylward here, who is not only a man of rank and property, but one well versed in the ways of the ton, offers a greater compliment to you than I could ever pay, unaccustomed as I am to a fashionable existence." This delicate reference to Aylward's title was not lost on Alicia who had already realized that except for the scandal involved in breaking off with Lord Chalfont, she stood to gain far more by becoming

Countess of Woodbridge than she did as the future Marchioness of Kidderham. She gazed pensively at the large Chalfont emerald that now graced her left hand.

Alistair, noting her speculative expression, did his best to hide a triumphant grin. Truly, things were proceeding better than he could ever have dreamed. It only remained to concoct an explanation for Alicia's change in plans that both Alicia and Aylward could live with.

Lord Aylward hastened to intervene. "No one could be a greater admirer of the lady in question than I, Chalfont. I hold her in the highest regard and, with your permission, of course, shall continue to do so when she is your wife." The earl turned and made as if to leave the terrace.

It was a noble speech, but one Alicia, who had suddenly glimpsed a brighter future for herself, was not willing for him to act upon. "Stay a moment, my lord." She stretched out an imploring hand to him. "Do not leave so abruptly. Surely ..." she paused, unwilling to let him leave yet even more unwilling to risk her spotless reputation.

It was the moment Alistair had been waiting for. "Alicia, I honor your dedication to a long-standing agreement between our two families. Your willingness to sacrifice your future happiness for the sake of duty does you great credit, but I cannot stand by while you suffer. It is as obvious that you and Aylward were meant for each other as it is that we will not suit, and I hereby release you from all obligation."

Alicia hesitated, not entirely pleased by the ease with which the marquess relinquished her and concerned lest the least breath of scandal attach itself to her name.

Correctly divining her thoughts, Alistair strove to reassure her. "Calm yourself, Alicia. I shall put a notice in The Morning Post that owing to unfortunate experiences in the late war we have decided that we shall no longer suit and that the engagement has been broken off by mutual consent. How does that strike you, Aylward?"

The earl, unable to believe his good fortune, stood stock-still for some minutes, too bemused to reply, a beatific smile on his face. Then, coming to with a start, he replied, "Perfectly unexceptionable, but you are too generous, too—"

Alistair waved away the earl's thanks. "You have done us both a favor. Alicia is correct in thinking she deserves better than a life with me." The irony of this was lost on the happy couple who were gazing at one another with mutual delight.

Leaving them to their newfound felicity, the marquess strode back into the ballroom, scanning the crowd for a mop of bright red curls, but it was nowhere to be seen.

Harriet had indeed left Lady Margrave's elegant town house. Cursing herself for being a coward, she had pleaded a headache and asked Charlie to take her home the moment she had caught sight of Lord Chalfont entering the ballroom. She had thought that the marquess's absence had given her the opportunity to regain the equilibrium that had been so upset by his revelations in the carriage on the way home from St. Albans, but she had been thoroughly mistaken. To be sure, life had seemed very empty without him, but in a way it had been more peaceful; and while it was true that she missed his energizing presence, she at least was not subject to the strange fits of breathlessness that overcame her every time she saw him.

Harriet had begun to hope that this embarrassing condition had remedied itself while the marquess was in Oxfordshire, but the instant she had laid eyes on him at Lady Margrave's, she knew she had been utterly and completely wrong. Not only did she feel her cheeks flush and her heart pound, but her knees threatened to buckle underneath her, and her stomach seemed to be turning somersaults. Whatever was ailing her? Totally disgusted with herself, Harriet had plucked at Charlie's sleeve and declared herself seriously unwell.

Ordinarily Charlie would have questioned such an odd state in someone who as far back as he could remember had never suffered a headache in her life, but he had just caught sight of the determined approach of Miss Wolverton and her formidable mama, and he himself longed to be anywhere but this particular ballroom. Miss Wolverton was a plain, earnest young woman whom Charlie, in a mistaken moment of pity for the eternally partnerless miss, had once asked to stand up with him. He had been paying dearly for this generous gesture ever since as he found himself hounded from one ballroom to another and it looked as though he were about to be forced to pay again.

Such a golden opportunity for escape was not to be questioned, and he hustled his sister out of the ballroom and into their carriage with dispatch. Too wrapped up in thoughts of his own close call, he had been silent during the short ride home and Harriet had been able to escape to her bedchamber without any comment.

Arriving in the safety and privacy of her own boudoir, she threw herself, fully clothed, onto the bed and stared fixedly at the embroidery on the counterpane. This foolishness must stop immediately, my girl, she scolded herself. It is bad enough for you to behave like such a ninny, but it is even worse to suffer weakness when he, if he thinks of you at all, looks upon you as an intellectual companion with whom he can discuss the issues of the day and nothing more. Harriet would not allow herself to acknowledge the fact that having striven all her life to enjoy precisely that sort of relationship with a man, she now longed for something quite the opposite. The situation was impossible. She could not go on like this. There was nothing for it but to avoid contact with Lord Chalfont altogether for she could not trust herself to remain unaffected when he was around.

Having come to this conclusion, Harriet decided that the only solution lay in putting as much distance between her and the marquess as possible and she resolved to return to Buckinghamshire at the earliest opportunity. She would inform Rose tomorrow that she was to begin packing. After all, she had done her duty and supported Elizabeth. Her sister's marriage date had been set at last and there was no further need for Harriet's presence.

There was gentle scratching on the door. 'Thank you. Rose. I shall not need your services." Harriet dismissed her maid who, hearing of her mistress's early return, had come to ready her for bed.

Rose smiled slyly to herself. The rest of the household might ignore her mistress's pale face and listless behavior, but it had not been lost on her. And now, it was reported that Lady Harriet was suffering from the headache. She, Rose, knew it was no such thing, but rather the return of a certain marquess that ailed her mistress. Having correctly divined the cause of Harriet's general lack of interest in life during the marquess's sojourn in Oxfordshire, the maid had made certain that she knew the moment the Marquess of Kidderham had returned to town and thus she had heard from a stable boy, bribed with delicacies from the kitchen, the instant his lordship's traveling carriage had pulled up in Mount Street. If there had been any doubt in Rose's mind as to her ladyship's attraction to his lordship it was now thoroughly dispelled, but what was she to do about it? Rose racked her brain, but to no avail. There was nothing to do but trust in the course of true love and stand ready to be of service to her mistress in whatever way she could. Rose made her way back to her own room under the eaves in a thoughtful mood.

Meanwhile, Harriet was entirely mistaken in her belief that the marquess remained totally unaffected by her. In fact, as he prowled the darkened streets later that night trying to work off some of his restless energy, he could think of nothing but Harriet. The heady feeling of freedom and the elation at having successfully terminated his engagement to Alicia had long since subsided to be replaced by a nagging sense of doubt and uncertainty, which was as unsettling as it was unusual.

Heretofore, Alistair had never stopped to wonder what any of his many inamoratas had thought of him or how they had felt about him. Though ostensibly he had been the pursuer and they the pursued, he had never approached a female until he had seen that particular look in her eyes that invited his addresses. Now he was cudgeling his brain trying to remember if he had ever seen that look in Harriet's eyes, and he could not, in all honesty, say that he had. It was a lowering thought indeed.

To be sure, he had seen the dark blue eyes sparkle with curiosity and interest, but had there ever been anything more, anything to indicate that she longed to spend the rest of her life with him as much as he longed to spend it with her? Alistair was not at all certain. In the carriage he had told himself that she wanted him as much as he wanted her, that her body was responding to the need in his just as strongly as he longed to draw her close and feel one with her. Now, examining it all with the cold clear light of objectivity, he began to wonder if his own desires had colored his interpretations of her response to him.

"I don't know, I don't know," he muttered to himself as he paced one street after another in an agony of indecision. Finally, unable to think anymore, he simply wandered from Mayfair to Whitehall, along the river to Westminster, and back to Mayfair again until he was at last exhausted enough to rest, if not to sleep.

But by the time he had reached home, the sky in the direction from which he had just come was growing pink. There was no time for sleep now. If he were going to put an end to this hideous state of uncertainty, he would have to seek out Harriet as she took her early morning ride in the park, for that was the only chance he had of seeing her alone, or at least with only her groom for company. The marquess ordered a pot of coffee and some hot water and then, stripping off his evening clothes, he plunged his head gratefully into the steamy washbasin that Richards had brought him.

An hour or so later, freshly shaven and somewhat revived by quantities of hot black coffee, he was dressed immaculately in a superbly cut coat of blue kerseymere, his snowy cravat perfectly tied, his top boots gleaming as though he had arisen and dressed in a most leisurely fashion. Mounted on Trajan he made his way slowly to the park, keeping a weather eye out for an enormous black stallion with a red-haired rider. Once in the park he rode back and forth along Rotten Row trying to catch a glimpse of Harriet while at the same time trying to appear as though he had nothing more on his mind than the fineness of the morning.

At last he caught sight of Brutus trotting sedately along the edge of the park. Harriet had arrived some time earlier, but her senses heightened wherever the Marquess of Kidderham was concerned, she had quickly identified him and was now doing her best to avoid him without seeming to do so. But she soon heard the thundering of hooves behind her and knew herself to be unsuccessful in her attempt. There was nothing for it but to allow him to catch up with her and then deal with it as best she could.

Biting her lip nervously, Harriet waited for Lord Chalfont to come alongside her and greeted him with as much equanimity as she could muster, which was not a great deal. In fact, she could not even bring herself to meet his eyes as she inquired after the success of his journey into the country.

"Thank you. I had a most rewarding trip which I found to be extremely enlightening, but it was not all I had hoped for."

"Oh? And why was that?" Completely forgetting her resolution not to become involved in any sort of conversation with Lord Chalfont, Harriet made the mistake of looking at him. She regretted it the moment she had done so for having looked into his eyes, she could not look away again. Their curious amber color reminded her of warm sherry, and the expression in them was disturbing in the extreme, being at the same time both caressing and demanding, expressing admiration, yet at the same time asking questions she was not prepared to answer.

"It was not all I had hoped for because you were not there to talk to, to help me think things through," Alistair responded, still fixing her with his enigmatic gaze and not giving her a chance to recover herself.

"Oh?" Harriet's voice rose to a squeak. One gloved hand clenched at her breast as if to quiet her thudding heart. This was dreadful! He had no right to stare at her in that unnerving fashion. She wished he would stop. No, she wished he would not. What did she wish? Harriet could not think when she had ever been at such a loss for words.

A curiously tender smile quirked the corner of the marquess's mouth. He was enough of a man of the world to sense her unease and to be able to take some credit for it. This was promising, for it meant she must be a little attracted to him. Before his rescue of her, Harriet had never exhibited shyness or self-consciousness in his presence, quite the contrary. But since their embrace in the carriage she had been uneasy in his presence. Good. That meant there was hope for him.

"Lady Harriet, I feel I must tell you that Miss De Villiers and I have broken our engagement."

"What?" Occupied as she was trying to regain control of her composure, Harriet was shocked out of her self-absorption by this piece of news. "I mean, I am sorry to hear that."

"I am not."

The blue eyes looking up at the marquess widened in surprise.

"Come now, you, more than anyone must have seen how ill-suited Alicia and I were to one another. It is the best for both of us. We would only have succeeded in making one another miserable. Besides, Aylward adores her and will be able to give her everything that she wants."

"Aylward?" Harriet echoed in wonderment. Who would have guessed that her little plot would have been so successful so quickly? She could have hugged herself at her own cleverness.

Mistaking her surprise for dismay, Alistair suffered a pang of jealousy stronger than he thought he was capable of feeling. After all, Aylward had been a more constant companion to Harriet than to anyone else until Alicia had caught his attention. Had Harriet cared that much for the earl then? No! It was impossible. He would not believe it. Having gone this far, he was not about to lose heart. "Yes." He persisted. "And Alicia appears to feel that he will be all that she needs. I expect they will make a match of it and be very happy. And now, at last, I am free to live my life as I please without having to answer constantly to ... well, that is all behind me now. What is more important is that now I am at liberty to ask you if you would do me the very great honor of becoming my wife."

"Your wife!" Harriet exclaimed in astonishment. Her head was in a whirl. Things were moving too fast even for her to react to. The marquess free of his confining engagement to Alicia was one thing, but marriage was quite another. "But I never had any intention of getting married. I prefer to remain in control of my own life," she responded mechanically, too overwhelmed by the surprising turn of events to think before she spoke.

"I know you did not, but I need you. You are the one who started me on this budding political career. Now you must share it with me."

There was something about the word must that set alarm bells ringing in Harriet's head. "I do not see that I am obligated to do anything." She replied with dignity. "Why can I not do the same thing without being married to you—just as a friend?"

Seeing he was getting nowhere, Alistair jumped down from Trajan and tied him to a nearby tree. He strode over to Harriet and held out his hands to help her dismount. "Come, let me explain it to you."

Harriet eyed him suspiciously.

"I promise I shall not force you to do anything against your will, but I find it extremely disconcerting to carry on such a conversation on horseback." He tied Brutus to the same tree and turned to catch her as she slid to the ground.

"Now"—he led her to a little grove of trees—"it is more than your friendship I want, Harriet, and you know it. I love you. I have since the moment I saw you, and there is nothing I want more than to spend the rest of my life with you. If you do not believe that, then I shall just have to spend the rest of my life convincing you."

"But, but—" Harriet did not know what to say. One part of her could think of nothing she wanted more than to spend her life with him, and another part of her was more afraid than she had ever been in her life.

"But what, sweetheart?" He prompted gently.

"But Mrs. Gerrard."

"Mrs. Gerrard?" Alistair echoed blankly.

"Yes. That is where I first met you, after all. I know that someone like Alicia who is only after your title and your fortune would not care if you had other interests but I would." Overcome with sudden shyness, Harriet looked down at her gloved hands.

He could have laughed with relief. "Harriet, my love." He reached down and tilted up her chin so she was forced to look him straight in the eye. "I told you once before that I was at Mrs. Gerrard's the first time because I had just announced my engagement to Alicia and I felt my entire life closing in on me. I felt as though from then on I would cease to exist except as Alicia's escort, someone to order as she saw fit. Then I saw you, enchanting and vital as you are, and my whole world changed. You made me see that there were still things I could do to make a difference in the world, and I wanted nothing more than to please you, to keep seeing you and warming my spirit at the fire in your sweet sympathetic soul so I came back again and again."

"But it was not only to see me. Kitty made certain that all of us were well aware of the attentions you were paying to her. She said that you were most adept at lovemaking."

The marquess had the grace to look sheepish. "My thanks to Miss Kitty. I make no excuses for what I did beyond my frustration at the thought of the life I was facing. But I think you will discover, if you were to ask Kitty, that after the second or third visit I ceased availing myself of her, of her ... ah services precisely because I was falling in love with you."

Alistair pulled her closer to him. "Harriet, we were made for each other. I know that. We share the same interests, the same beliefs, the same conviction that we should devote ourselves to making this world a better place, and"—he gently traced the line of her lips with one finger—"the same passion."

Harriet pulled away from him. "But I do not want passion. All my life I have fallen into scrapes because of my enthusiasms, and I refuse to continue that way. I wish to live calmly, continuing to help where I can, to be—"

"As coldly perfect as Alicia?" Alistair interrupted her, taking advantage of the opportunity to pull her back into his arms. "Harriet, you cannot help who you are. You are spirited, sensitive, and loving. The life you envision for yourself is no life, for life cannot truly exist without passion. I know you are afraid. I am afraid. I am afraid to care so much for someone after all these years of avoiding it. I am afraid to risk the suffering I should endure if I were to lose that someone. I did not ask to feel this way, but now that I do, I am willing to accept it, and I beg of you to do the same."

"No. I cannot. I shall—" Harriet began nervously, only to be silenced as his lips came down hard on hers, possessive, demanding, willing her to respond to him. The butterflies that had been fluttering wildly in her stomach since she had first seen him seemed to break free and spread to every part of her body, turning her limbs to water, robbing her of her will to resist. Slowly, languorously, she gave herself up to his embrace as his lips slowly traced hers, moving down the line of her jaw to her ear.

"I love you, Harriet," he whispered as he gently buried his hands in the bright red curls, tilting her head back so he could kiss her more deeply still.

Her mouth opened under his until she could feel their breaths mingling. Her body throbbed where it met the hardness of his chest and his thigh, and she could not help recalling Kitty's vivid descriptions of his lovemaking. Suddenly, her body seemed to have a mind of its own that had very little to do with intellect or the life she had envisioned for herself. All it wanted was to feel those warm, strong hands caressing her everywhere as Kitty had described in such detail, to surrender utterly and completely to the desire she felt in him and in herself.

Alistair looked down into the blue eyes dark with passion under half-closed lids. "I love you, Harriet. Tell me you love me. Please tell me you love me." He slid his hands from her hair, down her sides, caressing the delicate curves and pressing her close. "I want you, Harriet, and I shall never stop wanting you until the day I die. Please say you will be with me."

It was no use. Harriet felt drawn to him as inevitably as she had when she had first looked at him across the schoolroom, laughing at her, challenging her. She had not fully realized that her response to his teasing had been fueled in some way, even then, by her attraction to him, but she admitted it to herself now. She longed for him as much as he did for her. It was only fear of losing herself, of losing him, that held her back. Slowly her customarily buoyant attitude began to reassert itself. What was there to lose? Life had been so very dull without him that it did not offer much of an alternative to the unknown of life with him that she was now facing.

"Very well."

"Very well, what?" He teased, covering her face with gentle kisses.

"Very well, I shall marry you. But I want you to promise me one thing."

He stopped, suddenly serious. "Anything you wish, my love, as long as you will spend your life with me."

"I want you to promise me that if you ever go Mrs. Gerrard's you will take me with you."

Alistair gave a shout of laughter. "I always said you were incorrigible. Yes. I promise. But since you are far more likely to go than I, I shall hold you to the same promise. Is that fair?"

Harriet nodded.

"Say I promise you, Alistair."

"I promise you, Alistair, because I love you," she replied as he again swept her into his arms to prove to her just how much he loved her.

About the Author

Like many of you reading this page, Evelyn Richardson fell in love with the Regency period when she first discovered "Pride and Prejudice" stuck at home on a snow day in junior high school. She has followed that interest through college (where she wrote her honors thesis on Fanny Burney) and graduate school, and continues to indulge herself with membership in the American Society for Eighteenth Century studies and writing Regency set historical novels. Evelyn has also been a librarian and library administrator for many years, which is reflected in her meticulous period bibliography and lists of reference resources. Living in the Boston area, she has access to, and haunts (electronically or in person) several of the country's major research libraries. Even before studying eighteenth-century literature in graduate school, Evelyn Richardson decided she would have preferred to have lived in England between 1775 and 1830. Now living outside of Boston, she enjoys access to the primary sources that allow her to explore the details of the period and immerse herself in the same journals her heroines enjoyed which for her, as a longtime reference librarian, is the best of all possible worlds.

Author Website: www,evelynrichardson.net
Author Hometown: Lexington, MA